"I don't mind marriage. In fact, I welcome it. In my culture, a man is not considered a true man unless he is married, regardless of his age. But *I* want to choose my bride. I want marriage on *my* terms and on *my* time." Dev's eyes narrowed, focusing in on her.

She felt a certain heat start low in her belly. It had been a while since she'd run across a man her body felt worth rousing for. The glitter of his gaze told her they were coming to the crux of his proposition now.

"I want you to accept my aunt's request for a painting, but I want another painting as well. One that only you can provide. One that might not enhance my reputation but ruin it should the portrait become known." He leaned back against the plush gray squabs, giving her space to breathe, space to think, his eyes intent on her person.

D0644658

Author Note

This is primarily a story about giving ourselves second chances. Dev and Guinevere have a chance to find happiness again after having lost it, but it requires them to move beyond the obstacles of their past and the artificial barriers erected by society.

Secondarily, however, this is a story about carving out a place for oneself in a world that doesn't currently have a convenient spot for you—a story line that is as relevant today as it was then. Dev is a man of the British Empire who is caught between worlds. He represents the growing debate in the British Empire of the nineteenth century about what it means to be British and who is British. It is also Guinevere's story and the rising debate regarding what place there is in decent society for a woman who is unattached to a man while also rejecting the reduced roles within society available to unmarried women.

I hope you enjoy Dev and Guinevere's story and that it prompts some self-reflection on your own journeys.

BRONWYN SCOTT

—

The Art of Catching a Duke

If you purchased this book without a cover you should be aware that this book is stolen property. It was reported as "unsold and destroyed" to the publisher, and neither the author nor the publisher has received any payment for this "stripped book."

ISBN-13: 978-1-335-72389-5

The Art of Catching a Duke

Copyright © 2023 by Nikki Poppen

Recycling programs
for this product may
not exist in your area.

All rights reserved. No part of this book may be used or reproduced in any manner whatsoever without written permission except in the case of brief quotations embodied in critical articles and reviews.

This is a work of fiction. Names, characters, places and incidents are either the product of the author's imagination or are used fictitiously. Any resemblance to actual persons, living or dead, businesses, companies, events or locales is entirely coincidental.

For questions and comments about the quality of this book, please contact us at CustomerService@Harlequin.com.

Harlequin Enterprises ULC
22 Adelaide St. West, 41st Floor
Toronto, Ontario M5H 4E3, Canada
www.Harlequin.com

Printed in U.S.A.

Bronwyn Scott is a communications instructor at Pierce College and the proud mother of three wonderful children—one boy and two girls. When she's not teaching or writing, she enjoys playing the piano, traveling—especially to Florence, Italy—and studying history and foreign languages. Readers can stay in touch via Facebook at Facebook.com/bronwynwrites, or on her blog, bronwynswriting.blogspot.com. She loves to hear from readers.

For the department: Joshua, Nichole, Fred and Patrick, Sam, Emily and Harjit. Love to you all.

Chapter One

London—late April, 1825

Political London attended Lady Shelford's afternoon salons for the intellectual timbre of the conversation. Guinevere Norton came for the men and sometimes for the women. Today, she was looking for her next client and they were all 'auditioning' whether they knew it or not. The Shelfords' drawing room with its conversational clusters of furniture, where seven or eight groups could gather independently to discuss various topics of the day, was the perfect place to employ her unique talent: Guinevere Norton knew how to undress a man or a woman using only her eyes.

In fact, she was employing that rather naughty skill right now with just the slightest lift of her eyes over the rim of the delicate Sèvres teacup—a very innocent prop for what some might consider a very indecent pastime.

Best of all, the target of her current efforts, Lord Bilsham, was entirely unaware. While he was busy expounding on the need for more oversight in London's orphanages, she'd taken off his coat, discarded his green paisley waistcoat, stripped off the high-pointed shirt that partially hid the jawline slowly but inevitably losing the battle to middle-aged jowls and found the Lord beneath—the Lord she would paint before the very last of his youth was gone. In his older years, he would come to see the portrait as a memoir of sorts.

The truth was, the man was running to fat. He would be there soon, within a year, maybe two if he was lucky. The extra weight was already settling in around his chin, his middle. But her paintbrush could fix that, for a price. Bilsham might not be a Greek god beneath his clothing—frankly, most men weren't—but his pockets would put Midas to the blush. For that reason alone, Guinevere's fingers itched to paint him. She was already calculating the money; there'd be the public portrait and then there'd be the private one she'd coax him into later.

Bilsham was exactly the type of man she came to Lady Shelford's for—middle aged, rich and endowed with a strong sense of his own importance if nothing else. Lady Shelford's entertainment drew the right sorts and today she was going to walk out of here with a commission to paint an elegant portrait or two. Bilsham drew a rare breath and she moved in for the close.

Guinevere put down her teacup and leaned forward, china-blue eyes wide, her hand making the bold but slightly tentative journey to rest on his sleeve. It was a gesture that fell between audacious and ladylike, much like herself. 'Lord Bilsham, your concern for the children of London is touching indeed. I am told you are on the board of directors for a foundling home in Chelsea?'

'Yes,' He preened at the attention. 'We have forty children at the home and are working on an apprentice programme for both boys and girls.'

She deepened her smile. 'Marvellous, no doubt all thanks to your efforts as the board's leader and visionary.' His chest puffed up at that. 'What a legacy you'll have established for those who follow you.' Gwen thought she saw the first hints of a humble blush beneath the points of his collar. 'Have you ever thought of having your portrait done for the hall at the orphanage?'

Bilsham prevaricated now that it had come to a commitment. 'That seems like an unnecessary extravagance when there is so much need. I'm afraid it would look arrogant.'

This was the hard part, selling people something they viewed only as a luxury, but Gwen was ready. 'Certainly not as something self-serving, but as a way to commemorate your time in office—an inspiration, even, to others who come after you as governors of Chelsea House regarding the merits of philanthropy.' The idea of a portrait as a lesson-cum-legacy in civic generosity hit just the right note with Bilsham. She could almost see in his eyes the exact moment when what had been a luxury a few minutes ago became a moral imperative.

'What an excellent idea, Mrs Norton, when you word it that way.'

'It is why I paint, Lord Bilsham.' Gwen gave him a confidential look, her voice low and personal, 'So that the present can be preserved. Paintings are not luxuries only, they are keepers of our most personal histories.'

She took a card from her reticule, her name and address in bold, straight black letters, and handed it to him.

'It would be an honour to assist you when you're ready to proceed. I am at the studio most days from ten until four.' The light was good that time of day. She did her best work during those hours, but, most of all, it gave her a convenient excuse for not paying calls and doing the other tedious things ladies did to pass the day during the Season.

It saved a great deal of trouble for her and for others by not having to deal with her presence in polite female gatherings. The men of London might have learned how to accommodate her, but the women had not. Her birth and her marriage had made her a lady, one of them. But her choices had not. It raised the question London had been debating the last four years when it came to Guinevere Norton, née Parkhurst: could an earl's granddaughter and the widow of an earl's second son actually be set outside society? Or did her antecedents require a certain acceptance of her eccentricities? Those eccentricities being her address on the outskirts of where good society lived, her intent to support herself through her art, and then there were those years abroad with her husband in Italy living quite differently than one did in England.

Bilsham took the card with some aplomb. 'The honour would be all mine.' He tucked the card into the pocket of his waistcoat with due respect, understanding that it was indeed some privilege to receive the offer. Gwen did not take many clients, it made her exclusive and, by the same rule, one did not choose the elusive, controversial Guinevere Norton, she chose *you*. It was part of the mystique she'd so carefully cultivated and part of what kept her in London's good graces.

She touched Bilsham lightly on the sleeve once more as she rose. 'Lord Eden and Mr Marley were pleased with the portraits I did recently of their brides.' They were, perhaps, more pleased with the portraits that would never hang in the family galleries. Eden's bride had worn only her veil, strategically draped to take advantage of the light. That one had quite possibly been her best work yet, not that Bilsham would ever see it.

Still, Eden and Marley were on the orphanage board with Bilsham. Their references would sway him the last bit of the way. She'd done enough for now. Gwen left Bilsham and moved across the room towards the door. Her work here was done. It was time to make her exit. She might have time to stop and pick up her new brushes which had arrived that morning at the stationer's. Just the thought put a spring in her step. There was nothing like new brushes! The silky feel of untouched sable, the firm bristles of pigs' hair...

If the thought of new brushes hadn't been so absorbing, she might have seen him coming. But they were and she didn't. Halfway down the front steps of Lady Shelford's town house, her mind filled with the inspiring vision of flat heads, filberts and fans, she collided with a solid mass of man coming up the same steps as quickly as she was going down.

She went down hard all the way and it hurt. The thud of stone meeting tailbone was never pleasant. 'Watch where you're going!' In her surprise at being suddenly overset, she might have shouted, just a bit. She'd made an impact on him, too, but he was going *up* the stairs. He merely caught himself with his hands and righted himself with a chuckle.

'I definitely would if all of my destinations were as lovely as you.' The words carried the nonchalance of a practised flirtation in the tones of a seductive, sibilant tenor which was probably easier to listen to in other circumstances. A hand reached down to help her and Gwen stood, her gaze riveted by green eyes that shimmered like aventurine quartz when it caught the sun.

Her stomach gave an entirely appreciative but unlooked-for feminine flip at the sight of a handsome man, green-eyed and sable-haired with sun-kissed skin. There was only one man on the town that met that description, although she'd yet to meet him except through rumour; something she made a point of *not* putting too much credence in. Rumours were generally known for their exaggeration. But the clues were there. Might this be *him*?

'Allow me to introduce myself, although I suppose I already have.' Those green eyes gleamed with mischief and humour, and something else—supreme male confidence. 'I'm Dev Bythesea.'

So it *was* him, the Duke of Creighton's heir presumptive newly arrived from India. Technically, he was Viscount Everham, a courtesy title from the Duke, although if rumour could be believed, Bythesea preferred not to use it. That was just one of the little controversies associated with him. Society had talked of nothing else since news had circulated that Creighton had sent for him at last. She offered her hand to shake. 'I'm Guine-vere Norton.'

'*The* Guinevere Norton? The painter?' His eyes showed genuine interest. 'This is a serendipitous en-counter indeed. Ganesha is smiling on me most assur-edly today. You are exactly who I came to find. Rafe told me you attended the Shelford salons.' Rafe. That would be Lord Eden. So, *that* rumour was at least true. They were friends. If Eden had told him that, it made her wonder what else might Eden have shared? 'Your reputation precedes you, my lady.'

'As does yours.' She offered the response as a warn-ing. She was experienced enough in dealing with flir-tatious gentlemen to know it served no purpose to let them be too familiar. She kept her tone cool, aloof. 'Is there something I can do for you, Mr Bythesea?' His name was so *entirely* English, a potent reminder that he was a product of the Empire, the son of a man who'd made his fortune abroad in the far reaches of that em-pire and who was also a nephew to a duke. He was 'home' now to take his place among Britain's great-est peers.

'I don't mean to be rude, but I am on my way to col-lect an order.' She kept her tone polite but aloof, unwill-ing to invite any further enthusiasm or familiarity from him. She did not want to give the impression that she was open to impromptu appointments in the street. Her reputation was carefully curated and protected by every action she took. She would not have it unravelled by a chance meeting with a man already labelled as quite the decadent and he'd only been here a month.

He was not put off. He chuckled, an easy rumble that began low in his chest, an intimate sound just between them. He smiled charmingly. 'I can see I am doing it too brown. Rafe did warn me you were not a woman easily impressed with words and flattery.' Green eyes danced, entrancing. It was hard to look away.

'I can see he was right. Let me get straight to the point. I have a proposition for you, Mrs Norton.' He gestured towards an elegant dark, lacquered carriage waiting at the kerb, drawn by a pair of matched blacks. 'Perhaps we might discuss it on the way to your errand? My carriage is at your disposal. It is the least I can do after mowing you down.'

She arched a brow his direction. 'No,' she corrected, seeing the offer for what it was. 'Let us be clear, Mr Bythesea, *I'm* the one doing *you* the favour, not the other way around. You're the one with the proposition that needs listening to.'

'Shall I take that as a yes?' He offered his arm and she took it. Why not? It looked like rain overhead and she wasn't about to turn down a carriage when a deluge threatened. Besides, a handsome man with a proposition was always an interesting combination even if she wasn't in the market for what he might be offering.

The carriage was as elegant and new on the inside as it was on the outside, the interior equipped with plush grey cushioned seats and immaculately clean glass-paned windows draped in grey curtains of a darker shade. Bythesea took the back-facing seat and stretched out, his long legs spanning the length of the interior. Those legs certainly drew the eye—perhaps he knew that? Perhaps he'd done it on purpose? He was dressed for town in dark trousers and half-boots. She let her gaze move up those long legs with an artist's objective but curious eye, imagining them instead in tight breeches and tall boots. How would such an arrangement paint? Such attire would complement the sheer, imposing masculinity of him. Although in his case, less would be more. She considered him, her gaze removing his neckcloth, thinking about the peek-a-boo glimpse of tanned skin beneath.

'Where to, Mrs Norton?' He broke into her reveries, his laughing eyes guessing too easily the general trajectory of her thoughts, perhaps because his own thoughts were willing to go where most dared not openly go. She'd have to remember that. Dev Bythesea was apparently no stranger to boldness.

'The Strand, please.' Gwen infused her tone with an ounce of primness.

'Rafe—Lord Eden—says you do that—undress people with those magnificent blue eyes of yours. Don't worry, your secret is safe with me.' He chuckled, unfazed. 'Do I meet with your satisfaction? I hope so because that's part of my proposition.' He leaned forward, the breadth of his shoulders filling the space between them, lending a sense of intimacy to their conversation. He smelled of patchouli and spice, a scent that was masculine in the extreme to her senses.

'Shortly, my aunt, the Duchess of Creighton, will approach you about doing my portrait. The invitation may already be sitting in your post.' Knowing his aunt's reputation, it probably was. If so, he'd been right to move as quickly as he had. There'd been no time to waste. 'She feels such a piece will enhance my matrimonial prospects,' Dev supplied.

Gwen arched a dubious brow. 'Are those prospects in danger?' The last time she checked, ducal heirs were not hard pressed for brides.

He gave a wolfish grin. 'They are not as imperilled as I'd like them to be.'

'I'm not sure I understand.' She wrinkled a brow, trying to divine where he was headed with this.

'My reputation is somewhat questionable, Mrs Norton, as I'm sure you're aware. My father was the Duke's brother and there was no expectation that he or his future children would ever inherit, but fate was not kind in that regard.'

No, it had not been. The current Duke had produced prolifically, but only daughters. Still, he'd had *two* brothers. But one, the next oldest, had died along with his very young wife without issue three years ago and the Duke's youngest brother, Bythesea's father, had fallen victim to a fever the year following.

The tragedies were common knowledge among the *ton*. Society had made sure *everyone* knew. The Creighton dukedom's family history had experienced a resurgence in popularity the moment the heir had been sent for—a nephew no one had yet seen until he stepped off the ship.

Bythesea continued, 'With no expectation towards the inheritance, my father was free to marry as he wished and he chose the daughter of a local raja. He had a successful trading career with the East India Company and then struck out on his own when his interests diverged from theirs. I was brought up in the business and worked alongside him, but I sold my shares before leaving. Still, that leaves me with two marks against my name. I've dirtied my hands in trade and I'm half-English, an inescapable fact that is stamped on my features and in my skin for all the world to see. Never mind that my mother is a rani, a princess in her own right in *my* country.'

His country. She made a note of that. He didn't think of himself as an Englishman—at least not entirely despite his surname—nor did he give the impression he thought that much of a loss.

'My aunt wants a portrait that will mitigate those two black marks, that will make me appear more *English*.' The emphasis he gave the word left no doubt as to how he felt about that.

'What do *you* want?' She still wasn't sure what her role in this was and they were nearly to the stationer's. The coach turned down a narrow street.

'Not *that*. I don't want a wife chosen by my aunt from families who despise everything I am, everything I value. They will never respect me.' He gave a wave of his hand, dismissing generations of England's finest bloodlines, 'I don't mind marriage. In fact, I welcome it. In my culture, a man is not considered a true man unless he is married, regardless of his age. But *I* want to choose my bride. I want marriage on *my* terms and on my time.'

His eyes narrowed, focusing in on her. She felt a certain heat start low in her belly. It had been a while since she'd run across a man her body felt worth rousing for. The glitter of his gaze told her they were coming to the crux of his proposition now.

'I want you to accept my aunt's request for a painting, but I want another painting as well. One that only you can provide, one that might not enhance my reputation, but ruin it should the portrait become known. Rafe says you'll know exactly what to do.' He leaned back against the plush grey squabs, giving her space to breathe, space to think, his eyes intent on her person.

So, Eden *had* told him about the other portrait. They must be good friends indeed, more than the old school chums from India talked about among the *ton*. Still, she wasn't pleased Eden had said anything without her permission. Eden must trust Bythesea implicitly to breach the contract for secrecy he'd made with her. But by doing so, he'd put her in a position where she couldn't plead ignorance.

'I *can* do it, but it won't help your cause. Those paintings, the ones Lord Eden mentioned to you, are meant to be seen by no one but their buyer. They're private, for the viewer only. It's part of the contract and nonnegotiable.' It was one stipulation she insisted on not only for the sake of the viewer's reputation, but for her own as well.

Bythesea, shrugged, undaunted. 'I only need it for leverage, to ensure my aunt allows me to choose my bride.'

'And if she calls your bluff? What if she dares you to display the portrait?' Gwen could not have that. It was why she picked her subjects and not the other way around. She picked people who would be discreet.

'She won't. She treasures the dukedom too much to risk it, especially with rumours already being what they are.' He gave her a pointed look. 'I'm sure you've heard them. They were circulating the moment I stepped foot off the ship, all of them steeped in ignorance and myth.' There was a touch of anger to his words.

Gwen nodded. She knew the rumours of which he spoke. London abounded with speculation not only about his antecedents, but also about his rather liberal upbringing and what such an upbringing might lead to. Would he keep a harem in his exotic town house on Evans Row just off Berkeley Square in the heart of most decent Mayfair, a house no one had been invited to in the month he'd been in London, which only fuelled more rumours, these about the decor of his home.

What was he hiding there? Did he live decadently behind closed doors? Did he roam his home in silk trousers and a turban? She knew first-hand how unfair and inaccurate such baseless conjecture could be. When she'd returned to England after Christophe's death, people had talked endlessly about her choices and not to her advantage.

'The risk is not only your aunt's,' she reminded him, 'but mine as well. I've built my career on discretion.' If she took this offer and he exposed his private painting, her reputation would be in tatters.

'I have no intentions of giving you away,' he assured her as the carriage pulled to the kerb outside the stationer's. He put a hand on her arm as she prepared to exit, his touch sending a jolt of awareness through her that she'd not felt for a long time. His voice was pitched low, his gaze serious at last.

'There is *no* risk to you, I give you my word. My father and I did not build a trading fortune on double dealings or a lack of trust. My word is my bond. I swear by the gods, I would not betray you.' He removed his hand as a footman opened the door, but his gaze burned into her, lingering until the very last moment, 'Take your time, Mrs Norton, I'm in no hurry.'

She stepped down to the pavement, aware that he had followed her out of the carriage. She wished she knew what he'd meant by that—taking her time shopping or deciding? Or perhaps he referred to both. She had a feeling that nuance and entendre were *de rigueur* when one dealt with Dev Bythesea. He'd certainly keep a woman on her toes, or if that woman wasn't careful, keep her on other body parts, *his* and *hers*.

Dev Bythesea would certainly be a handful for any woman. There was some appeal in that, especially since the handsome Mr Bythesea could probably do with a touch of humility. He wasn't arrogant, but he was supremely confident in his charms.

He held the door open to the small shop and allowed her to pass before him. She turned to glance at him, eyes meeting. What a pleasure it would be to paint that face, that body, with no need for improvisation. She let a smile play on her lips, coy and secret, as she passed. 'I think I *will* take your proposition, after all, Mr Bythesea.'

A thrill of excitement began to hum through her,

shoving aside the warnings of her better judgement. It had been ages since she'd had a moment of recklessness and thrown caution to the wind. Why not embrace it? She would paint him and in a few weeks he'd be gone, but in the meanwhile it would feel good to feel alive. Surely no real harm could come from that. It was an invitation she could not refuse.

Chapter Two

She smelled like an invitation to sex, all sweet jasmine, as she swept past him, delivering her pronouncement with a sly smile. He breathed the scent of her in, once, twice, finding a citrusy bottom note hidden among the jasmine, and then the tempting scent was gone, overwhelmed by the tang of the shop's stronger scents: the turpentine and oil of paints mixing with the alum and tannins of iron gall inks to create the unique pungency of a stationer's underlaid with the woodsy linen scent of paper.

Dev trailed after her, hoping for another waft of jasmine and taking time to study her. Women seldom intrigued him for long. They were puzzles to be solved and, once solved, his interest moved on. But for the moment, Guinevere Norton held all of that interest, his mind wanting to unravel her, to understand her, this properly dressed, properly mannered woman with the improper occupation. What a riddle she presented.

She paused by a jumbled table to sniff at a vial of ink. These smells might very well be an aphrodisiac to Mrs Norton, so rapt was the expression on her face as she moved through the little shop. She stopped to run her fingers over the bristles of a fan-shaped brush, lavishing the same loving care on the brush as another woman might lavish on a length of expensive silk. The very act intrigued him.

This was not a shop most women would find appealing. It was small, crowded. There were no pretty displays to draw the eye, no eye-popping colours, or orderly presentation of goods. No attempt had been made at tidying. That the shop described itself as a stationer's was something of a misnomer in Dev's opinion. Shelves and tables were piled haphazardly with artists' supplies, paints and brushes and sketchbooks occupying the same space, but Mrs Norton seemed to enjoy the jumble, to understand it, even. She knew what she was looking for and where to find it. Thank goodness, Dev thought, looking about. There was no clerk.

At last, a clerk finally materialised from the back room, where Dev could only imagine the chaos, which might explain why it had taken so long for a clerk to emerge. The clerk was as haphazard as his shop, necktie askew, jacket dusty, but he beamed at Mrs Norton. 'I have your order at the counter. You will have to tell me how you like the bristles on the new filbert.'

To Dev's surprise, she smiled back and the two of them engaged in a conversation about brushes: liners, riggers, filberts, fans. It might have been conducted in a foreign language for all he understood.

The conversation pleased her, that much was evident. The smile she gave the clerk was wide and generous, her blue-eyed gaze pleasant. She was at ease with this dishevelled clerk in a way she'd not been with him in the carriage. There, her smile had been merely polite, her gaze sharp. Their discussion had not been as much a conversation as it had been a negotiation, a measure-taking. Of him. Was he worthy of her talents and, most of all, her trust?

But this—being here in this cramped little shop—was a chance to see her in her 'natural habitat', as it were, and he thought he saw things in her that others might miss in more artificial settings—like Lady Shelford's political salons perhaps.

Such people would see the quintessential English-woman, a woman of moderate height who was neither tall nor short, a woman with the prized pearly skin of a well-brought-up gentlewoman, the deep sea-blue eyes and flaxen hair to go with it, not a single strand out of place in the neat chignon gathered at the nape of her long neck.

She wore a plain but fashionable and well-tailored blue dress, chosen, no doubt, to bring out her eyes; just another part of the image she so carefully curated as a respectable woman of some means, an *acceptable* woman, a woman who was always impeccable in appearance and manner, a woman above reproach, a woman who was used to being in control.

The age-old urge to disturb such perfection surged. He wanted to mess her up, run his fingers through the immaculacy of her hair, to pull it loose, to stir the surface of that cultivated façade and see what lay beneath, for surely something did. He'd seen glimpses already:

her sharp, direct wit in the carriage, the essence of sensuality she'd captured in Rafe's private bridal portrait. Mrs Norton's art demonstrated quite aptly she was no shrinking violet, no innocent. She'd tasted the world. She understood the realm of men and women. She smelled of it. *Sensual jasmine.*

The clerk said something and she laughed. Dev wondered what it would take for him to make her smile, to make her laugh like that? He was intrigued enough to want to accept the challenge. It would be an interesting pursuit. It might take the edge of ennui off the prospect of his aunt's portrait and the Season that lay ahead.

'Have you seen our latest item? It's just in from Italy and I know how you like Italian things,' the clerk was saying excitedly, leading Mrs Norton to a cluttered table. From amid the detritus of brushes in cans and tubes of paint strewn about, the clerk retrieved a box of veneered oak. The lid was trimmed in marquetry, the edges painted with ink and gold and the centre of the lid bore a painting of birds and branches in subtle browns. The clerk lifted the lid and Mrs Norton actually gasped.

'Oh, there's a place for everything!' she exclaimed softly, her hand moving lovingly over the supplies contained within: chalky pastels, oils, a place for brushes.

'And look at this.' The clerk pulled two drawers out, one from each side of the box, with dramatic flair. 'There is this as well.' He undid a strap in the lid and revealed a secret space.

'For sketchbooks. How wondrous.' Her eyes actually sparkled as she studied the travelling artist's case.

'I thought of you immediately when it came in, Mrs

Norton. If you'd like, I could add it to your order,' the clerk offered.

Dev did not think she'd decline. He'd seen the look on her face, but she shook her head. 'Oh, no, Mr Witty...' she gave a light laugh '... I'd have to save up my commissions for such a luxury. Perhaps if it's still here by Christmas, I might treat myself.' Did Mrs Norton have financial difficulties?

She finished her shopping and paid for her order. Dev stepped up to carry her packages and was rewarded with a brief look of surprise, 'Why, thank you, Mr Bythesea.' Was she not used to such courtesies or did the opportunity for them simply not arise? It begged the question: were there no gentlemen in Mrs Norton's life? The questions were starting to mount, adding to the mystery of her, and his own interest ratcheted.

At the kerb, he angled towards his waiting carriage, but Guinevere Norton hung back. Dev held out a hand in invitation. But she had misunderstood his intention and thought he meant to part ways here. 'Shall I take you home?'

Again, another surprising demur. 'There is no need. I can take a hack. You've already been too generous,' The last was said for politeness's sake. She'd previously established he'd not been doing her a favour. This was a dismissal.

'It is no trouble, I assure you.' He had nothing else to occupy himself with this afternoon until he met Rafe at their club later that evening. He found himself quite loath to part company with the enigmatic Guinevere Norton who was a cool customer when negotiating portraits, but who'd warmed considerably over Italian ve-neered wood art cases.

'It is for me, though.' She gave him one of her sang-froid smiles, reverting back to the woman he'd collided with on the Shelfords' steps. 'I have other appointments, Mr Bythesea.' Unspoken understanding passed between them. Ah, then perhaps she did have gentlemen in her life, after all. It would not do to arrive home accompa-nied by one man when she was expecting another, who, if he arrived early, might already be waiting. For the business or the pleasure of her company?

There was nothing to do under those conditions but acquiesce. Dev hailed her a cab and helped her inside, settling her packages at her feet. He made her a small bow. 'Until next time then, Mrs Norton.' He waited for her cab to drive away before he climbed into his own carriage and gave the desultory command for his resi-dence. The afternoon seemed to have lost some of its newly acquired lustre.

He was nearly to Evans Row when the afternoon took on a different sheen, this one of trouble. The car-riage came to a stop a street from home. 'What seems to be the problem?' he called up to his driver, Oscar, a fine coachman on loan to him from his uncle until he could find another.

'There's a traffic snarl, Sir,' Oscar replied, gestur-ing with his whip. 'Something up ahead—it looks like a wagon or two are blocking the street.'

Dev grumbled, 'Delivery men should know to use the alleys, for this very reason.' London traffic took some getting used to, even when one was used to the crowded markets of India.

'It appears to be in front of *your* house, Sir,' Oscar interrupted and Dev felt a twinge of guilt. Was *he* responsible for this snarl? He searched his mind, going over his mental schedule. He didn't think he was expecting anything, although he was still in the process of setting up house and deliveries were a near-daily occurrence. It was possible he'd overlooked something for today. But surely the delivery men would have gone around to the mews? Unless the delivery hadn't been ordered by him, but someone else less concerned with how their actions affected others.

A seed of worry planted itself in his mid-section. 'Oscar, I think I'll walk the rest of the way.' Dev helped himself down from the carriage and set off at a jog that became ever faster as he neared his town house. By the gods, those wagons *were* outside *his* house and those men were going in and out, carrying pictures and sofas and boxes full of assorted bric-a-brac. He grabbed the delivery man closest to him, noting his livery for the first time. 'What is going on here?' but he knew. These were men from the Duke's household and so were these wagons.

'Her Grace's orders,' the man replied nervously when confronted by Dev's stern expression and imminent displeasure.

Dev let the man go, it wasn't his fault. He adjusted his tone. 'Move the wagons around back, we need to clear the street.' He was already moving up the steps and into the black-and-white-tiled hall where the Duchess of Creighton stood in the centre of the activity, giving orders to rival a battlefield general.

'Aunt, what is the meaning of this?' He retrieved a silk banyan from the floor—one of his favourites, in fact—and carefully dusted it off, dismayed to see it thrown aside so callously. 'I thought we'd decided I'd handle setting up house on my own.' Which had been its own bone of contention.

She'd wanted him at Creighton House, but he'd insisted, arguing that English men his age, *heirs*, kept their own residences until such time as a change in domestic arrangements was required. If she insisted on Anglicising him, he would not let her pick and choose the rituals.

'This isn't about setting up house, Everham, this is about your portrait.' The Duchess of Creighton carried on, oblivious to the numerous infractions she'd committed in being here, starting with trespassing and, from the looks of his banyan, likely extended to breaking while entering. He wondered how his other things had fared. It would be a shame for them to have survived an ocean voyage packed carefully in straw only to meet their end at the indifferent hands of his aunt.

Dev dodged two men hefting a sofa through his hall. 'I don't need sofas and tables, Aunt. I have furniture that *I* like'—beautifully carved teak *takhts* and *sandooks* of ebony and rosewood that he'd brought with him from his grandfather's palace. The pieces were ornate, featuring arches, lattice work, intricately carved finials and exquisite inlays, all of the finest products and far more comfortable than English furniture.

His aunt narrowed grey eyes at him, 'Those pieces

are not fit for a proper English drawing room. What marquess or duke will want his daughter married to a man who expresses such decadence at every turn?'

'So, this *is* about setting up house,' Dev was quick to point out as he strode to the drawing room, prepared to see chaos. He was not disappointed. His teak *charpai* with its carved legs and vibrant cushions was pushed out of the way up against a wall in order to make room for the cluster of heavy English furniture now grouped about the marble fireplace. His *peerees*, low stools, joined the *charpai* along with a low table. Only the turquoise carpet had been allowed to remain, quite possibly because so much of his aunt's furniture covered it.

'The light is good in here. I thought Mrs Norton could paint you in this room.' His aunt swept past him, leaving the scent of gardenias in her wake—a pleasant-smelling but neutral flower once one got past the pretty petals, not at all an aphrodisiac like jasmine. 'I've invited her to come tomorrow and make a preliminary survey of the space so she can begin her sketches. There's no time to waste.'

That was another of her strategies. She simply forged ahead as if one hadn't spoken when one said something she disagreed with. Few had the temerity to gainsay her and he was one of them.

Dev raised an eyebrow in challenging enquiry, knowing full well Mrs Norton had not even received the summons yet. 'Has she accepted the commission? I hear she is quite selective and that her clients are chosen by her, not the other way around.'

'I sent the summons this afternoon. She will accept.

She has yet to paint anyone as regal as a duke's heir. This will be important for her. If gossip is true, she attempts to be financially independent from her family and in-laws. She can't afford to say no, not to us or to the future business our custom might bring her.'

Dev supposed that explained why she'd not bought the art case. He could imagine Mrs Norton sorting through her post this evening and seeing the note from his aunt. Would she see it as an 'important opportunity'? How would she take the summons when she was the one who usually did the summoning, all pride and financial consideration aside?

It would have been interesting to see how his aunt's request played out without his intervention this afternoon. He wasn't so certain Mrs Norton would have accepted. One might argue that she would be compelled to accept out of financial need based on what she'd revealed at the art shop, but Dev thought Guinevere Norton was a woman who always gave herself a choice. She did not paint herself into corners with no escape.

Two men came to remove the *charpai*, 'No, leave it,' Dev instructed sharply. 'Take these instead, I don't want them here, portrait or not.' He gestured to the newly placed furniture, then faced his aunt. 'This is my house and I will furnish it as I see fit.' He was careful to take some of the bite from his tone.

He might not want to be the Duke's heir, he might not have wanted to be dragged to England, but his aunt and uncle were family as sure as his grandfather and the aunts and uncles and myriad cousins he'd left back home, just less familiar to him, but no less deserving of his respect. Family was family, and family was everything. The concept had been drilled into him at a young age in his grandfather's palace and in his father's home. It was something both worlds agreed upon.

Dev could accept that as long as there was still room for disagreement. He would not be his uncle's puppet any more than he'd allowed himself to be his grandfather's. He would be the Duke if he must, because the law required it, but within that, he would be his own man.

His aunt's grey gaze went steely with impatience over his resistance. 'Everham, you simply don't understand how things are done here. You must trust in me and in your uncle to guide you. I've brought out five daughters and seen to spectacular matches for all of them. You must allow me to do the same for you. When I say you cannot pose as a maharajah reclining on that decadent day bed in a silk banyan...' she waved to the offending furniture in the corner '... I mean that no decent family will have you. Decent families don't want to be reminded they're marrying a little further down the ducal family tree than anticipated. They want their daughters to marry an *Englishman*. Horses, hounds, country estates and long lineages.' *Not half-foreign sons of third sons.*

A part of him felt sorry for his aunt, that the dukedom had come down to this—an heir who could have gone his whole life without coveting the very thing she'd spent her adult life nurturing and protecting.

She'd spent her health on five pregnancies, each to no avail in her opinion since they produced only daughters who could not inherit. She'd spent years working alongside his uncle to see the dukedom thrive economically in changing times, acting as a hostess to his uncle's political ambitions and now acting as a nursemaid in his uncle's final days. This was the work of her lifetime and it would all be handed to him.

'I am cognisant of the honour you and Uncle do me,' he said truthfully. Life was about family, but it was also about duty. Still, if a man could only marry once, he would choose the bride. It might be different if he were at his grandfather's. His grandfather had a circumspect sixteen wives and twenty-three concubines, much more restrained than some of his other counterparts and ancestors.

Of course, rampant polygamy was definitely a myth. Only royalty who had to look to the succession had multiple wives. Most Hindus did not. His father, Englishman that he was, had only the one wife and Dev had been raised in between worlds, allowed to choose which traditions he'd embrace until the choice had no longer been his to make.

'Bring the trunks,' his aunt snapped at a footman in the Creighton livery. 'I've brought the ducal robes. I must insist on them.'

Dev smiled, understanding an agreement had been reached. He would wear the robes and she would leave his furniture be. This would be the way of it for the rest of his life—a series of compromises, the constant tug of war between give and take in the hopes that in the end he would be true to himself and to those who were counting on him.

As his aunt drew the velvet robes from their careful packing, Dev wondered—did Guinevere Norton compromise? Or did she make economies like eschewing art cases so that she didn't have to? His father had made such economies in the beginning when he'd established his own trading company and with it the right to live as he chose and do business as he chose. Those economies had been his father's key to freedoms, just as, perhaps, those economies were the key to Mrs Norton's independence.

His mind was far from ducal robes, focusing itself instead on Guinevere Norton and her economies. Was she even now at home, sifting through her post, finding his aunt's summons and perhaps sparing a thought for him, maybe even a smile as she recalled their afternoon? He could imagine too well the way her luscious mouth would quirk at the corners before fully giving way to that smile.

He'd only been in her company for an afternoon and already he knew her smiles communicated a thousand messages. There'd been the smiles she'd given him, all calculating consideration as she weighed his words; the smiles she'd given Mr Witty, all friendship and openness in their shared love of art supplies; and there would be the smiles she gave him tomorrow. Dev would see to it that she did.

If he couldn't bring himself to look forward to the portrait painting, he could at least look forward to seeing her again. It had been a long time since someone had captivated him so thoroughly from the outset. There was potential there. She might be just what he needed—a final fling before settling down with a demure English rose, assuming she could be persuaded. That would be the intriguing part—giving chase and determining if Mrs Norton could indeed be caught and, if so, what would be her terms? It was a most provocative challenge and one that he would enjoy.

Chapter Three

Gwen arrived, well-worn artist's case in hand, sharply at eleven the next morning at the town house on Evans Row. Despite her outward calm as she raised the knocker, she acknowledged that a certain amount of curiosity accompanied her on this visit. This *was* the home of the early Season's most talked-about and anticipated gentleman. Rumour about it abounded in whispered conversations behind fans so often that even Gwen had heard them. While rumour in general was mostly the product of hyperbole, those exaggerations often originated in a kernel of truth. Which kernels of truth lived inside Number Five Evans Row?

From the outside, the home bore all the traditional markings of a wealthy English town house: a tall, three-storey redbrick façade; long windows with white shutters, framed from the inside with symmetrically drawn back curtains, looked down on the street. It was not exactly what the home of a ducal heir-in-waiting's home should look like: discreet, hardly the stuff of rumours.

Her knock was answered by a proper butler who escorted her through a proper white-and-black-tiled hall, notable only for its sparseness, to a small sitting room that looked out on to the street. The room was done in a most proper English decor. Pale blue striped paper featuring dark pink cabbage roses adorned the walls between white-painted wainscoting, crown moulding, chair railing and a white carved fireplace mantel. The furniture was elegantly ladylike with spindly legs and upholstered in a matching pale blue.

Gwen took a seat on the blue sofa, studying her surroundings. There was nothing to find fault with about the room. It was neat and clean. *Ton*nish London would be disappointed. She let her gaze take in the room, looking for clues about the man she would paint. Every room told a story whether it meant to or not. But as her eyes drifted over the white, carved mantel, the windowsills and end tables, the conclusion was the same: bareness.

There were no pictures on the walls, no bric-a-brac on the tabletops, not even a vase of flowers on the mantel. Bareness told its own story—a story of roots not yet planted, of a persona not yet determined. Perhaps it was to be expected. He'd only been in town a short while. Imbuing a space with genuine personality took time.

Gwen gave the space a final survey, her toe tapping beneath her skirts with impatience. She told herself her impatience was due to wanting to see the rest of the house. What would it look like? But another part of her knew better. She was impatient to see not only the house, but the man as well. Would he disappoint today, too? She was prepared for that. Second impressions were often quite different than first.

Yesterday had been filled with the thrill of first encounters. Would that thrill still be there or would he simply be a man today? As ordinary as his house? Would her stomach still flutter? Would her pulse still race with that unlooked-for jolt of awareness. Did she want it to? What would disappoint her more? The absence of that jolt or its presence?

The door opened and Dev Bythesea stood there, dressed in dark trousers and a grey frock coat worn open to reveal a green and grey paisley waistcoat shot with silver thread and a striking forest-green cravat that drew one's gaze immediately to his glittering eyes and dark, inky curls, curls just long enough for a woman's hand to enjoy mussing them, the sight of him enough to send a wave of physical awareness through her. The thrill was, most unnervingly, still there.

'Good day, Mrs Norton. My apologies for keeping you waiting. My aunt and I had…details…to discuss.'

She suspected 'details to discuss' was a polite way of saying he and his aunt had been arguing over something? Her? The portrait? She'd detected an undercurrent of conflict yesterday when he'd mentioned his aunt and certainly he'd made no bones about his preference to eschew the title when it came to addressing him. She had the sense he'd not come willingly. *'In my country…'* he'd said. No, definitely not willingly. A duke under duress unless she missed her guess. 'If you would come with me, Mrs Norton? We're ready to receive you.'

The Viscount and the Duchess were waiting for her.

Gwen stifled a smile as she followed Dev Bythesea down the empty, corridors of his home. She did marvel sometimes at how high she'd flown to reach a point where such meetings were common to her day.

She was the granddaughter of an earl, her claim to tonnish society had been tenuous since birth. Her father was an earl's *third* son. She'd wed an earl's bohemian second son who had loved art and her. Society hadn't quite known what to make of him: love him because he was easy to love or disown him because he fit none of society's moulds. They'd absconded for Italy after the wedding and she'd never looked back until she'd had to, seven years later.

After Christophe's death, she'd learned how to marry her talent for painting with the ability to provide independent financial security for herself and now here she was, preparing to conduct a commission with a duchess.

Some might say it was the high point of her career, that she'd 'arrived'. The *ton* would say it was only because they'd very generously allowed it. And by unspoken correlation, they could take it away with a single rumour. Everything she did must be done with care to ensure that never happened. They'd be taking away much more than her ability to paint.

In the public drawing room, the Duchess might have been the one sitting for a portrait. She sat posed in dark violet silks against the grey upholstery of the sofa included in the cluster of furniture nearest the door, every aspect of her person and the space she occupied elegantly arranged to enhance one another.

Those intent on catering to the highest-ranking peer

in the room would have stopped their visual peram-
bulations and looked no further. *Who* they'd come to
see was right there in front of them. But those intent
on *what* they'd come to see would look deeper into the
room. They, like her, would see beyond the carefully
orchestrated space the Duchess controlled. They would
see the low, wooden furniture with its carved legs and
intricately curved arms and backs, the brilliant colours
of the throws strewn about them.

'Mrs Norton, allow me to present Her Grace, the
Duchess of Creighton.' Bythesea did the honours and
Gwen sat, careful to position herself to take in the room
beyond the Duchess. This room was at war with itself;
the conventional English grouping at this end was at
odds with the foreign amalgamation gathered about the
fireplace at the other end. Perhaps it wasn't the room
that was at war, Gwen amended. It was the people in
it: Bythesea and the Duchess. The room was merely
their battlefield—at each end of it stood their fortresses
carefully arranged.

'I am so pleased you've decided to take the commission and that haste is no issue. We want to reveal the portrait at the end of May. I have a small ceremony planned,'
the Duchess said in polite but direct tones. Gwen arched
a brow in subtle contest over the wording. There'd been
no decision. This had been a command.

'I have some ideas about how and where my nephew
should be painted.' She gestured for the stoic footmen
standing sentinel between the long windows to fetch
something. 'I've taken the liberty of bringing the ducal

robes as a reminder to everyone of what my nephew will inherit.'

Gwen nodded patiently. This was how it always went with clients whether they were duchesses or not. Everyone was suddenly an artist when it came to their portrait. But behind her, she could feel Bythesea bristling. Ah, she thought, this was what the 'discussion' had been about. He did not want to wear the robes.

'I thought we could paint him here by the pedestal with the bust of the first Duke of Creighton as a reminder of our illustrious lineage,' the Duchess concluded. 'The Viscountcy itself goes back to the Conqueror.'

Gwen smiled politely. 'Of course. It's all very impressive.' *And very English*, she amended silently to herself. Robes *and* a distinguished lineage—such Englishness could not be thrust into anyone's face more thoroughly, *or* obviously. The Duchess was not making subtle allusions.

'I will take your ideas under advisement,' she told the Duchess, using the opportunity to rise and move the conversation under her control. 'I would like to see the rest of the house. I find it's helpful to see a subject's surroundings in order to understand the person better, his likes and dislikes, if there's a favourite item or theme.'

The Duchess rose, too, but Bythesea was quick to intervene. 'I would be glad to offer a tour, Mrs Norton. Aunt, stay here and enjoy some tea. You've worked so very hard these past few days.' The temptation to argue crackled between aunt and nephew, but the Duchess was too well mannered. His aunt merely nodded and allowed him to usher their guest from the room.

Bythesea's hand dropped to the small of her back as he escorted her through the corridors of the home, stopping before each closed door to open them and allow her to tour through the rooms. There were the public rooms on the ground floor, then up the grand staircase to the private rooms: a music room, another sitting room—the house seemed full of them—a dining room with a table long enough to seat twenty, a ballroom with a shrouded chandelier, bedchambers that overlooked the gardens. Each room like the one before: immaculately English with its wallpapers and curtains, upholsteries and linens, but devoid of any sense of itself.

There was no uniqueness here. That was unlikely to change. There wouldn't be any time. This was not meant to be a permanent residence. Dev Bythesea would move to the ducal town house when his uncle passed and that would be in no more than a few months. It was hardly worth the effort to establish a unique presence throughout the house. But surely there would be a pocket or two that were his. A man needed a retreat, after all, especially one who was so far from home.

'Shall I show you the library?' Bythesea asked as they stood in yet another guest chamber, 'Or have you seen enough?' The question was laced with challenge and Gwen answered it with a sharp, curt response.

'That depends.' Gwen turned from the window. 'Is it like all the others? If so, I think I've seen enough, unless you want to show me something useful, Mr Bythesea.'

'You mean private, not "useful".' He crossed his arms over his chest, the action causing the seams in his sleeves to strain in their attempt to contain the muscles within.

Gwen fixed him with a hard, professional stare. 'This tour is to get to know you so that I may paint a portrait that accurately reflects you. A portrait is more than the person in it. However, you seem determined to undermine my efforts. I can't decide if this tour is meant to frustrate me or to take another jab at your aunt.' Either way, she would be the one who paid. If she turned out a mediocre portrait, her reputation would suffer.

He eyed her speculatively. 'Yesterday, you promised me a portrait that would ruin me, not a masterpiece.'

She smiled coolly. 'I promised your aunt a portrait as well. I will deliver on both and how the two of you use them is up to you.' If the drawing room was anything to go on, the portraits would become another set of weapons. 'It's none of my business, as long as you don't expose your portrait as we agreed. However, what *is* my business, quite literally, is producing quality work. Each piece serves as a recommendation for the next. My livelihood depends on it.'

His eyes narrowed as he contemplated her blunt dressing down. 'Very well, then, in that case what would you like to see next?' he asked in deceptively silky tones that might be taken by the unwary for a sign of acceding or perhaps by other more sophisticated parties as seduction.

Either way, the words were a trap she refused to walk into. Did he expect her to blanch at his nuance and retreat? Or did he expect to derail her with flirtation, conflating business with pleasure? That last made her temper flare. Did he think she was so easily manipulated?

She levelled a stern blue stare at him, 'I would like to see your bedroom, Mr Bythesea.' It was a gamble, but if there was any room that would offer insight into the heart of Dev Bythesea, that would be the room, she'd wager her commission on it.

He arched a slim, dark brow. 'We've only known each other a day, Mrs Norton,' he dared to banter, dared the conflation that made her temper flare.

'I'm sure that's never stopped you before.' She marched past him to the door and stepped into the hallway. 'Your bedroom if you please, Mr Bythesea.'

He gave her a smug smile, his hand once more at her back. 'This way, if *you* please.' He led her down the hall to a set of double doors at the corridor's end and ushered her through. The moment she stepped inside she knew her instincts had been right. This room *was* different. It was alive in ways the other rooms were not, *could* not be.

This room was indelibly *him*, an abundance of sensual appeals like the man himself, so many in fact that she hardly knew where to look first. Her eyes moved to the windows draped in miles of rich russet silk, tied back with a thick gold braid to reveal the light beyond. She stepped to the centre of the room, forcing her gaze to collect itself, to take in the room piece by piece.

An embroidered cloth featuring geometric shapes on its elaborate hem draped the mantelpiece of the fireplace. Beside the fireplace was a low chair like the ones at the far end of the drawing room, a table beside it bearing a carved rosewood trifle box. She could see him sitting there of an evening, legs stretched out before him, gaze contemplative as it rested on the flames.

Her eyes moved on to the stunning cabinet of ebony with its painted panels and at last to the bed, a tall four-poster affair of carved teak dressed in silken russet covers and pillows in orange and saffron. It made her hand ache in a desire to touch the soft material, to feel the silk run through her fingers like water, fluid and cool. It beckoned to her more passionate senses, tempting them to imagine what it would be like to lie among those sheets, to savour the decadence of them.

'Well, well, is that a blush I detect?' His gaze had followed hers and divined the direction of her thoughts too easily.

'Tell me about the furniture,' she said, putting her composure and attentions back together, drawing her eyes away from the bed. She focused on the cabinet. 'Tell me about that, it is exquisite.'

'It is.' He walked towards it, stroking its surface with his hand, 'This is a *sandook* from my quarters in my grandfather's palace.' His voice dropped, all teasing and sophisticated innuendo gone, replaced by something that bordered on awe. She noted it all. He loved this piece because he loved his grandfather, because this piece reminded him of a life he'd left behind most likely for ever. 'These panels tell the story of Shiva and Sati, the greatest of all love stories.' She did not miss the reverence with which his long, elegant fingers traced the panels.

'Tell me,' she said in a voice only slightly louder than

a whisper, drawing on the privacy of the moment and the quiet intimacy of the room.

'I will tell you a summary,' he corrected, sliding her a mischievous glance. 'It's a long story and we haven't got all afternoon. It begins not unlike your western romances. Sati marries Shiva, the great god, against her father's wishes because they are madly in love. But then her father holds a *yagna*, a great ceremony of sacrifice to honour the gods. He honours all the gods but Shiva.' His hand moved to another panel. 'Sati is overcome with anger at the insult done to her husband and in her rage she throws herself into the fire and dies.' His head bowed for a moment as if he were lost in another memory.

'That's awful. Forgive me if I don't find romance in jumping into the fire.'

He slid her a glance and a patient smile, 'Ah, but that's *not* the end. Shiva is devastated and there are consequences to his grief during the many years he spends in mourning. The universe suffers during that period. There's a lesson in that for all of us about the selfishness of being ruled by personal passions at the expense of the group, I think. Suffice it to say Shiva is eventually reunited with Sati. After a series of rebirths, she is reborn as the goddess Parvati.'

He chuckled. 'See, your western stories stop too soon. They would have stopped at the fire. In those stories, death *is* the end. Even those Church of England weddings vows, 'until death do we part', assumes an ending. Not so for us—there are no endings, only beginnings. Birth leads to death; death is the gateway to life. There are no finite lines, there are no breakings, only unending circles. *That* is the real moral of Shiva and Sati's story. The hope of love is eternal.' His long fingers lingered on the final panel. 'All life is a cycle,' he said softly. 'They were destined to be together and nothing, not even death, could stop that.'

His words brought her up short. She'd not expected that. The obliging, duty-bound heir was also a romantic. If only he were right and his words were truth instead of fancy. But she knew better. Such hope was a fiction. Christophe was gone. He would never be hers again. She'd had four years to accustom herself to the idea and it still seemed foreign, strange, to wake alone, to listen for his feet on the stairs to the studio, but to know that he'd never arrive.

'It sounds complicated.' Love had not been nearly as complicated for her as the aftermath of living without it. Gwen moved away from the cabinet, hoping a change in locale would change the conversation and the trajectory of her thoughts.

'Isn't love always complicated?' He followed her to the door. They left the room, but not the conversation and the questions it raised. She suspected he was subtly probing and using the story to do it.

'I suppose it can be.' She tried for obliqueness. Perhaps he would take her vagueness as a hint that such topics were off limits in their painter–client relationship.

'Is it complicated for you?' He was probing openly now, his question confirming her suspicions. He had indeed been digging for personal information.

'I thought I was the one interviewing you,' she offered the pointed reply in warning. Loving Christophe had been straightforward. Living without him had been less so. Now, as a woman on her own, everything had to be negotiated and navigated for fear of ruin at every turn if she were not careful. At the top of the stairs, she paused and faced the Viscount before they descended, braced for yet another negotiation.

'Thank you for the tour. It will help me immensely when I think about how best to situate you for the portrait.' It always helped to lead with a compliment, an appreciation. 'Let me be clear, however, before we go any further. Painting is often an intimate undertaking, but it is a one-way intimacy. Subjects don't often grasp that. You, as the subject, must necessarily be revealed, but I do not. My personal life is off limits.' It was not the first time she'd had that conversation with a client.

Such a conversation was usually met with a stiff response of, 'Yes, I understand entirely.' But today her reproof was met with hard green eyes and a rather solemn but ominous response.

'I must most sincerely disagree. The artist and the client are intertwined in their creation. The artist cannot help but be revealed, Lady Gwen.' He managed to make it sound like another challenge as they descended the stairs to re-join his aunt. Well, so be it. She knew how to guard herself and her heart these days. It was a challenge Dev Bythesea would lose. He would find she invited no one into her sanctuary.

Chapter Four

Ah, sanctuary at last. Dev stepped inside Number Forty-Nine Pall Mall and drew a breath that was both relief and relaxation as the door of the Travellers Club shut behind him, sealing out the hubbub of the street and settling the noise in his mind. He passed his outerwear to a waiting footman and indulged himself in a moment of silence by standing in the entry hall, eyes closed, letting the quiet of the club wash over him after a hectic day of appointments—appointments scheduled *for* him, not *by* him.

Little of what had taken his time up today had been self-instigated and therein lay the source of his disgruntlement. His aunt had shuttled him from place to place as if he were one of her debutante daughters. It was a habit he'd have to gently disabuse his aunt of in good time.

But here, in the hallowed halls of the Travellers Club, he was his own man: not the Duke in waiting, not the grandson of a raja, not a man expected to pluck a wife from the bouquet of fresh English roses descending on town for the Season.

Here, he was just himself, a man like the other men present: men who'd seen the world, who were interested in the possibilities presented by that world, who enjoyed discussing their travels and their plans. Here, he was among like-minded men, not just like-minded in shared interests but also like-minded in the implicitly understood burdens of the responsibility he carried because they carried those burdens, too, often at the expense of being themselves as well.

'The usual, my lord?' a footman enquired in hushed tones when Dev opened his eyes. Dev nodded, not bothering to correct the eager young man in his form of address. He knew a losing battle when he saw it and he didn't want the young man to get in trouble with his superiors for not showing the right degree of deference.

'Yes, please. Has Lord Eden arrived yet?' It had become his custom to share a drink or two late in the afternoon with Rafe before Rafe returned home to his new wife—Rafe, who'd been his link to London and his anchor to India. He'd needed that friendship greatly in the month he'd been home.

Rafe was a man with whom he could discuss his experiences and who would understand his perspective without needing to be told because Rafe had lived it, too, had known only life in India until he'd gone to Oxford and then stayed in England to run the London end of his father's shipping business. Dev had missed his friend terribly when they'd parted at the age of eighteen. But now, a decade and a half later, he was savouring the reunion.

'No, not yet,' the footman informed him before moving off to procure the 'usual'.

'Very good, I'll wait for him in the coffee room.' Dev rolled his shoulders, feeling the last of the day's tension leave him as he stepped into the high-ceilinged room decorated with masculine elegance and a nod to Greek antiquity evident in the plaster cast of the Phigaleian Marbles retrieved by club member Charles Cockerell at Bassae. The room was moderately populated this time of day and Dev immediately spied a vacant clutch of leather club chairs in a corner where two men might manage a little privacy and conversation.

Dev made his way towards the chairs, stopping briefly to acknowledge a pair of his uncle's friends who were eager to enquire after his uncle's health. He stopped one more time to greet a new acquaintance of his own—the Duke of Cowden, Finn Tresham, whom Dev had taken an instant liking to when they'd first met. They were of a similar age and situation, both of them young heirs to weighty titles.

The difference between them was that Finn Tresham was on the other side of it, having inherited last year and taken a bride, a woman he esteemed greatly and who was already with child as a sign of that esteem, while Dev was the heir waiting for the inevitable and a man still in want of a future duchess.

Cowden rose to shake Dev's hand. 'You are just the person I was hoping to see, Everham.' He gestured to the man with him. 'Have you met Viscount Taunton yet? Taunton, this is Everham, the man I was telling you about. Taunton is just up to town. He likes Somerset too much, misses all the good gossip tucked away in the country.'

Cowden laughed and it was clear the two were long-time friends. 'I've hatched a plan I want to run by you, Everham. Not today, though. I could see your mind was elsewhere the moment you entered the room. But I'd like to talk soon. It's a venture I call the Prometheus Club.'

Dev smiled, genuinely intrigued. In their previous conversations, he'd been impressed with Cowden's investment sense. 'I am definitely interested. I'll look forward to it, in fact.' He turned to Taunton, 'Will you be joining us?'

Taunton laughed and waved a hand. 'Hardly. Prometheus gets his liver eaten out nightly. I haven't the stomach for Cowden's schemes. I prefer to cheer for him from the sidelines.'

'Prometheus was the Titan of foresight,' Cowden argued, unfazed by Taunton's dismissal. 'We'll meet this time tomorrow, Everham, and talk.'

The thought of business, real business—not this appointment keeping with tailors and teas—appealed to Dev. It put a spring in his step as he reached the chairs in the corner. He missed the day-to-day excitement of running the company with his father's partner. Each day had been full of challenges to tackle, people to meet, prices and goods to negotiate.

The import–export business was a puzzle in constant need of solving. Trade was a political tool, an economic tool as well as a diplomatic one. If used correctly, trade could accomplish almost anything. It was why the East India Company had been so successful. The Company might not have wielded trade with the most effective nuance, and certainly not without prejudice, but it had understood the power of it. So had his father and that had accounted for his father's success.

The waiter arrived with the *maireya*, a fruity, spiced wine, that Dev personally stocked at the Travellers for his convenience as a small taste of home. Rafe arrived only a moment later, sending the waiter off for another drink. 'No brandy?' Rafe commented, folding himself into the chair opposite. 'How are we going to convince London you're English if you don't drink brandy?' He chuckled, but he was only half-joking.

'You sound like my uncle, only he isn't joking in the least,' Dev took a grim sip of the *maireya* at the mention of his uncle. There were no laughing matters left to the Duke of Creighton, just an indeterminate but small amount of time. Whether it was a few weeks or a few months, the end was undeniably near.

All teasing faded from Rafe's countenance. His gaze grew solemn. 'How was he today?' The Duke was at his best in the afternoons and Dev spent every afternoon from one until four with his uncle, poring over the estate books and meeting with solicitors at his uncle's bedside to better understand the arrangement of the dukedom's holdings.

'Thankfully the estate is in better shape than he is.' Dour wryness was the best he could manage. 'Some days are better than others, but those days are only false hopes. Still, we are determined to make the best of them and the time he has left.' Dev took a large swallow of *maireya*, hoping to dislodge the thickness in his throat. 'Dammit, but I wish I had been summoned earlier.'

There'd been two years between the death of his father and Dev's summons to England, two years of knowing the inheritance was inevitable, only the issue of 'when' had not been determined. If not for his uncle's illness, he would still be in India, waiting. Foolishly, needlessly. Waiting would not change the succession. In hindsight, Dev thought he should have taken ship immediately. Staying in India had been akin to an ostrich burying its head in the sand. Valuable time had been wasted.

Rafe furrowed his blond brows. 'Is the estate in that poor of a shape? I was under the impression that Creighton ran a tight ship.'

Dev shook his head. 'He does and it will make the transition as seamless as it can be. It's that I would have liked to have known him better. He is my father's brother, the last connection I have to my father's family. They are my family, too, even though I haven't got to know them.' Yet.

He *would* get to know his aunt, his five female cousins, their spouses, their children, and he would extend the protection of the dukedom to them. They were his family now, along with a handful of more distant cousins, including the other Bythesea male of note, a second cousin by the name of Aldrich.

Dev gave a rueful smile. 'At least I'll get to say goodbye, though. I didn't have time to say goodbye to my father, not in any meaningful way. I don't even know if he knew I was there at the end. The fever took him so quickly. The blessing of consumption, if there is one amid the pain, is that there's time, time to plan, time to say goodbye and, in my case, time to get to briefly know an uncle whom I grew up half a world away from.'

For him it was a time of arrival and a time of departures all wrapped into one tricky package containing the emotion of reuniting with family and the politics of succession, the delicate balance he'd spoken of with Mrs Norton today: greetings amid farewells, blessings amid curses.

Rafe raised his glass. 'To the Duke of Creighton—may he have one more summer in the sun.'

'To last summers,' Dev replied.

Rafe fixed him with a serious stare and moved the conversation to its next logical progression, understanding the other implication of Dev's words. 'Your aunt still means to see you married before Creighton passes?'

'She is insistent. The Season begins in earnest in a week. Her fear is that if the Duke dies before I marry, mourning will disrupt courtship and a wedding for at least a year, if not longer. Unfortunately, she's not alone in her thinking. Matchmaking mamas will not be eager to see a duke go languishing for a wife if it can be avoided and the Crown would understand the need for haste. It does not like such a thinly populated family tree leaving a cradle empty longer than necessary.'

Dev slid the stem of his glass between his thumb and forefinger thoughtfully, 'My aunt and I disagree on what "longer than necessary" means. I mean to marry. I agree with her on the importance of a marriage and an heir to secure the family. But I disagree that speed should override a considerate choice.

'She'd prefer I marry the first girl who happens by with a suitable pedigree. *I* will choose my bride and she will be someone I find agreeable in a variety of ways so that we might start our marriage with something more than a title between us. That takes time. But my aunt does not care who the girl is as long as it's quick and she's from a good family and has the ability to be a duchess. Any deb will do.'

Dev swallowed the last of his *maireya*. 'I'd be more discerning if I were her. After all, my wife will supplant her and will take over all her hard work. She should at least be capable.'

Rafe chuckled. 'I don't envy you the battle. Her Grace is formidable. How did the portrait session go? Did the ducal robes fit?'

'The robes are a tight fit, metaphorically speaking, but the session was…intriguing.' A waiter hovered nearby, enquiring with a discreet arch of his brow if another glass of *maireya* would be required. Dev gave a shake of his head. He never had more than one glass. Alcohol was frowned on in his grandfather's palace— even the *maireya*, reserved exclusively for royalty, was drank sparingly. As a result, growing up, Dev had never acquired a taste for excessive drinking.

'Guinevere Norton is an interesting woman. She's one thing my aunt and I agree on, although for different reasons. *I* chose her on your recommendation regarding her other work.' He had plans for that other work. It would buy him time to find a wife he could live with, grow with. Perhaps even someone he could love. 'I showed her my bedroom today,' he added the last with a mischievous grin.

Rafe laughed and waved for another brandy. 'If I didn't know better, I'd say that sounds like quite the portrait session, but I *do* know better. Mrs Norton cannot be seduced and certainly not that quickly.'

'Why? Do you doubt my skill?' Dev probed with a joke. This was exactly where he wanted the conversation to go. He was fishing for information on the interesting artist and Rafe ought to know at least something about her that might offer him insight on what his chances were. 'Or is it that she's a consummate professional with a reputation to protect?'

She'd been very clear on that today with her scolding, which hadn't really been a scolding as much as it had been a warning when he'd had time to think about it. He'd got close to something she'd wanted to protect today and she'd wasted no time in driving him away from it.

Rafe took a fresh snifter from the waiter's tray. 'Yes, to all of that, except doubting your skill.' His eyes were mischievous. 'I'd usually never doubt your skill, but it will be nothing to her. You will waste it, like waves smashing themselves against a rock jetty, only to ebb back into the sea.'

Dev eyed his friend. 'You know that only makes me want to try more.' The idea of an affair with Guinevere Norton was growing even more appealing, exactly what he needed to say goodbye to bachelorhood and settle into marriage. A woman who could resist his charms?

It wasn't arrogance talking, it was empiricism. Most succumbed and rather too easily despite their early airs to the contrary.

What a challenge it would be, especially if that woman was already intriguing in her own right. His interest in her just doubled. 'Besides, your metaphor is flawed. In the battle between water and rocks, water wins. Water eventually wears away the rock,' he added smugly.

Rafe set aside his glass and leaned forward, all seriousness. 'You're thinking of an affair with her,' he accused gently. 'You've not heard what I've said, my friend. She is not a game, not some merry widow to be the subject of a wager in a club betting book. She would not thank you for it for one. Second, she has brothers, four of them. Third, you will lose. Not even I would wager on you. Her heart simply is not available. She loved her husband desperately and, for all intents and purposes, she does not intend to love again.'

Ah, so that's what she'd been warning him away from this afternoon: her heart, her private grief. Dev sat back in his chair, contemplative. He could respect that. His mother had mourned his father terribly. She, too, had sworn off love and marriage, but both had found her again. He'd been pleased to see her married to his father's business partner before he'd left and even more pleased to see the affection that had blossomed between them as result of their long-standing friendship.

'Never is a very definitive word,' was all he said. His mind was teeming with questions. He'd sought information to answer questions about Guinevere Norton, not to spawn more of them. 'What else do you know of her?'

Rafe shook his head. 'I know only what everyone else knows. She's the widow of an earl's second son. She paints portraits for select clients and she lives discreetly. That discretion and independence makes her something of a difficult mystery for society, so society likes to pretend she doesn't exist.'

'Except when they want a portrait done by one of their own,' Dev put in.

'Yes, except then. Then, she gets to be one of us. But for the rest of the time, she lives in a borderland. She is hard to know and that has mostly been her choice, her decision.' It was much the same price for independence his father had chosen to pay in breaking away from the East India Company, a company that would have worked him to the bone, but made no place for his son. There'd been no place for a mixed-race family in the East India Company, just as there was no easy place in the *ton* for a woman like Mrs Norton.

'Because she didn't want to fit into any of the "knowable" categories available to a widowed woman?' Dev could surmise that much on short acquaintance. She was not the sort who would be happy tucked away in the country or the sort to flit from party to party in town, drowning her grief in entertainments. There was only the grieving widow or the merry one. Nothing in between.

Rafe nodded. 'Once, there were women who would have befriended her, but only if she toed the line.' He finished the last of his drink. 'If you want to know any more about Mrs Norton, you'll have to ask her yourself.' Dev would definitely ask his own questions, but he wasn't sure asking would secure answers.

They rose: Rafe off for home and the charms of his new bride and Dev for a round of evening activities with his aunt where he'd no doubt meet a collection of suitable young misses in town early in hopes of getting a jump on their counterparts, and him.

Dev took his coat from the footman at the door, feeling the burdens of his world settle on his shoulders once more as assuredly as his coat. Evenings were for his aunt's ambitions, afternoons for his uncle's estate, but his mornings, starting tomorrow, were for Guinevere Norton. It was something at least to look forward to in this Season of duty, a bit of pleasure to balance the responsibility.

Chapter Five

She had elegant, efficient hands with long slim fingers that never stopped moving, never stopped directing the pencil across the paper, sometimes in short strokes, other times in broad sweeps, but always with intention and purpose. Each stroke heightened Dev's curiosity. What was she drawing? What did it look like? More importantly, what did *he* look like under the ministrations of her pencil? The drawing would be a reflection of how *she* saw him, just as his thoughts about her hands were a reflection of how he saw her: elegant, efficient.

He'd made quite a study of Mrs Norton in the half hour she'd been sketching him—the long fingers, the short furrows that formed at the top of her nose when she knit her brow, puzzling something out. Both very pleasing features. There were, however, two disappointments hanging in the balance against those features: first, that she'd said very little as she drew. He'd been hoping for some meaningful, insightful conversation that might shed further light on her story. After Rafe's remarks yesterday afternoon, his curiosity about her was hungry and wanted to be fed.

The second was that she'd chosen to sketch him at his aunt's end of the drawing room with its cluster of English furniture. Perhaps she wasn't as interesting as he'd hoped if she gave in to the Duchess so easily. Yesterday, he'd thought there was a likely chance she'd stand up to his aunt given how she'd not allowed his aunt to have her way with the portrait.

Then again, she'd refused the Italian art box. Perhaps she needed his aunt's money more than she needed his good opinion. He'd been disappointed in women before, women who had been promising on the surface but with nothing beneath it, their purported boldness only a mirage.

She looked up from her sketch pad and redeemed herself in a single short sentence. 'I think that's enough here. I'd like to move to the other end of the drawing room and do some sketches there.'

Dev grinned, aware that he felt relief. 'I thought you'd never ask.' He fell into step beside her as they covered the distance to the other end of the room. 'I was afraid I was to be reduced to a complete Englishman.' He slid her a sly look. 'I was afraid you might be reduced, too.' How would she respond to that rather bald and slightly unflattering truth?

'Because your aunt is the one paying for the portrait?' she replied coolly. 'You do not know me well, then, Mr Bythesea. I will always be true to my art, not the pay or the patron. If I blew every which way a patron desired, I would have no sense of myself at all as an artist and, without that "voice", I would have no reputation. I would soon find myself out of business, nothing more than a mediocre dabbler, of which this world has plenty.'

He recognised the caution in that. His aunt would not sway her decisions any more than he would. He was also a patron of sorts in regards to this portrait.

'Your aunt wants an English portrayal and you want an Indian portrayal, mostly to shock her, I think.' She slid him a sideways look in confirmation. 'I am not on your side or on her side, Mr Bythesea. I am on art's side, the side of posterity that uses art as history, as a marker of moments. I will paint the truth, which is neither entirely hers or yours.

'This portrait will keep your family's history, but it will also attest to a broader history, marking a place in time where a self-made man who had no real expectation to it ascended to a dukedom. More than that, this man is a man of mixed blood, which speaks to redefining what it means to be British at this point in time. One can be British and not live in England. By those terms, one can be British and not look like an Englishman.'

His step slowed, his mind stunned by the insight of her comment. 'That is quite perceptive, Mrs Norton. You may have missed your calling. You should have been a politician or a diplomat.'

She gave a laugh, throaty and mysterious. 'I think many artists already are.' They reached the arrangement of *takhts* and *sandooks* at the far end, the drawing room doors open to the gardens to catch the spring breeze. It caught the scent of her, wafting the air with jasmine. In the distance, a fountain burbled in the garden. He closed his eyes for a moment, letting the sweet ache for home fill him. He could almost imagine being back in his grandfather's palace.

'If you would sit here, please?' She gestured to an ebony *takht* with curved arms and he sat, letting her capable hands unknowingly smooth away the ache for home as she arranged him: adjusting his shoulders, straightening the fabric of the heavy robes, turning his head, tilting his chin. 'You have a very capable touch.' He caught a breath of her jasmine scent up close and closed his eyes, unable to resist indulging.

'Oh, no, you don't,' she scolded. He didn't need his eyes open to know she leaned over him to make a final adjustment. His mind could imagine her very well, those competent hands at his shoulders once more, perhaps her breasts impersonally brushing the white miniver fur of the robes as she straightened him. 'There's to be no drifting off.'

He opened his eyes slowly, catching her gaze with his as she stepped back. 'Perhaps some conversation would not be amiss then. Shall I tell you what I was thinking?' He tracked her as she retreated to her seat and took up her pencil and tablet once more.

'You may tell me anything you like, Mr Bythesea.'

Really? He was almost tempted to try that out, to tell her something scandalously true, that he'd liked the feel of her hands on him, that her touch was enormously capable which boded well for other touch-based exploits of a more intimate variety.

She would scold him for it, though, in those crisp

tones she'd used in the carriage on the way to the stationers and then again on the stairs yesterday when she'd drawn the line that would define the nature of their relationship as artist and client. Well, lines were meant to be crossed.

He opted for half of what had been passing through his mind. 'I was thinking how your perfume reminds me of my grandfather's palace.'

She looked up from her sketching, her pencil never stilling. 'Tell me about it—did you spend a lot of time there? You've mentioned your grandfather before.'

He suspected it was a prompt she used often with clients. How convenient it was to fill the time with talk of anything but herself. Did she think he was so egocentric as to not notice the ploy? How it made her a bystander, a wallflower even—something that was otherwise improbable. She was not the wallflower type. She made an impression on a man, something Dev was sure she tried to control. But he would not call her on it today. For now, with the soft spring breeze and the scent of her jasmine lingering in the room, he was too happy to regale her with tales of home.

'I spent summers at the palace. It was outside town and it was cooler. We lived in the city, my parents and I. My father needed to be close to the docks and warehouses, but summers were unbearably hot so he'd send my mother and I off to Grandfather's.' Dev smiled, his mind wandering back over those years.

'Please, tilt your chin to the left, don't move,' she scolded softly. 'You may continue.'

He readjusted his head, careful this time not to get

caught up in the memory. 'The palace was a world unto itself. There was an enormous wall about it for security reasons, of course. When one arrived, the wood and iron gates had to be opened. They took several men to operate. Then, once opened, they were immediately shut again as soon as the guests passed through.

'The palace was very exclusive. And quiet. A city boy recognises such things. At the palace there was only birdsong and fountains and hushed voices. Except for the zenana where the women and children lived. I have fond memories of playing there with my cousins when we were very young.'

In those days, he'd never thought such summers would end, that they would all be together for ever: he and Aahan, Reyansh and pretty, dark-eyed Aanchal, who'd wept when he and the other two had outgrown the zenana. They'd promised to come back and tell her all about their adventures in the outside world.

What he wouldn't give to be such an innocent again, for those days when he had no thought of inheriting a dukedom half a world away, when his only thoughts had been about making Aanchal smile. But that was another lifetime ago and now Aanchal was Reyansh's.

'You must miss it very much.'

'I do. I miss the palace. I miss my family. I miss myself most of all,' Dev confessed. 'I liked who I was there, I knew who I was there. But I will never be that person again. It was hard to leave him.' Their eyes met in the moment, something akin to understanding flickering in her gaze as if she truly grasped what he meant.

She dropped her eyes back to her tablet. 'Sit still,

please. You've lowered your shoulder.' She began to draw again, picking up an earlier thread of the conversation. 'The palace sounds like a true retreat, then.' It was an encouragement for him to go on, but Dev thought he'd talked enough about the palace and it was her turn to be prompted to some disclosure.

'Italy is known for its hot weather as well. Did you have a retreat for the summer months?' The question caught her off guard and she looked up this time not for the sake of her art, but out of surprise. The faint smile of memory teased at her lips.

'We had a villa in the hills above Florence. There was a loggia from which one could see the Arno in the distance and enjoy the breezes,' she offered, perhaps before the shock of surprise settled and she realised what she'd done, for in the next moment, she was notably busy with her sketching, as if she'd said too much, or as if she wanted to suppress the memories that followed. Intriguing. Dev felt compelled to push on, to keep her talking.

'You miss Italy. I hear it in your voice.' Dev gave her no chance to deny it before he took the leap across the line she'd so carefully drawn yesterday. 'Was there no possibility of remaining?' They were no longer talking about buildings and breezes, but of things much closer to the heart, to the person.

She was on the defensive, her answer cool, polite, yet not without its own revelations even as she sought to reinforce her walls. 'I have four brothers, Mr Bythesea, all of them older. So, no. There was no possibility of remaining. Just as I am beginning to believe there is no possibility of you sitting entirely still. Every time you say something, your shoulder drops.'

She would be a difficult sister, he thought. Brothers would want to coddle and protect her while she would want none of that. Was that why she'd gone to Italy? To outrun over-protective brothers? What had they thought about her choice of husband?

'I shall make a trade with you, then. I'll sit as still as a stone if you tell me about your brothers.' If she would not say more about Italy, perhaps she'd at least elucidate him on the status of her family. After all, that was hardly a secret.

'Fair enough,' She gave him one of her polite smiles—unfortunately *not* one of the smiles she had given Mr Witty. Perhaps she recognised this was the more impersonal topic. She could choose to tell him, or he could just look up the family in *Debrett's*. But then she flashed him another smile, this one a warning. He barely registered it before she dropped the stunner. 'They're called the Four Horsemen.' Rafe had forgotten to mention that.

'I take it the name isn't just because they're equestrians?' Dev replied drily, careful to keep his shoulder still. 'Hellraisers, are they?' That earned him a laugh.

'That's putting it mildly.' But she smiled as she said it. She was fond of her brothers, then.

'Do they have names?'

'Caine, Kieran, Stepan and Luce—short for Lucien.' He liked how she smiled when she said their names. It was another of her memory smiles. She cared for her brothers despite their overbearing natures. 'They would not hear of me living so far from family alone. Two of them came to Florence to actually ensure I returned after...' She paused here, perhaps sensing that what she'd meant as an impersonal story had strayed into the personal. She cleared her throat. 'Dying, it turns out, is quite an elaborate undertaking.'

Did she mean the pun? he wondered and decided she had not as she continued.

'There were a thousand loose ends to tie off and a woman alone is not always best situated for handling them. That's the truth, although it's only true because men make it so. Overbearing my brothers might be, but they handled...everything and everyone afterwards. The gallery, the villa, the house in town, the solicitors, the well-wishers who came scavenging for crumbs.' She gave a small laugh. 'For bohemians, my husband and I had managed to acquire quite a bit to be disposed of in our years there.'

He could well imagine those details—property to sell, things to pack. A life to say goodbye to, all the while being on stage. He'd tried to spare his mother as much of that as possible, tried to give her the privacy grief required.

'Coming to England was a bit like that for me,' he offered. 'I sold my interest in the trading company to my father's partner, so there was paperwork to process in the divestiture. And I will likely not see India again. I certainly won't see my grandfather again. When I took my leave of him, we both knew it was for the last time. My mother will write, of course, and we'll have correspondence, but it is not clear to me if she will ever come here or if I will ever go there. It's a risky business for dukes to go gallivanting about the globe when there's a succession to secure.' If his uncle Alistair had stayed put, things might be very different now.

'How do you stand it? Being so far away? Knowing you'll likely never go back to the place you loved? The people you loved?' she asked quietly and Dev heard the wistfulness beneath the question, the longing for what had been and what could never be again. He understood that kind of hurt, it was like an ache that one learned to live with because one didn't want to live without it, to forget it.

Dev let out a sigh, hoping it didn't disrupt the line of his profile. 'For every farewell, there is a new beginning. I am able to meet family I might never have met. You are back with your family and you have a portrait business. Surely, these are good things?' He doubted her family knew about all the aspects of her portrait business, though. It would, no doubt, shock the Four Horsemen to learn their sister was engaged in something that rivalled their own decadence.

'They are good things, in their own way.' She was back to her polite smiles, masking something far deeper. Her pencil stopped and she fixed him with a cool gaze. 'I thought we'd agreed that my personal life was off limits.'

He grinned, not caring if his shoulder dropped or his chin lowered. 'We did not agree on that at all. In fact, I remember clearly saying that I disagreed.' He rose from the *takht*. 'I believe our time is nearly up for today. Will you show me what you've done? I admit to being curious.'

She shut the sketch book definitively. 'Absolutely

not. These are just sketches and useful only to me in their current state. They will mean nothing to you. Besides, have you forgotten that your opinion holds no sway here?'

Dev made her a small bow. 'How could I forget when you seek to remind me of that at every turn? I shall see you out. I would say "until tomorrow", Mrs Norton, but I am wondering if I might see you sooner than that? My presence is required at the Camford soirée tonight. I would like you to accompany me, for the sake of your art, of course. It would offer you a chance to see me in my British surroundings and perhaps you can recruit new clients.'

She was going to prevaricate, make some sort of excuse, he could see it in her cool eyes. What was it Rafe had said yesterday about discretion being her choice? So, he left her no room to refuse.

'I'll call with my carriage at eight. Good, I'm glad that is decided. It will make the evening much more enjoyable for me, I assure you.' While everyone was watching him, he would be watching her. Artists weren't the only ones who learned from observation. He was already looking forward to what he might glean. What might she accidentally reveal if he was observant enough?

What had she got herself into? One did not have to be incredibly observant to realise Dev Bythesea had manoeuvred her into accepting the invitation and none too subtly. The invitation had been a rhetorical question at best and her acceptance had been explicitly presumed.

Now, here she was, sitting at her dressing table, having her hair put up and her Italian silk pressed into perfection for an unintended evening out.

'What do you think, My Lady?' Her maid, Eliza, set down the hairpins and stepped back. What Gwen thought was that she could have said no to Dev Bythesea's invitation. She *could* have refused just as she'd refused the carriage ride home from the stationer's. When she said no, Dev Bythesea *did* relent. He did recognise when the game was over, as opposed to escalated.

But she hadn't said no today. She'd *allowed* him to get away with it for reasons she didn't want to explore too closely. It was too late to get out of it now. Besides, sending a note at this point would be the coward's way and Dev Bythesea would know it. She would not play the coward with him.

Guinevere turned her head to one side to catch the effect of Eliza's work in profile. Eliza had done her hair in a soft Celtic knot that lay at the base of her neck, incorporating a series of braids and twists and setting them off with a gold clasp in the shape of laurel leaves.

'I think it's lovely.' She smiled in the mirror to her maid's pleasure. The poor girl hardly had a chance to dress her for evenings since she chose so seldom to go out socially of a night.

'I'll wear the carnelian pendant with the matching earrings.' A simple, elegant stone displayed in a gold setting, the ideal match for her Italian silk, a well-cut, timeless gown unencumbered by the passing annual penchant for various flounces and furbelows. 'But we'll put the jewellery on after the gown,' Gwen reminded the excited girl, 'so that it doesn't snag on the fabric.'

That was Eliza's cue to fetch the gown from where it hung on the wardrobe and help her into it. It was a carnelian red to match the pendant and it would no doubt be one of the oldest gowns present this evening. She'd had it made it for a gallery showing in Florence six years ago. Another lifetime ago. But she would not think about that tonight.

She would think, instead, about tonight. After all, that was the whole point of having permitted him to manoeuvre her into this—to force herself to move forward, to take one more deliberate step between her and a past that could not move into the future with her if she meant to live again.

Tonight was about moving forward, at least with business. She could recruit new clients, continue to build her base and it would be helpful to her portrait to see Dev Bythesea among his peers. How would being among them diminish him or enlarge him? How would a crowd change him? These were important considerations in rendering an accurate portrayal of the man.

Eliza fastened the necklace about her throat and Gwen's hand closed gently over the gem. Carnelians were for courage, the Romans believed. She would need some of that tonight. Dev Bythesea was living up to her initial assessment of a challenge in every way. He refused to be put into his place. He'd refused to play by the rules and leave her private life alone. As a result, she'd shown him more than she'd meant to today.

Mentioning her brothers had been one thing, but

she'd not intended to disclose about the villa, that place where she and Christophe would escape to, where they could be alone, where they'd dreamed some of their most intimate dreams, had some of their most intimate moments, where she'd done her first nude—of him, of Christophe. The villa and its memories were hers alone and yet she'd let Dev see how much it meant to her.

And she hadn't stopped there. She'd let him see how she *felt* about life, about loss. She'd even allowed him the knowledge of her address, the right to pick her up at home. Those allowances had been a definite blurring of the lines today between business and something more informal.

The question was why had she allowed it? There'd been inquisitive men in the years since her return to England, men who had thought to court her. She'd become an expert at rebuffing them. Why was Dev different? Because he understood her, she supposed. His experiences mirrored hers in ways an English gentleman who'd never left English soil could not understand or appreciate.

When he'd talked today of his life in India, the loss of who he'd been there, she'd felt as if he'd walked through her own mind and seen her thoughts. How she ached for Italy, for the woman she'd been there: loved, cherished, free, never confined. To be with Christophe meant there were no rules, nothing to clip her wings. He'd shown that first nude of hers at the gallery opening, proudly proclaiming her talent.

She'd not had to hide, not the way she did here in England where there were nothing but rules that had to be followed. She'd had to remake herself. Dev understood the cost and the necessity of that. Which was the best reason she could come up with at the moment for why she'd agreed to attend the soirée with him, even though every practical fibre of her being argued against it. She should not become too attached to her subject.

There was a scratch at her door. 'My Lady, Viscount Everham's carriage has been spotted down the street,' came the footman's hushed report. She gathered a wrap and a small reticule from where they'd been laid out on her bed and hurried downstairs. She would meet Bythesea on the front step. She might allow him to pick her up but no one was allowed into her house. This was *her* sanctuary.

The invitation into his life tonight did not necessitate reciprocity on her part and she had no intention of offering it. She'd given him too much already, including her address. But there'd been no way to avoid that once he'd announced he'd send his carriage.

She was out the door just as his carriage rolled to the kerb. If he'd had any ulterior motives in issuing his invitation with the hopes of glimpsing some small piece of her world, she'd just put those motives into check. *She* was her own gatekeeper, of her past and her present. She decided who had access to her life, she decided when to grant that access and to what. Dev Bythesea would need more than bold charm and sharp green eyes to overcome her defences.

Chapter Six

She was right to have those defences up. They'd only been at the Camford soirée for half an hour and Gwen could already see the veracity of her choice. She might have agreed to come on the grounds of it being good for business, but *she* would not fall prey to that charming smile or the dangerous sparkle of those aventurine eyes. She'd had time to steel herself against their powers and thank goodness for that. One only had to be in his presence a short time to recognise that Dev Bythesea in dark evening clothes was a lion among the tame toms and tabbies of London.

It was, admittedly, a rather visceral image, but it was the most apt comparison Guinevere could conjure as he prowled the Camford drawing room. It did not take an artist's eye to note that he was taller, broader, than most of the men present. More confident, too. Simply more of everything.

Which should not have been the case, Gwen remarked to herself as she stood alongside him for another round of introductions. He was the outsider and yet it seemed to her that he'd managed to reverse the roles, making the others present earn the right to his attention. Such a skill would stand him in good stead in the months to come.

'Mrs Norton, this is a pleasant addition to the evening.' Bythesea's aunt joined the small group at the long windows, a tall, elegantly urban gentleman on her arm. Her smile was polite, but her eyes were cool as they swept past Guinevere to land solidly and with meaning on her nephew. Gwen was not sure his aunt was entirely pleased to see her, or perhaps there was another source for the woman's displeasure.

Bythesea met his aunt's gaze evenly. 'I thought it might help with the portrait if Mrs Norton accompanied me.' He nodded across the little circle to Lord Bilsham. 'Mrs Norton is doing Bilsham's portrait as well later this summer, for the orphanage.'

His aunt gave another polite smile and interrupted before the conversation could move on. 'Where are your manners, Everham?' She gave her head a short, nearly inconspicuous tilt towards the man with her. 'I think introductions are likely in order.'

'Quite right.' Bythesea's own smile was tight and another inscrutable look passed between him and his aunt. Guinevere sensed an undercurrent of tension rippling between the threesome, tension that she was not entirely part of. If his aunt was displeased to see her here, she was at least not the whole sum of that displeasure.

'Mrs Norton, gentlemen, this is Mister Aldrich Bythesea, my second cousin.' The words were infused with all the perfunctory politeness required of introducing family, but none of the warmth. Of course, how could they be? Bythesea didn't know his cousin, yet there was coldness beneath his words, not neutrality.

If Aldrich Bythesea noticed the ice, he gave no sign of it. He inclined his head to the group and smiled most charmingly. 'Call me Bish, if you please. No one calls me Aldrich, that's a vicar's name.' He winked broadly at the group, 'I have no aspirations there, if you take my meaning.' There was general small talk after that until Bythesea disengaged the two of them from the group and they found their way out of doors into the Camford gardens. The evening was delightfully cool after the heat of the crowded drawing room and decidedly more private.

'This is a pleasant change.' Guinevere sighed gratefully as the evening air washed over her face. 'I've quite forgotten what this kind of evening can be like. So many people to meet and impress.'

'You should have plenty of enquiries for commissions after tonight with Rafe, myself and Bilsham singing your praises.' Bythesea flashed her a smile as they strolled the lantern-lit pathway leading towards the famed Camford fountain. There were other couples out taking the air as well, but no one within earshot.

'Do you think I lack for work?' she teased, but it was only a partial tease. She might need to work for her funds, but she could provide for herself as long as she was conscientious. 'I may not have a duke's fortune at my disposal, but I do well enough. Let me remind you, I am doing a portrait for a duchess,' she added cheekily, nearly tripping on an uneven paver and stubbing her toe. 'Ouch!'

'Pride goeth before a fall.' Bythesea laughed, reaching to steady her. 'Please, take my arm. I won't have you falling on my watch. Last I checked, it was quite expected that a lady take a gentleman's arm and you haven't taken my arm all night,' he scolded. 'People will say the fault is mine.'

So, he had noticed. She'd hoped he wouldn't. She hadn't wanted to, hadn't wanted to create for others the impression of closeness between them. 'I did not want anyone to mistake our association for something more than business. If I did not take your arm, it was for your benefit as much as mine,' she put the reason to him bluntly.

'You would not take Bilsham's arm if he were to stroll the drawing room with you?' Bythesea queried, clearly not convinced of her argument.

She shook her head, trying to ignore the pain in her stubbed toe. 'It's different. Lord Bilsham is a married man and has been for years.' She did tread carefully with her words here, not wanting to offend Bythesea. Bilsham had a reputation as an upstanding gentleman. There was no room for rumour there.

Bythesea arched a dark brow, a wry smile hovering on his lips. 'In short, Bilsham poses no risk to your reputation because he's boring?'

'Precisely.' She winced and Bythesea noticed.

'Come sit by the fountain, then, if you won't take my arm. Your toe will feel better in a few minutes.' They sat and he tossed her a mischievous grin as he leaned close, his toilette of patchouli and spice gently exciting the air. 'I'd rather be dangerous then. I don't want to be boring, Mrs Norton, not even if boring makes me acceptable.' He grimaced. 'Boring is hardly a rousing endorsement of the marital state. Why would anyone seek it out if it was nothing but ennui until death do us part. Surely, by all accounts, your marriage wasn't boring.'

That made her smile, perhaps against her will. 'No, life with my husband was never dull. It was one adventure after another from the moment the priest announced us man and wife.' Her smile widened. 'We went straight from the wedding breakfast to a yacht that sailed us to Italy. I'd hardly been anywhere besides London and Sussex. Here I was, eighteen, married and on my way to Italy. It seemed like a fairy tale and it was. I was a different person in that life. I was never boring.'

'But now? Are you boring now?'

She trailed a hand in the water of the basin. 'Things are different now. I must live quietly if I am to live freely.'

He leaned close again. 'They are perhaps different only on the surface. Beneath that, though, your passion still lives, I think. You're a woman who paints secret nudes for the *ton*.' His voice was a delicious whisper at her ear, sending an unwanted tremor skittering down her spine, a tremor of…desire? No. She was on guard against *that*. Awakening? Perhaps. She had been asleep for so very long. But that was just as dangerous. She didn't want parts of her awake. Wakefulness brought pain. 'I don't count that as boring.'

'What about you?' she asked recklessly, unnerved

by his line of questioning and what it awoke in her. She was desperate to redirect the conversation. 'Why is it that you've not married already?' He was thirty-three, plenty old to have been married. Surely he must have considered it.

He gave a dry laugh. 'That's a story nearly as long as Shiva and Sati's and it's not for tonight. But in short, once my uncle Alistair died and I knew the dukedom would come to me eventually, it simply seemed better to wait. It was clear at that point that my bride would need to be an Englishwoman of a certain background.' He paused. 'I think, given how things have turned out, it's best that I had not married yet. It would have been difficult to bring my wife here.'

Gwen was not so easily put off. 'But your uncle died only three years ago. Had no one captured your heart before that?' She couldn't imagine the ladies of his district not setting their caps for this handsome man with a thriving business and wealth.

Dev gave her a patient smile. 'You are generous in thinking I must be quite the catch. In that regard, India is not unlike England. Whether I am here or there, I am still a man caught between worlds. It makes me a rather dubious matrimonial prize.'

It was exactly an answer to her question, Gwen thought. She sensed there was more to it. Who had turned him away? But he'd already made it clear that would not be discussed tonight. In truth, it ought to be irrelevant to their business, and it was certainly proof to just how far afield their conversation had wandered.

She closed her hand around the carnelian pendant.

Courage. But for what? To resist? To maintain her firm line of not mixing business with pleasure? Or the courage to relax a bit, to engage in getting to know Dev Bythesea, and perhaps if the opportunity arose, to play a little, to flirt with this man who saw the world as she did, who understood what she felt.

To have such a companion would be like old times. But not old times because it wasn't Christophe she'd be having those conversations with or be flirting with. A spark of guilt threatened. Was it disloyal to Christophe to seek those special things that had been such a part of who they were together with another?

She recognised her mistake too late. 'Your pendant is lovely.' His gaze dropped to her decolletage, drawn there by her hand. Did he think she'd done that on purpose instead of reflex? 'May I?' His hand removed hers, his fingers warm on her skin as he held the pendant. 'Carnelian. Very pretty. This is a beautiful setting.'

'It's for courage,' she said softly, 'according to the Romans.'

'Ah, is it?' He smiled and released the pendant, his fingers skimming her skin. 'Not so different than the Hindus then. The carnelian is a chakra stone—the *muladhara* chakra. A chakra is a source of inner energy,' he explained. 'The *muladhara* chakra is the source of balance and security, not unlike courage.'

She was needing all that courage at the moment. This—sitting near a fountain, talking quietly in the semi-darkness and partial privacy of the garden—was nice. Sincere. In these moments she felt as if she didn't have to manage impressions, to present a face, to hide, and she sensed Dev Bythesea felt it, too—that for a few moments he didn't have to perform, didn't have to manage his impressions either, but instead he could just *be*.

'It must be difficult for you to always be on guard, everyone watching you, meeting a new family and expectations to meet on all fronts.' She spoke her thoughts out loud, not realising how non sequitur they might sound to him. They'd been discussing chakras and carnelians and her thoughts had leapt to feelings of the moment, feelings that were not engendered by their conversation topics but by whom she was with.

He laughed in the darkness, his laughter blending with the burble of the fountain. If he found her conversational offering divergent in the extreme he gave no sign. 'There is so much I could say to that. I could talk all night.'

Part of her wished he would. She liked listening to him. He had intriguing insights and different perspectives. At least, that's how she explained it to herself as opposed to 'he was a good storyteller and she liked the sound of his voice'. That explanation sounded too desperate and lonely.

'Being the focus of social attentions is new *and* old,' he said and she waited for the story that would follow, another piece of him to add to her drawings. 'Life in the Raja's palace is peaceful, but there is also a fishbowl quality to it. The Raja's grandson is always under scrutiny, especially when he is also an Englishman's son. A person's behaviour reflects on his family. This is not the first time I've been "on guard" as you say.'

He leaned close, the whisper of a smile on his lips,

'But we're not on guard now, are we? You and I, here in the garden,' No, but she ought to be, yet a part of her made war on her common sense, wanting to be off guard for just a while longer, and that part of her won, perhaps because she wanted to show empathy, wanted to offer understanding or perhaps something more was at work. Whatever it was, she found herself talking about things she'd not shared for years.

'A fishbowl is quite apt,' Gwen said thoughtfully. 'It was like that for me when I came back from Italy.' Back. Not home. Italy was home, the life she'd made with Christophe was home. England was not part of that—something she and Dev had in common, she realised. 'Everyone was watching me: my parents, my brothers, my husband's family. I am sure much of it was motivated by kindness and concern. People wanted to plan my life, make decisions for how I would live. I think they wanted me to know I'd be taken care of, but in exchange they wanted me to act a certain way.'

'And you had to decide who you would be now in this new world.' He reached for her hand and she let him take it because it seemed natural to do so as they discovered yet another similarity in their experiences.

'I decided I would be myself, that I would not turn my back on who I'd become in Italy. I'd left England as an eighteen-year-old bride, barely out of the school room and most definitely untried. In Italy, I'd grown into adulthood, discovered myself. I did not want to give that woman up. But even in trying to save that woman, I've had to keep her under wraps. She is not entirely free despite the cost of that decision to save her. If I'd given her up, I could have retired to the country and lived in quiet gentility on an estate offered from my husband's father. He would have owned me then.'

The Earl would have had leverage with which to win any argument should they come into conflict. She would have had no voice. Her own family would have taken her in, but that, too, came with caveats, most particularly that she would marry again, well and soon, in order to not overburden the already stretched coffers of an earl's third son with four sons of his own.

'Now they don't know what to make of you.' Bythesea nodded towards the drawing room to indicate that his comment encompassed more than her family. 'You and I have that in common as well. Those people in there don't know what to make of me either. Am I an outsider because I was raised abroad? An insider because of my impending inheritance? Am I a man they can use, a man they should marry their daughters to, or a man to ignore?'

He gave her a considering look full of honesty and naked truth. 'I imagine it is the same for you—what do they do with an earl's granddaughter who married an earl's second son, but who refuses to go quietly into the country or remarry but instead prefers to support herself through her art? Art which is too good to ignore, art they *want* to hang in their galleries because it features them at their very best.'

She gave a light laugh, hiding her surprise at having been so well understood, too well, actually. How was it that a man she'd known for a handful of days saw her so clearly when the society she'd moved in for four years did not? 'As you say, we have certain things in common.' She was aware their hands had intertwined, their fingers lacing together as his thumb ran over her knuckles in a slow, thoughtful motion.

'We, you and I, must always be on guard, always considering the face we put forward, not just for society, but with our families. Perhaps with them most of all,' he added wryly.

'Speaking of families, tell me about your cousin. Your aunt did not seem entirely pleased with him tonight.'

He sighed and looked down at their hands with a shake of his head. 'Aldrich Bythesea is a walking cautionary tale about what happens to dukedoms that only sire daughters.' He glanced up, the playfulness gone from his gaze. 'He is what I protect the succession against. He's the next male heir should I die without an heir or if I die before inheriting.'

The splash of the fountain was the singular sound in the background as she thought through that. 'But he can't inherit,' Guinevere said. 'Not all of it.' A benefit of being part of a third son's rather large family, was that one was well-versed in how the family tree grew. Her grandfather's earldom would go to her uncle, her father's oldest brother, and if he were to die before inheriting, it would go to her uncle's son, her cousin, Phillip. And then, if the worst happened, and her uncle and Phillip were dead, it would go to the second son, her uncle, Marcus, and then his son and so on. She called on that knowledge now.

'You're right. Without me, the Creighton dukedom

will cease to exist. Bish isn't a direct male heir. All he can aspire to is the Viscountcy. He can be Everham, but never Creighton. If I fall, it all falls with me,' he said quietly.

It was a weighty concept and they sat with it in the still solemnity it deserved beneath the night sky. 'That certainly gives more onus to the portrait and your aunt's haste,' Guinevere offered after a while. This was more than it had looked on the surface. On the surface, it had appeared to be simply the age-old dance between parental figures and reluctant bachelors, the final, forced push to the altar to do one's duty. Men were often just as compelled to wed as women even if the reasons for it were different. But beneath that veneer, something far greater lurked than the personal preferences of one man. She thought fleetingly of Bythesea's story of the mourning god, Shiva, and his selfishness.

She felt his grip tighten on her hand. 'I must marry, but *I* want to pick the bride and I do not know if I have the time left to me to find her or even if she exists.' She'd never heard desperation in Dev Bythesea's voice before, never heard anything less than confidence, but she heard a tremor, a thread, of desperation now.

'There is still time for the portrait to do its work. We will find you the bride you want,' she vowed solemnly, feeling suddenly moved to great depths by his words. 'The right woman will see your aunt's portrait and will know she's the woman for you.'

'Assuming she's among the small pool of debutantes coming to town.' He gave a dry chuckle. 'It's a little bit like the story of Cinderella, isn't it? Only I have a por-

trait and not a glass slipper to fit to a lady.' He paused
with a sigh. 'I think that poor Prince also had succession issues to deal with, although the story doesn't explore him much. No one ever talks about the pressure
on men to marry. I think there should be a fairy tale
about princes.'

He gave her a wry smile, but they didn't laugh. It was
not a remark made in humour but in dead seriousness.
To laugh would demean it.

A long, awkward silence followed. What did one say
to that? It was a telling comment about how deep their
conversation had gone, how personal it had become. It
was a warning that the conversation had gone too far.
She needed to put an end to it.

Guinevere swivelled her ankle, testing her stubbed
toe in its slipper, and found the pain gone. 'It's late and
I have a very pressing client tomorrow.' She smiled at
her jest to lighten the mood. 'Might we go before I turn
into a pumpkin?' Before the intimacy of the fountain
coaxed any more secrets from her, or any more pieces
of her past, pieces she usually kept locked away, and
definitely before she developed something more than
objective empathy for the man she painted.

'On one condition…' he rose and held out a hand to
her '…you take my arm on the way back inside. The
gods have already warned you once.'

Gwen laughed and slipped her arm through his.
Fate had been tempted in more ways than one tonight
and she had no desire to tempt it further. This sudden,
fierce, attraction to Bythesea had caught her by surprise
from that first day on Lady Shelford's steps and she still

didn't know what to make of it, especially now when the attraction was more than physical. Perhaps physical she might have understood, might have managed, might have ascribed to mere loneliness. But this was so much more. This was an attraction of the mind, of the soul.

She simply wasn't ready for it. She might never be ready. Her free hand reached again for the carnelian pendant. Maybe she simply wasn't brave enough for that sort of an adventure any more. She'd lost much when she'd lost Christophe. To try again to find someone with whom she might share such a connection, if it was even possible, meant to court great risk for what would likely be an impossible quest.

Dev was sure to disappoint eventually. She'd already found a great passion and lost it in her lifetime. The odds were against her finding two when so many people rarely found one. Even if she did find it with Dev, he was not for her. He would leave her in order to do his duty. On such grounds, it made it very hard to convince herself to give up the safety of her harbour and venture the seas of romance even with a man like Dev Bythesea at the helm.

Chapter Seven

Damn. The odds had very nearly been in his favour. He'd been one storm at sea away from a viscountcy. Bish tossed back a drink at Mackey's off St James's, a mediocre club for mediocre men who couldn't climb the ranks into the hallowed halls of White's, or Brooks's or the Travellers, where his cousin was no doubt sitting in a fine leather seat right now, drinking whatever it was he drank—rumour had it *wasn't* brandy, but something strange and foreign—surrounded by the *ton*'s finest.

Bish checked his watch and rethought. Maybe not. It was just a bit past midnight. Perhaps his cousin hadn't made the club yet. Perhaps he'd lingered elsewhere with the lovely portrait artist and was lingering with her still. Bish signalled for another drink.

Some men had all the luck and some men, men like himself, only had part of it—the part that made a man hungry for more, the part that made a man realise that for some men luck had to be manufactured. What his cousin had been handed on Fate's silver platter, Bish would have to serve to himself.

He took the drink from the waiter and took a small, considering sip. Where did one go from here? His cousin's arrival was certainly a setback. He'd known from childhood the dukedom would never be his as the grandson of his great-uncle's brother. He was an appendage to greatness, a limb on the branch of the great Creighton tree, but a limb too far from the main trunk for it to be useful for anything beyond invitations to London's parties. Which was no small thing in its own right. Opportunities, to be fair, were indeed made in such ways.

Bish knew he lived better than most. He'd attended Oxford. Sat for the law where his quick mind and his good looks had served him well. Now, he was an esteemed barrister with offices at Greys Inn. In time, he'd ascend the bench as a justice of the peace because of his family connections, even if he didn't have an illustrious career. But he wanted more and there was the Viscountcy dangling before him, the juiciest carrot of them all. What did he care if attaining it destroyed the dukedom? *That* was never going to be his anyway.

Now, his cousin was here, though, the current Duke teetering on life's cliff in a daily battle against the inevitable. One might conclude that time had run out for Bish, the heir secured and hence the succession. Bish swirled the brandy in his glass. A man wishing to claim a title had to prove his worthiness to it. When the current Duke died, his cousin would have to put forward his petition as the heir presumptive.

It *should* be a pro forma matter. These things were hardly ever contested and his cousin was the oldest son of the previous heir presumptive who was directly related to the current Duke. That part, on the surface, was fairly straight forward. *Unless* Bish could show that Dev Bythesea wasn't. It wouldn't even matter if his claim wasn't true, it only mattered if Bish could make the Committee of Privileges believe it to a large enough extent. Muddied waters were all he needed.

He sat back in his chair, his eyes closed, his sharp mind running over the three claims needed for an heir to secure the succession. One, he must be over twenty-one. There was nothing Bish could do there. Bythesea was thirty-three. Second, he must be a member of the Church of England and, third, his parents must have been legally married before he was born. It was the last two Bish would play with. He'd spent his adult lifetime preparing for this moment, for these arguments and now the moment was here.

It would have been so much easier if his cousin's ship had sunk, but it hadn't, so Bish would have to make his own luck with the tools he had. He'd seen the men to-night at the Camford soirée. They'd not been sure what to make of his cousin. He could use that uncertainty. It would be easier to muddy the waters of his cousin's claim if men didn't like him or were frightened of him and what he might mean for the future of the peerage.

Perhaps the Committee of Privileges and the Lord Chancellor would decide his 'concerned' enquiry would be an answer to their very proper Church of England prayers and provide a reason to keep Dev Bythesea from the title, especially if Bythesea could be socially discredited—a man too scandalous to be welcomed.

Never mind that the aristocracy was full of its own eccentrics. What one might tolerate from an insider was far different than what one would allow from an outsider. Especially, if it meant making the lucrative Creighton dukedom extinct. While a sufficient portion would stay with the Viscountcy, there would be plenty of land and money that would revert to the crown to be divided up or reallocated.

Bish chuckled to himself, imagining it. It would be like a feeding frenzy he'd seen once—sharks ripping apart a fish in the water, fighting one another in their avarice. Those who emerged with scraps from the feast would be grateful and further favours would be forthcoming. He began to make a list of things to do in his mind: discredit his cousin by fomenting scandal, start circulating rumours—even baseless ones had teeth. Then, do his research so that when the time came, the teeth had come in on those rumours. In short, sow dissension, doubt and disturbance among the already questioning ranks of the *ton*. It was one of his favourite strategies.

Dev would wager a cask of *maireya* Mrs Norton had to be running out of strategies for keeping him at arm's length. It had been three days since the Camford soirée and their surprisingly intimate discussion in the garden. In that time, she had busied herself sketching him and various objects around the town house, keeping her conversation businesslike in the extreme. No doubt because she'd realised in retrospect that she'd said more than she would have liked in the Camford garden, enough, in fact, to have crossed her own self-imposed lines and now she was eager to re-establish them. Today, she was doing that by sorting rather too energetically through the shelves of his library.

Ostensibly, she was searching for tomes that might show to advantage in the portrait while, in her words, sending a message about the diversity of his education which encompassed *both* eastern and western canons. But personally, Dev thought she was using the search to mask other reasons emotionally closer to home.

'You're stalling,' he drawled, hitching a hip against the long reading table where her selected books were piled. He glanced at the book she added to the stack. 'You already have the *Iliad*. We don't need the *Odyssey*, too. I think we have enough.'

'Not yet, I want to be sure.' She turned back to the shelves. 'I need a few more books with olive-toned covers and perhaps red. It's not just the titles that have to be right, but the colouring, too,' she insisted with professional briskness.

He pushed off the table and moved towards her, taking the book from her hands and setting it aside. 'I need you to answer a question for me. Is it me that unnerves you or was it our conversation the other night that has set you on edge?' Perhaps it was both, but he'd let her decide what she was comfortable confessing to.

For himself, the conversation at Camford's had certainly been *something*. He wouldn't say it had bothered him, that sounded too negative, as if the conversation had been disturbing. He'd not been disturbed as much as he'd been aroused by it, by her, by exploring the facets of who she was in the little gems of information she had advertently dropped. He suspected that was what was haunting her now.

She'd given away too much of herself and she didn't understand why or didn't want to admit to why—that she felt it, too, this attraction that simmered so potently between them, that drew them not just physically, but in other ways as well. Would she act on it? Was that part of her dilemma, too, as her loyalty did battle with her husband's spectre? If so, he could not help her there. How could he compete with a ghost that had the advantage of being viewed through the rose-coloured glasses often afforded the dead?

Her gaze arrested and lingered on his at the question. 'Why would you think that either was unnerving? If I seem brisk, it is because we have a deadline to meet. You said yourself you felt time was of the essence. I am merely trying to expedite that.' She moved away from him with a swish of her skirts and began sorting the books on the table.

'I think we are finished here. Tomorrow, we can work at the studio.' Would that make her feel more comfortable? To be on her own ground? Safe ground that was hers, but not hers in the way her home was. She'd not wanted him to step one foot inside her home. Had that been for propriety or protection?

'Your library is most impressive, Mr Bythesea. Thank you for sharing it with me.'

'Is that all you find impressive?' If she wasn't going to answer the question, he wasn't above pressing the issue with a little innuendo.

'Besides your audacity?' she said sharply, gathering her things. 'I think you may have confused notice for attraction. I notice you, Mr Bythesea. I notice your green eyes, your long legs, the charm of your smile, because I am an artist. It is my job to notice them in order to understand you and how best to portray you on canvas. Do not mistake that for personal attraction.'

'Call me Dev, or Devlin if that's more comfortable. There should be no more "Mr Bythesea". If you're going to deliver such scathing scolds, we should definitely be on a first-name basis.' Dev laughed, knowing that was the opposite of what she expected. She expected a man to be chastised by her strong words.

'Devlin? Is that your full name?' That had got her attention, proof that his comment wasn't as far from the mark as she would make out. She was attracted to him, interested in him. He'd not mistaken that.

'It was a compromise between my mother and my father. She wanted Dev, which means immortal and charming to some, poet or god to others. My father wanted something that retained a sense of my English heritage as well, so they settled on Devlin. What about Guinevere? Ballrooms are full of girls named for Greek mythology and flowers, but, as English as it is, there are not so many Guineveres.'

'My mother liked the King Arthur stories.' Some of the tension he'd sensed in her eased. 'So, the story of my name is fairly straightforward.'

'See, sharing isn't so hard.' He offered her a smile and held the library door for her. He'd taken to seeing her out on these visits instead of turning her over to a footman. Perhaps it was because he was loath to see the best part of his days come to an end before it was even lunch. Perhaps she would stay longer if he did not question her so fiercely, yet such questions weren't entirely for his benefit alone. She'd locked herself away so thoroughly he was convinced she was not only hidden from the world, but from herself as well.

'Information is power, Mr Bythesea,' she cautioned.

'Dev,' he prompted.

'Information is power,' she repeated, ignoring his request, 'as are words. Names. With them we breathe into existence things perhaps best left unspoken, left unborn.'

She was warning him away and he refused to be shooed off. 'Or left for dead? Like the past?' They reached the front door and he helped her with her wrap, letting his hands linger at her shoulders, letting his voice linger at her ear as he heard her own breath hitch in the tiniest of gasps. *Noticing* him, no doubt.

'Don't fool yourself, Guinevere, the past is never really dead. It lives in us no matter what we tell ourselves. We cannot outrun the past any more than we can outrun who we are. Who we are is who we have always been and who we will always be.'

She shot him a look that bordered on scathing. 'You're quite the sage, Mr Bythesea but I must respectfully disagree. Good day.'

He let her leave without argument, knowing those were words she didn't want to hear, words she'd spent the last four years defying. If ever there was someone who wanted to erase the past, to make herself anew, it was Guinevere Norton. Did she realise that wasn't true, though? That she only wanted to erase part of the past, the painful part? Did she realise, too, that no matter how she dressed or the face she put on for society, she was still the same person inside who had loved fully and who, based on that love, had taken extraordinary risks?

That was the woman he wanted to know, the woman he wanted to find, not only for the sake of his own curiosity, but for her sake as well. One only needed to be in her presence a few days to know that a woman like Guinevere Norton should live life awakened. And, yes, he wanted to be the man who was responsible for awakening her, for bringing her back from the shadowland in which she'd confined herself.

She should not have brought him here. Dev was prowling her studio on the Strand with the same intensity he'd prowled the Camford soirée. Only this time, *she* was the focus of those sharp green eyes, she *and* her space. Guinevere looked up from mixing paint, watching him warily, waiting for him to spring with his questions and his probing as he had yesterday in the library. She'd thought she'd be safe here, the studio a kind of neutral ground. But nothing was neutral when it came to Dev Bythesea—odd for a man who spoke of balances. But where balance was a middle, neutral ground to her, balance was simply the tension between extremes to him, a juxtaposition of opposites. She knew better now that it was too late.

He stood with his back to her, his gaze fixed upon the view of the Thames out the long windows she paid extra for in rent and which were well worth it. 'Your studio is beautiful, Mrs Norton. Does your family approve?'

'About as much as your aunt approves of your home furnishings. Tolerate is the word I would choose. Not approve. As long as I behave decently, it is something they can pretend does not exist.'

'Then your studio is doubly impressive since you must sustain it on your own along with your residence. Not many women alone could afford to do so,' he complimented, but she sensed a probe hidden within it.

She put down her brush. 'Is that your way of asking how my husband left me situated after his death?'

He turned from the window and instinctively took up the subject's perch on the chair she'd arranged to catch the light. 'It is something of a curiosity point for me. You are a puzzle in that regard. I thought you would buy the Italian art box.'

She set aside her palette and moved to situate him, trying to ignore how her hands revelled in touching him, revelled in feeling the power of him beneath the cloth of his coat, the hard strength of muscle, or the straight line of his jaw where it met the angle of his chin.

'My independence is worth more to me than the ability to purchase extensive wardrobes and luxury items on a whim. I do well enough during the Season and in the early spring. But autumn and winter, people are not focused on portraits. I must budget carefully for the lean times. Rent does not stop even if commissions do.'

'But surely, you have your widow's portion.'

'That's hardly a subtle enquiry.' She stepped back to

survey her arrangement and to select one of the books from his library.

'Does it need to be? I thought we decided we needn't be on our guard with one another.' Precisely because of that, she needed to be on watch. He would have all of her secrets out at that rate.

'That portion must last me the rest of my life. I do not touch it and will not touch it until I must. It is for when the day comes there are no commissions or I cannot paint.' That day had come too soon for Christophe. She switched out the book for another, ignoring the memories such a statement coaxed to the fore. 'There, I like the red leather cover better and who can argue with Plato?' She strode back to her easel, feeling more protected with the barrier between them.

'Such a statement suggests you mean to spend your life alone. You do not intend to marry again?' The feeling of protection had been a misnomer. His questions rode roughshod over her silly barriers.

'Why would I marry? My brothers will further the family ambitions with their marriages. I am no green girl who must wed, nor do I have a dowry that makes me a candidate for most men,' Gwen offered her sanguine, rational answer.

'Those are reasons other people marry. Why not wed for yourself? Why not wed for love?'

Dear heavens, the man did not pull his punches even when warned away. Gwen dabbed her brush thoughtfully in the white paint on her palette, mixing it with the green. 'I have already married once for love. I do not think it is likely I will do so again. I have already had my great love. It would not be fair to someone else, to make them compete with that.'

'Companionship, then?' Dev suggested. 'Perhaps it needn't be a great love.'

'Companionship is nice, but why would I settle for that when I know there can be so much more? That I *had* so much more?' She fixed him with a probing stare. 'That seems rather hypocritical coming from you with your story of Shiva and Sati. You are a romantic at heart, Dev Bythesea, and I doubt you would settle for mere companionship if left to your own wishes.' She gave a wry smile, seeking to shock him, perhaps. 'Besides, I may have many forms of companionship without marriage if I choose.'

She had chosen that once, soon after she'd returned. It had satisfied certain wants at the time, but she'd not been keen on repeating it. No one had appealed to her in that way since. Until, well…until now, she supposed. As much as she might deny it, she did feel some attraction to Dev Bythesea that transcended the 'notice' she'd spoken of yesterday. But how much of that attraction was generated by his efforts or by her desire? 'Passion is not love.'

Dev's eyes rested on her for a long moment, his green gaze thoughtful enough to make her fidget. What did he see? What had she inadvertently shown him? 'You loved your husband deeply, and he loved you the same, he must have for you to believe so strongly that you will not find such depth of feeling again in this lifetime.' He paused and she waited. 'That is a wondrous thing to have experienced, but all the more tragic to have lost because of its wonder, its rareness.'

There he went again with his balances. 'The great pleasure must be balanced with great pain? Is that it?' Gwen smiled.

'Yes, but that's not where I was going with it.' Dev chuckled and she had to remind him to adjust his shoulder. 'Do you think, having experienced such an incredible relationship, that it holds you back? This idea that nothing else will ever measure up so why try?'

'I did try.' Would that shock him? Probably not. His grandfather had sixteen wives. 'Once. I have not been compelled to try again.'

'What happened?' Dev asked quietly. The sincerity of the question was more shocking in its simplicity than her revelation. He'd turned the tables on her yet again. Where most would have at least looked askance at her admission and found it scandalous, he did not. His concern was for her, for why the affair had failed, nothing more.

'I'm not sure, really. There was nothing technically wrong. He was kind, solicitous, patient. He was a widower, too. He was older, though. Still, he understood my loss. He didn't pressure me about my life in Italy or my painting. It should have been enough.'

But it hadn't been. His lovemaking had left her unaffected, unmoved beyond the comfort a warm body in bed beside her. 'I knew I wanted more and I knew, too, that I would not find it, not with anyone.' Christophe had become the stick against which all men, all attraction, all romance, would be measured. All would fall short. She'd stopped looking, stopped hoping for the impossible.

Dev nodded, thinking for a moment. 'Is it really all that surprising the affair failed? Sex in itself is not moving on, Gwen. It engages the body only in a physical exercise. It does not necessarily engage the mind, or the heart, not unless *we* allow it. And you did not.' No, she hadn't. Perhaps she feared what would happen if she did, of what she might lose again if she were to find what she was looking for.

A slow grin spread across his lips that was answered by the warm heat of attraction unfurling low in her belly. Oh, he was dangerous to tempt her like this and she was wicked to allow herself to be tempted by images of such exercise. 'Do you think your husband would want you to remain locked in the past? To not allow yourself true pleasure?'

'Perhaps it's not his memory that keeps me there but my own, by my own choice. Perhaps I don't wish to leave the past just yet,' she answered, drawing her gaze back to the easel and applying her brush as if covering the canvas would also cover up her errant thoughts, stop them from interrupting the existence she'd carved out for herself.

'I've upset you,' Dev said. 'That was not my intention.'

She hazarded one more look over the easel. 'Wasn't it?'

'Maybe you need upsetting.' He smiled. Did nothing anger him? She'd like to upset *him* for once.

There was a knock at the studio door, a messenger with a note for Viscount Everham. Dev broke the seal with an irritated flick of his thumb. 'It's from my aunt,' but she watched the irritation on his face change to something sterner, darker. He rose abruptly. 'I must go, immediately.'

'It's not your uncle, is it?' Fear for the Duke's health gripped her.

Dev shook his head. 'No, it's worse. It's my cousin.'

Chapter Eight

It was worse than she thought. She was becoming infatuated with him. It was time to be honest about that before it got out of hand. Guinevere studied the sketchpad in her lap, taking in the half-formed profile of Dev Bythesea. How long had she been staring? She'd thought spending an evening in would help her refocus her thoughts and regain perspective. It had not.

She should not have brought her work home with her. She should have left him at the studio. As if she could lock him out of her mind when she closed the studio door. But he was fast becoming 'not the usual' client.

It had been simple in the beginning. He was just a client. Actually, he wasn't even that. His aunt was the client. He was merely the subject. All she had to do was paint him, sell him to an audience of aristocrats so that he could make a good marriage and continue the dukedom. It was hardly any different than what she'd done for countless debutantes whose parents wanted their daughters portrayed in a certain light. Nor was it any different than the portraits she'd done for the sake of posterity, like the one she'd do for Bilsham at the orphanage. And yet it was not like anything she'd done to date.

Now she was sitting alone with her thoughts. That was *his* fault. Dev made her think too much, made her pay attention to things she'd rather not pay attention to—not just in the world, but in her mind. He made her think about Christophe, made her think about the past, about the present, about her choices, her losses. Most of all, he made her think about the future, something she resolutely did not do beyond safeguarding her funds.

She'd succeeded so far in avoiding the long empty road of the future because she focused on each day, roping them together like pearls on a string until they became a week, a month and then another month, quite by accident and without intention.

She focused on each day, each painting, so that she didn't have to think about this year or the next rolling out before her without Christophe beside her, with her mind haunted with memories of how it had been, and how it would never be again. It was the only way to manage the loneliness without it overwhelming her, although tonight she felt as if she were losing that battle.

Damn you, Christophe, for leaving me alone.

Angry tears threatened. She swiped at them before they could smudge the sketch. He'd left her alone in ways that transcended his physical absence from her life. When he'd died, he'd taken her dreams with him. Not just dreams of art and love, but dreams of a future that involved a family, motherhood and children.

She and Christophe had not been in a hurry for those things, those were dreams for a later time, time they'd thought they had.

To reclaim those things without him meant she'd have to open herself to love, the risk of loss. She simply could not do it now that she knew what that loss felt like, how it left a person hollowed out. She could not bear losing another beloved spouse or, heaven forbid, a child, a living creation of that love. It would be too much, even if it were possible.

Perhaps it wasn't possible, though. Perhaps children had never been in the cards for her. After all, she and Christophe had been married seven years without incident. Even if they'd not been deliberately trying, they'd certainly taken ample opportunity and they'd not always been careful. One would think Mother Nature would have caught them. Now she'd never know because Christophe was gone from her. *Damn him.* Damn Dev Bythesea, too, for making her think about such things again, remember such things, *feel* such things that she could reasonably do nothing about without considerable risk to her own heart.

You could have done something. You needn't be alone tonight, the voice in her head reminded her gently but honestly. *Dev asked you to join him at the Birdwells' musicale.*

A note had come just as she'd returned home that afternoon, apologising for his abrupt departure and asking her to the musicale. *I want to see you*, it said. That one line had sent a tremor through her, feeding her infatuation, underscoring the not-so-undesirable tension that rippled between them when they were together.

This had not been an invitation issued to make up for the morning session cut short. Nor had it been offered as a courtesy to grow her client base. *He* wanted to see *her*, be with her on a level that had nothing to do with business or his portrait. Her curiosity had wanted to go. What had his cousin done? No doubt this summons was about telling her just that.

If she went, she would know. Perhaps he was counting on that, on her curiosity getting the better of her. But her practical side argued caution. What message would she be sending him if she dashed to his side? That she was willing to overstep the bounds of the client–artist relationship once more? That she had nothing to do but answer his beck and call? If she overstepped her own rules now, what other bounds was she willing to overstep?

Even if dashing were possible, there was still one problem. She'd not been invited to the Birdwells. She wasn't their sort. They were quite…conservative…and widows who painted and had lived abroad were not on their guest list no matter what their antecedents or who her in-laws were. To show up would be to cause a scene. Either because she'd be turned away on her own, or because she'd have to invoke Viscount Everham's name to gain entrance, which would cause all nature of undue speculation neither of them would find useful.

So, she had stayed home. To work on preliminary sketches. To sort through her thoughts. Gwen set the sketchpad aside. It was getting too dark to work. She'd need to light more lamps if she wanted to continue. She rose and went to a carved, wooden beverage cart that looked like a little carriage done in the Italianate style and poured a small glass of *vin santo* from the decanter as was her nightly custom. Beside the *vin santo* was a decanter of the clear *grappa* Christophe had preferred.

How many nights had she and Christophe ended the evening this way, beside a fire, in a drawing room, the world quiet about them, a sipping glass of their favourite drinks in hand and conversation about anything and everything? They'd talked of art and love, sex and philosophy, but most of all they'd talked of what was in their hearts.

Dreams had been spun amid the midnight shadows. What conversations those had been. They had awakened more than her body, but her mind as well. They'd taught her about the world, educated her in a way no finishing school ever could.

From the door to her little drawing room, the clearing of a throat drew her attention. 'Mrs Norton,' her footman said awkwardly, 'there's a gentleman here to see you. I've told him you don't receive at this hour,' or at all, frankly, hour notwithstanding. Any receiving she did was for business and it was done at the little parlour at the studio. 'However, he insists.' He held out the salver with the single card on it.

Gwen glanced at the clock on the mantel showing it was nearly ten. She could guess who it was before she took the card. He would have given her an hour to make her presence known and when she hadn't arrived, he had decided to take matters into his own hands. If Dev Bythesea's mind was made up, he would find a way to get what he wanted. Tonight, that was her. A tremor ran through her at the realisation. He could have talked to anyone, to Eden or perhaps his new friend, the Duke of Cowden, but he'd chosen her for better or worse.

If she turned him away, he would ask why the next time she saw him. In fact, he wouldn't ask. He would simply tell her, confront her with her own cowardice. He would make her own this moment, this choice. 'Bring the Viscount in, Reginald. I will see him.'

She smoothed her skirts and made a plan. She would see him long enough to tell him it was inappropriate to be here and send him on his way to some place more appropriate, like his club or to Eden's. But one look at Dev and that plan was quashed.

It was his eyes that gave him away. They blazed like aventurine flames fuelled with anger and rage. Something had upset him. She pitied anyone who'd crossed his path at the musicale. To be the recipient of his ire would not be pleasant. But his ire was only the surface, the protective armour shielding something more— hurt. Whatever had happened today had left an invisible mark. She was something of an expert in those.

Suddenly, it did not seem as important to dismiss him, to teach him a lesson about calling on her outside of business as it did to offer succour. He wasn't as much a prowling tiger in this moment as a wounded one, protecting itself with its ferocity. He would not want sympathy from her. He would want compassion veiled in strength and wit.

'Whatever your cousin has done,' she remarked drily, 'I pity him, if there's anything left of him *to* pity.' She was rewarded with a harsh laugh, further proof that Dev Bythesea, the most composed man she'd ever met, was *hurting* and he'd come to her. She could not turn him away. She moved to the beverage cart. 'Come, sit. Have a drink and tell me all about it. *Grappa* can do wonders for the soul.'

Dev wasn't sure if it was the *grappa* that soothed him, or if it was the room with the gentle warmth of its fire on a chilly spring night, or if it was simply being in her presence as he sipped his *grappa* from a tulip-shaped glass. She was dressed for home in a comfortable, loose blue gown, her hair in a simple chignon. She was not expecting callers, nor was there any sign she'd been out tonight previously. It wasn't just his invitation she'd refused, then. That made him feel slightly better.

She wasn't upset over him rushing out today. She had good instincts, too. She'd not smothered him in overwhelming comfort the moment he sat. Instead, she'd let him sit in silence, let him enjoy the drink. She did not pester him with questions. She understood that a man would share in his own time, that he needed to be as one with his thoughts before he parsed them out in front of others.

That particular courtesy went a long way in alleviating the tension that had accumulated in him since leaving her studio. It was a courtesy a woman who understood men knew to extend. He doubted any of the debutantes at the musicale this evening would have such experience.

'The world seems more manageable from a chair by the fire.'

In the dark, in the stillness, with a beautiful woman who understood what he needed by his side.

Indeed it did. The troubles of the day seemed quite minor compared to the peace of being in this room. He liked that she'd not moved to light any extra lamps, to set the room ablaze with light, but had let the shadows do their soothing work. The only light came from whatever glow was cast by the lamp on the table near her chair and the fire. It was a soft, orange light, quiet and still. 'Do you like the dark?' he asked, curious.

'Darkness can be a good friend.' She sipped a golden amber liquid from a small glass.

'I find it strange that a painter would enjoy the dark when they prize the light.'

She gave a throaty laugh in the dimness, the sound of it sultry and low. 'Do you? A man of balance? What is the light without the dark, after all? Light is nothing without darkness. Rembrandt knew it. Light cannot bring emphasis to a subject without darkness. Before that, Da Vinci used *chiaroscuro*, dark and light working together to highlight the subject.'

He felt his eyes close as she talked, felt the last of his anger seep away, something else rousing within him, taking its place. Good lord, listening to her talk about artistic technique, her voice low, here in the dark, was making him hard. His reaction was as deliciously inappropriate as being here.

'I don't think you came here to talk about art, though,' she invited. Not pressed, *invited*. Another sign of an experienced woman who knew how to manage a man. He was welcome to discuss what was on his mind. He was not *required* to do so. She demanded nothing of him and in not demanding, he wanted to offer her everything.

In his relaxation, he'd slouched in the chair. He forced himself to sit up a little straighter. 'I should apologise for coming unannounced.' His error was more egregious than that, though. He wasn't here merely unannounced. He was here uninvited in her sanctuary, one that she'd taken great pains to protect. She'd met him on the front steps, by heavens, when he'd called for her. He'd not been meant to get past the front door. Still, tonight she hadn't turned him away.

'When you didn't come to the Birdwells, I had to see you,' he confessed. Simple words for a more complex thought.

'I was not on their guest list.'

He should leave it at that, but he couldn't. He pitched his voice low. 'Would you have come if you had been?' Would she have come for him? Because he'd requested it? After the events of today, he felt very much alone. How wondrous it would be to know there was someone he could call to his side. He would make sure she was on every guest list in London in the future.

'I don't know that your aunt would have liked that.' She flashed him a meaningful glance.

'I would have vouched for you. Viscountess Birdwell would not have denied me.' People didn't deliberately seek to upset future dukes, even dukes they weren't certain of yet.

'I am your painter, Dev, not your shield. If I go with you anywhere, I prevent others from getting close to you. It's difficult to meet eligible young debutantes with another woman attached to your side. Especially, when that woman is not welcome in all circles and has a certain reputation of her own. My presence does you no favours when you're trying to establish your own suitability,' she cautioned gently.

'I don't want them.' He ground out the words and tossed back the last of his *grappa*. That was a mistake. One did not 'toss back' *grappa*. He saw her stiffen at his words, no doubt picking up the implication behind them.

'Why did you come here tonight?' She arched a brow and fixed him with a hard stare, calling him to account in the dimness. 'If you came to talk, I can listen. If you came for…something else, you will not find it here.'

No matter how much good that something else might do them both, Dev thought.

He sighed, dangling his empty grappa glass from his fingers. 'My cousin is making trouble for my aunt and my aunt is making trouble for me.' His aunt had been frantic when he'd arrived at Creighton House this afternoon in response to her note. 'It seems my cousin is "concerned" about the succession, particularly my link in the chain.'

'How concerned?' She'd relaxed back into her chair now that he'd answered her question to her satisfaction. But he had answers of a different sort from her.

She *was* affected by him, by the attraction that sizzled between them.

'He wants to contest my suitability to meet the requirements of heir. He did not say it in so many words. He simply told my aunt he was worried over a vague "someone" not approving when the time came. He made it sound as if he were an ambassador bringing news to Her Grace about society looking to make a fuss. I doubt society cares that much beyond their guest lists. Society might gossip, but gossip takes little energy. Rousing itself to take on the Heralds' College is beyond society's level of interest.'

The anger began to thrum again against the peace of this room. He pushed it back. 'How dare my cousin do this? Can he not see this is a difficult time for my aunt? That she does not need him making trouble?' He drummed his empty hand on the arm of the chair, an outlet for his disapproval. 'And it is *he* who is making the trouble. He is the ambassador of his own cause.' Bish would bring down the dukedom for the sake of claiming the scraps from the wreckage.

'Sometimes that's the best time to make it,' Guinevere mused aloud. 'People can't handle any more on their plate so they give in and give up.' She turned her head to look at him as she lolled against the back of the chair and he sensed she spoke from personal experience. 'When Christophe died everyone came, friends, vultures, and sometimes it was hard to tell the two apart.'

It was the first time she'd referred to him by name. Previously, when she'd spoken of him it had always been by as 'my husband'. Perhaps that was her way of keeping him at a distance, at keeping her memories at a distance. Dare he hope it meant something that she mentioned him now? Was it possible that she was letting down her guard at last? That the mention was deliberate? Not an accident of drinks in the firelight?

She gave a soft, self-deprecating laugh in the dimness. 'Artists wanted to be sure they were paid. They wanted their money, they wanted their paintings back, their sculptures back. The landlord came wanting his rent, wanting his contract honoured, wanting me out of the gallery space so that he could rent it to another client. Everyone wanted something from me in those days. It would have been easy to lose everything.

'My husband's solicitors were honest men, but they were not interested in consulting a woman on business especially when there would be no more business for them once my husband's accounts were wrapped up. They wanted it all done quickly. Left unchecked, they would have taken the path of least resistance and sold it all.

'Thankfully, my brothers managed everything so that I left Italy with a decent sum sufficient enough to start my life here.' Then she added quietly, 'Without them I would have given up. I'd lost the man I loved. At the time, nothing else seemed to matter.'

The allegory was not lost on him. His aunt cared for his uncle deeply. Her energies were bent towards him, towards what he might need as his life neared its end. He mattered…the dukedom mattered. That was the sum of her world these days. She hadn't the time or energy for Bish's games. She would have ignored his cousin entirely if his latest contretemps didn't involve that succession. But without support, his aunt would not be able to put up a fight for long, even as formidable as she was.

'She has me,' Dev replied, but even as he said it, he wondered if that would be enough. After all, he was the source of the problem according to Bish. His support might mean very little.

'On what grounds does your cousin grumble?' Guinevere asked. A strand of hair had come loose and now she wound it about her finger in an absent gesture. The dark and the fire was working its magic on her as well. Their guards were going to sleep.

'That I am not Church of England. He doesn't say it directly, but he hints at it through "concerns" about that and about the recognised validity of my parents' marriage. Will Britain accept their marriage, he asks, and then follows up with statements like, "best to anticipate these things ahead of time so we are not surprised", to make it sound as if his insights are meant to be helpful instead of undermining.' Or direct threats.

'He has not lodged any official paperwork, though?'

'No, I suppose he doesn't want to show his hand outright until he absolutely must.' The longer Bish could wait, the better the chances would be that the Duchess would be overcome by grief and the reality that her husband was gone.

'How is your uncle?' Gwen asked quietly.

'I told Rafe the other day I hope he has one more summer in him. I think he might, but not much more than that.' He paused and set aside his *grappa* glass. 'Some days, I wish he would go, that it could be over for him. Consumption is not kind to its victims. Some days, it's all he can do to breathe. What is that worth? What is the quantity of such days worth to him? Selfishly, they are worth much to me. I need the time with him. I have questions. I want to know his vision for the dukedom. Yet, it would be better for him if it could be over.' He had not voiced such sentiments to anyone for fear they'd misunderstand, think he was anxious to inherit, to claim his 'glory' and wealth. But she would not judge. His opinions were safe here.

'The age-old debate.' She sighed in the darkness. 'How best to die? To linger and tie up loose ends, to say all that needs to be said even though lingering comes with pain, or to go quickly, suddenly, with no time to prepare, but also with no time to suffer.'

Insight flashed. 'Is that how Christophe went? Suddenly with no warning?' They were undressing one another with their words, laying each other bare with their questions.

'Somewhere in between, I think.' She gave him a sad smile, her own arm dangling over the side of her chair, her fingers trailing close enough to touch his in the space between. He let his fingertips flirt with hers.

'Tell me,' he whispered in the dark.

Chapter Nine

She wanted to tell him, here in the darkness where the night would wrap around her words, around them, giving them a space out of time into which she could whisper the truths she carried deep inside. His fingers brushed against hers and she hooked her little finger around his.

'It was August and it was hot. We were spending a few weeks with friends in Naples on the coast. We were all at the beach. It was a grand party, a day full of champagne and laughter, and kisses. One can live passionately in Italy without drawing any censure.' Gwen smiled softly, recalling the memories. That day had been beautiful right up until it wasn't. She'd worn a loose, gauzy white dress and walked barefoot with Christophe in the surf.

'I want to paint you like this,' he'd murmured at her ear. 'I want to remember you just as you are now, the world as it is now.' He'd closed his eyes. 'I am making a mind picture.' They'd laughed and kissed, the water lapping at their feet.

'After lunch, he and two of the other men took a small boat out. They wanted to dive and snorkel…' She paused. 'Do you know snorkelling? They've been doing it for literally millennia in Greece and the Mediterranean. But perhaps not everywhere?'

Dev chuckled. 'Yes, I know snorkelling.'

'Christophe loved to snorkel. He said it was peaceful under the water.' She paused and dropped her voice. 'Before he went out in the boat, he kissed me, told me he loved me, that our life together was the best of his.'

She paused again, this time to hold back the guilt. She should have known. Why hadn't she seen through those words? If she had, she could have stopped him, could have tempted him to stay ashore. The guilt pushed hard at her walls. Somehow, she should have *known* that he was saying goodbye.

'He was always saying extravagant things like that,' she whispered her defence in the dark. She'd adored that about him, the way he lived out loud with his words and his actions. If he felt like making love in the middle of an art showing, they'd sneak off and do it. They'd not been bound by rules.

'He did not come back,' Dev surmised. 'An unexpected accident, then? Something went wrong with the snorkelling?' He was inviting her to continue, to finish the story.

'No, he did not come back and, no, it was not an accident.' This part was harder to tell. No one wanted to hear it, or wanted to believe it, certainly not Christophe's parents, who were content to believe it was a snorkelling accident. Perhaps it was what they needed to believe for their own peace.

'That day, it was sudden. I had not awakened beside him that morning never thinking I would not go to sleep beside him that night. But I think Christophe had been planning it for a while.' She sought Dev's gaze and found it.

'He had received an unfavourable diagnosis a few months prior. He had tremors, a shaking palsy. He'd ignored them for some time, but he was noticeably struggling to hold a brush even before he sought medical help. Of course, there was no medical help, only an explanation: there was no cure. The tremors were from a neurological disorder and it was only going to get worse. He had good days and bad days.'

'So he went into the sea and never came back.' Dev's voice was soft.

'Because he could not bear witnessing his own deterioration, or forcing me to watch it and the unravelling of our lives. If he could not paint, if he could not conduct business, we had nothing. He decided to quit while we were ahead.' She took a deep breath, the old emotions starting to roil as she said the words into the night. 'I hate him for it.' The words were tantamount to heresy. What kind of person said such a horrid thing?

'Only because you loved him so much,' came the whispered reply.

The words broke the dam, a dam that had held for four years, a dam that had enabled her to leave Italy and cobble together the semblance of a life without Christophe, to live with her haphazardly strung pearls. She had cried before. She'd cried when he died. She'd cried for days afterwards, for him. But not for herself. Not for the life they'd had, not for all she'd lost. She'd feared if she gave her grief full vent she could be lost entirely, that she might never emerge.

She did not recall when she slid out of the chair to the floor, or Dev moving to her, taking her in his arms, offering the comfort of his embrace, or how long she cried. She only knew that when her tears subsided, he was there. 'This is not what you came for, to have me go to pieces,' she apologised, somewhat abashed over what had happened, the direction the evening had taken.

'Isn't it? I came for you because you did not come to me.' His hand ran up and down her arm in a soft, idle caress. 'Besides, I rather like this. You and me on the floor, in the dark, in the quiet. No one around, no need to keep our guard up, no expectations except being in the moment. Such a phenomenon has become quite rare in my world.'

'Mine, too,' she murmured, her body nestling closer to his of its own accord as it settled and calmed. She ought to put a stop to it. One did not behave with a client as she'd behaved with Dev tonight, baring her soul with such personal talk and sitting on the floor with him, bodies entwined as if they'd known each other for far longer. Yet she couldn't help but feel as if their very souls seemed to speak to one another in a way that made time irrelevant.

She knew the feeling—it had felt that way with Christophe. It was one more reason to put a stop to this. She wasn't sure she wanted to travel that path again, to feel that way again now that she knew what it also felt like to lose it, to have to live without it. Perhaps this was different, though. She'd not counted on losing Christophe so soon, but she knew from the start that she'd lose Dev. He could only give her moments, not a lifetime. He was meant to marry a duchess-quality debutante.

But not tonight.

She breathed in the spiced patchouli scent of him. She promised herself just a few more moments of peace. Then she would end this. She would turn it into a moment out of time and move on. But, oh, she thought as her head drooped against his chest, what a delight it was to be held, to feel that for once she was not alone.

He was not alone when he was with her, Dev mused. Awake or asleep. She was most definitely the latter at present. He could feel it in the soft heaviness of her body against him, the dead weight of the entirely relaxed, all tension released, perhaps devoured by the exhaustion of her emotions and tears. What a revelation tonight had been, both of her and of him, once more illustrating that their journeys were not so different, that they understood one another. The ease with which her body had sought comfort from his was merely an outer manifestation of that understanding. Where bodies entwined, hearts and souls had already entangled.

Dev shifted on the floor, leaning against the chair to relieve his back and adjusting Guinevere in his arms, careful not to wake her. She'd want to apologise, want to get off the floor and end this moment. He was not ready. He wanted to hold her, offer her comfort even in her sleep, wanted to ponder all that she shared with him and what it meant.

How long had she waited to tell someone about Christophe? How long had the want to share those last days been tamped down because no one wanted to listen? Christophe's family preferred a different rendition of their son's death and in that preference they'd left Guinevere alone in her grief; they'd made her an outsider in her own husband's family when she ought to have been a cherished insider, treated tenderly. No wonder she'd felt she couldn't go to them.

That had been the first revelation tonight. In the story of her loss and return to England, he saw that they were both fighting a battle to maintain their own autonomy: she in her desire to remain independent of two families who sought to control her and he with his aunt. He wanted to please his aunt, to ease her burdens, but not at the expense of his own self-worth. Guinevere was uniquely poised to understand the knifepoint of that dilemma given that she was similarly perched. She understood, too, the stakes in losing that battle.

Guinevere mumbled in her sleep and he murmured comfort to her. She was afraid to love again. That was the second, more personal revelation. She loved deeply, passionately, with all that she was. It was in her temperament to not hold back. And yet in giving her all, the pain was tenfold. It was no wonder that, in losing Christophe, she was reluctant to seek love again, knowing what lay on the other side of it.

How ironic that it was exactly the sort of love he wished to find for himself despite her cautionary tale of loss. She'd had that extraordinary love and did not want it again. He sought it, but was unlikely to find it given present developments. His marriage and his legitimacy as the heir were now both intricately tied up with one another.

Dev rolled his shoulders, acutely aware of the thin slip of paper tucked inside his evening jacket. It was this paper as much as the situation with his cousin that had sent him here tonight in a desperate bid to not feel alone. How odd that he felt less alone here in the dark with one sleeping woman than he had this afternoon as his aunt had ranted or this evening at the musicale in a crowded drawing room. He'd felt as if everyone in the room had been staring at him, whispering about him, not even behind his back. There'd been no effort at subterfuge. Dev feared what it meant: that Bish had refuelled the rumour mill.

It wasn't the first time. He was well aware London society had been discussing him for weeks now. But tonight's scrutiny had felt more intense. Perhaps it was because he was viewing that scrutiny through the lens of his cousin's threat to appeal the line of succession. London had been waiting for him to fail and now there was something tangible for them to sink their teeth into. They would be disappointed, of course. Bish had only smoke, no flame. Dev was confident the documents he'd brought would squelch Bish's attempts to bring down the dukedom.

It was the process that bothered him most. It would take a little time and in that span Bish would have the ability to grow rumours while London waited for the

Heralds' College's pronouncement. His uncle could die. His female cousins and their young families would be affected by whatever scandal Bish spun. When Bish stirred the pot of scandal, he embroiled them all and Bish simply did not care.

That was what made he and Bish different. He saw himself as an extension of the family, its representative. What he did reflected on the family and, likewise, what the family did reflected on him. It was one of the primary lessons his grandfather had taught him and his father had reinforced. It was also what made the balance between protecting the group and protecting his own self-sufficiency precarious. Whereas, Bish had no balance. He saw only himself and his personal gain. Bish did not care how this affected the family as a whole.

Such selfishness could not be tolerated, nor could it be allowed to go unaddressed. Dev did not relish one of his first tasks as Duke of Creighton being to mete out justice of the social variety to his cousin, but if he did not Bish would make more trouble. He'd learned that, too, from his grandfather.

How many times had he accompanied his grandfather on errands of justice, or sat in the throne room behind his grandfather's seat, listening and learning? He knew his duty just as he knew sometimes that duty was unpleasant. With the ducal robes came ducal responsibility.

Dev stroked Gwen's hair with a sigh. He needed her to start his other portrait right away. His aunt had preached strongly today about quickly seeking a marriage before 'anything else goes wrong'—those were her exact words and a reminder that as much as he wanted to remove burdens from her shoulders, he'd done quite the opposite in adding to them from arguing with her about where and how he'd live, to his desire to marry only after a thorough search for a wife with whom he could share genuine compatibility and passion.

He appreciated his aunt's sentiment, but it was likely too late. Certainly, a good marriage would go a long way to adding to his credibility. His bride's family would have reason to back him in a succession squabble. But that sort of family with a pristine and honourable name would be wary of jumping into a marriage with a duke who might not be a duke. They wouldn't be as sure as he that Bish had nothing more than baseless talk. All top-level families with marriageable daughters would be waiting to see how it played out before committing.

Dev yawned, feeling weary. The only families that would ally with him if Bish made good on his threat would be the more opportunistic sort, those willing to risk short-term scandal for long-term gain. He chuckled to himself and looked down at Gwen. Her brothers, the Four Horsemen, were hungry enough for a good fight. What would he give for a few more allies.

There was Cowden and Eden and both of them had long-reaching arms. But they had wives and soon they'd have young families to think about. They would have limits. They would never say so, but they didn't need to. Dev would never ask it of them, he knew better. He'd not put a friend in that position. But the Four Horsemen had no wives, nothing to lose and much to gain.

By the gods, that was midnight and madness talking. He laughed softly in the dark. When had his thoughts turned from a last fling with Gwen to matrimony? Gwen didn't want to be a duchess and he didn't want to compromise the independence she'd so carefully cultivated. Still, the thought lingered. He could show her it was safe to love again, that she need not be alone. A second happiness was possible.

He shook his head, trying to shed the fantasy. But to do that successfully meant he had to compete with Christophe, the perfect ghost, and win. He was starting to see what Rafe had meant when he'd said her heart simply was not available. Perhaps, though, Dev thought drowsily, it wasn't a matter of winning, but of showing her that it didn't have to be one or other, that there was room in her heart for both the old and new. Balance, not extremes. He could live with that.

He ought to wake her, or carry her upstairs and see her tucked in. He ought to go, which would require hailing a hack—a dubious prospect at this hour—or walking back to Evans Row, the safety of which was also a dubious prospect this time of night. Just the thought of the work such tasks demanded made him stifle a third yawn. He did not have the energy to get up off this suddenly most comfortable floor made warm from the fire burning nearby. Far safer to stay here, he reasoned as his head drooped to meet hers.

She was still in his arms when Dev awoke, a warm, bright light on his face. In those first, floating minutes between sleep and wakefulness there was, for him, a moment of absolute clarity where all thought was sharp and defined. This morning, that thought was peace. This was what peace felt like. It was a peace that came not from knowing everything around him was settled—he'd long accepted that kind of peace was impossible—it was instead a peace that existed because everything was not settled and calmness prevailed within him anyway.

Guinevere stirred in his arms. 'Good morning, sleepy. It seems we've drowsed the night away,' he joked, reluctantly letting her disentangle from his embrace as she stretched, her mind awakening with her body.

The questions started, followed by the apologies. 'How long?' she said, her voice trailing off as she realised the ineffectiveness of the question. What was there to say? There'd been moonlight outside when they'd begun talking and now there was sunlight. She stumbled to her feet. 'I am beyond sorry. You should have woken me.'

Dev laughed. 'I couldn't.' He rose, dusting at his trousers. 'I fell asleep, too. Despite the floor's dubious comforts, last night was, perhaps, the best night's sleep I've had since arriving in England. There is nothing to apologise for and I won't have you playing the martyr thinking I spent the whole night awake watching you sleep at the expense of my own,' he offered gently. She was struggling. She was remembering her manners, becoming the proper version of Mrs Norton again.

She strode to the door, looking about for her footman. 'I'll have a chamber prepared for you with hot water for washing.' She paused. He imagined her searching her mind for the proper protocols and finding none. She gave the order and turned back towards him. 'Will you stay for breakfast? The least I can do is offer a hot meal for having importuned you.'

She was magnificent like this—sleep-tousled, her thoughts as mussed as the rest of her. 'Hot water and breakfast would be lovely, and, to be clear, I am not importuned in the slightest, I assure you.' He flashed her a wide smile as the footman returned to lead him upstairs. There was a certain intoxication in knowing the always-in-control Mrs Norton was flustered...over him. Well, he supposed that made two of them. It was possible he might be a bit 'flustered' over her, too.

Chapter Ten

Flustered was an understatement. She was far more than flustered about what she'd done and what she'd shared. She was glad for the sanctuary of her room, with the door shut behind her. Here, she could reflect on what had happened and fully indulge her mortification without anyone to see.

Guinevere stripped out of her rumpled clothes, wishing she could strip away the memories of last night as easily. Sweet heavens, she'd fallen asleep in his arms after sobbing in them, after practically baring her soul to a man who'd been a stranger not so long ago. She'd told him things she shared with no one. To make matters worse, he was a client.

In the span of one night she'd violated every rule she'd set for herself and then compounded that egregious display of misconduct by inviting him to stay for breakfast. It was only eight in the morning. This did not bode well for the rest of the day.

Her maid appeared with hot water and went about her usual morning routine, going to the wardrobe to select a gown. If she noticed anything amiss such as yesterday's clothes on the floor and the bed unslept in, she had enough tact not to mention it. 'Perhaps the white muslin with the cornflowers on it?' Eliza held up the first selection. It was one of her favourites because of the wide cornflower-blue sash that brought out her eyes when she was so inclined to care about such things.

Are you so inclined this morning? the voice in her head whispered the question.

'The blue will be fine.' She nodded to Eliza and took a seat at her dressing table while Eliza laid out the necessary clothing. Yes, this morning she was so inclined to such things, she told herself fiercely. She would not go back downstairs looking shabby as if she were embarrassed by the night. It had happened. She couldn't change that, but she could suggest through her demeanour and her actions that it needn't change their relationship. She was still his painter and he was still her subject.

It wasn't as if they'd made love. Except that was only physical. They'd kept their clothes on, perhaps, but they might have made something far more potent than love. Sometimes shared stories bound people together more intently than a coupling in the dark. Well, whatever she'd breathed life into last night, she had to face this morning.

She had Eliza dress her quickly and do something simple with her hair. She didn't want Dev to think she was hiding up here or stalling. If she was lucky, she'd arrive downstairs ahead of him. But she wasn't lucky. When she returned to the drawing room, Dev wasn't there. For a long moment, she thought perhaps he'd decided against breakfast and had left, which was both disappointing and prudent. Then she caught a glimpse of movement on the veranda beyond the French doors. He'd gone outside.

Guinevere slipped out the doors quietly, wanting the chance to study him undetected as he gazed out over the lawn, his back to her. His dark hair curled against his neck, damp where signs of his morning ablutions lingered. He stood, long legs shoulder width apart, his stance allowing the eye to take in the slim taper of his waist between the length of his legs and the width of his shoulders—shoulders that were sans jacket, she noted.

He wore only his waistcoat and shirt, as if she needed any more temptation. She cleared her throat to announce her presence. 'I see you've found my loggia, or at least the best I can manage in England.'

He turned with a smile. His jaw was clean shaven and her heart jolted. The footman must have put out Christophe's razor for him. He put a hand to his cheek, reading her thoughts. 'I hope you don't mind?'

'Not at all,' she said politely. It was silly to mind. Why hold on to such things if not to use them? After all, she'd kept Christophe's brushes at the studio to use. This was no different. But it felt different, as if it were a sign of moving on, not just with her new life, but moving on with a new person. Whether she meant it to happen or not, Dev was here, in her private space. She had not turned him away when she'd had the chance.

'This is my retreat. I like to take breakfast out here when the weather permits.' She moved to stand beside

him and look out over the small green space with its little putti fountain at the centre and the geometric-shaped
knot gardens surrounding it, working the eye's gaze
outward to the squared boxwood hedging that framed
the perimeter.

'My attempt at an Italian garden.' She lifted a shoulder in a gentle shrug. 'There's not much space for such
things in this neighbourhood, although the neighbourhood is decent enough.' It was what she could afford
on her own income.

'I like it. The fountain is peaceful.' Dev smiled at her
as the breakfast tray was brought out and the wrought-
iron table on the veranda set. 'If I were a painter, I'd
paint you sitting on the fountain's rim, dressed just as
you are, a cornflower among the evergreens, a portrait
part-English and part-Italian, perhaps reflecting the
subject's inner turmoil.'

'We might make an artist of you yet.' She laughed at
the flattery, but not at the insight. It was disconcerting
to be known so well. 'It is true, it is hard for me to let
go of Italy. The house is full of flotsam, as my brothers
call it.' She gave another little laugh, hoping that keeping the conversation light would keep Dev from prying
loose any more stories from her.

He chuckled, too, studying her with a long considering stare of his green eyes, softness in his gaze. 'I
know a little something about flotsam, too. I brought
what I could with me so that I might be surrounded by
memories, by comfort.'

Dev ushered her towards the now-laid table, the simple gesture changing the locus of control. How easily he

did that—take over a space, putting himself in charge. No wonder society was so intimidated by him. But she wasn't. She was rather…*aroused* by that take-charge attitude and the body that went with it. It was, admittedly, nice for once to be taken care of in small ways.

He held her chair for her and she sat. 'I hope you don't find breakfast too meagre. In Tuscany, breakfast was also small and sweet.' She reached for the silver pot and poured steaming espresso into the small, white, demitasse cups fitted in their silver saucers. The strong aroma of coffee filled the space between them. 'I found Italian breakfast agreed with me.' She smiled and filched a pastry from the tray. '*Maritozzi* are my favourites. Try one, it's just a pastry filled with whipped cream, but it's delicious.' As if to demonstrate, she took a bite, letting her teeth sink deep into the roll. 'Mmm… This is heaven. No matter how a day is going, *maritozzi* always makes it better.'

'I'm sure it tastes almost as delicious as watching you eat it.' Dev grinned and reached forward, touching the tip of his napkin to the corner of her mouth. The gesture was gentle and intimate and she could not allow it. Lines had been crossed last night, but she could still retreat behind them.

Gwen trapped his hand where it rested at her cheek and shook her head. 'Dev, we cannot pursue this.'

He removed his hand. 'This? What exactly is "this"?'

Heavens, the man was infuriating. He was going to make her say it. Very well. Did he think she wouldn't? He should know by now that she was no wilting wallflower, afraid to speak directly. But perhaps that was what he wanted—for her to say the words out loud, to breathe life into them, make what existed between them real.

'Last night was a moment out of time, a moment of weakness for us both brought on by our vulnerability. It was understandable but that does not make it excusable or repeatable. To repeat such an interlude is to court scandal.' As well as other temptations she preferred to remain nameless. Repeating last night might lead to nights *not* spent on floors but in beds, nights *not* sobbing in his arms but sighing.

The path to such outcomes was not as long or remote as she might wish it to be. She could readily see herself walking that short distance with very little persuasion from him needed.

The only thing holding her back now was her own sense of restraint—a restraint based on the need to preserve her reputation from rumour and the memory of Christophe with its hard lesson that to love was to risk loss on a soul-wrenching level. And guilt. That, too, was holding her back, because unlike the brief earlier affair, this time she was allowing it to mean something.

'I must once more disagree with your assessment.' Dev took a slow sip of his coffee, unfazed by her ultimatums. What she'd meant as an end game, he saw as an opening. 'I see nothing wrong with two people finding solace with one another, sharing with one another. He leaned forward for a moment, dropping his voice. 'I was honoured to be the one you shared with last night. It was a privilege. There are few people in the world whom we can trust enough to truly be ourselves with.' He paused and sat back in his chair once more, contemplating his next words. His gaze stilled on her.

'Which was why I came to you last night,' he offered the words slowly. With a hesitant gesture, he reached into the small, narrow-slit pocket of his waistcoat and took out a slim piece of folded notepaper. He handed it to her. 'I am, apparently, to find such a person from this list. My aunt gave it to me last night.' Ah, so his upset had indeed been from more than the trouble with his cousin. She'd not been wrong there in sensing the upset ran deep.

Gwen scanned the fine script. 'There are only twelve names on it.' She recognised several of them by reputation only, girls all from good families, all very young. The oldest was twenty, a Lady Mary Kimber who was entering her second Season.

Dev gave a dry chuckle. 'Yes. Twelve. You can see my scepticism in believing I will find a paragon from such a small pool of candidates. I think it highly unlikely my soulmate is among them.' He was trying to make light of it, but his hand tightened about his demitasse cup and the light had gone out of his eyes.

Gwen leaned forward, her hand covering his free one where it laid on the table. It was a reckless gesture, an indication that she'd not yet retreated behind the lines of safety, that the intimacy of the night still lingered between them despite her earlier claims. 'What can I do?' Did he want her to offer an opinion on these girls? To guide him in some way? She had little to give in that regard. She did not move regularly in such circles to know more about them than their names.

He met her gaze with stern green eyes full of purpose. 'We need to start the portrait immediately. I need the leverage with my aunt. I need to slow down the clock on my nuptials so that I may have time to find a bride of my choosing.'

And time, Gwen thought, to win over his aunt should his choice not coincide with the Duchess's criteria.

Desperation flickered momentarily in his gaze. 'I need to find a bride who will give me at least a chance at happiness.' He waved a hand at the list Gwen held. 'These girls cannot give me that. I will be the Duke to them for ever, the outsider. Neither of which will endear me to them. They will quiver in fear around me, afraid to voice opinions of their own or to challenge my authority when it needs questioning. They will do nothing more than say yes and no and lie as stiff as a board doing that which is only a duty to them.'

He paused, checking his rising temper. 'I am sorry, I should not have spoken so bluntly or in such anger. I am sure they're all very nice girls.'

'They are, from what I know. But you are not wrong,' Gwen affirmed. 'I do not mind the bluntness. Such things are a natural part of marriage. Such things ought to be enjoyed. Those girls, and you, deserve better than duty.'

Dev nodded. 'Thank you for saying so. You are an enlightened soul. Perhaps that's why I seek out your company so much.' He gave a wry smile. 'But what I deserve or want does not factor into my aunt's plans. The dilemma still remains. I need time and, without the other portrait, I do not have it.'

Gwen offered an empathetic smile and put a pair of *maritozzi* on his empty plate. 'Eat,' she insisted. 'It will help. Truly.' Her insistence was rewarded with a laugh as he took a bite. She poured them another cup of coffee as he ate, his brow furrowing and eyes closing in the age-old gestures of a man in the throes of culinary ecstasy.

The sight sent a sharp tremor of want through her. He was impossibly handsome like this, on the verge of abandon, an enticing glimpse of what he might look like when he was fully unleashed in the throes of a pleasure of a different sort. She made a mental note of it, wanting to remember it. For the intimate portrait, of course, nothing more.

His eyes opened as he swallowed. 'You're quite right about these. I feel better already.'

'I told you,' she teased, pleased to see him visibly relax once more. They lapsed into silence then, each of them content to sip coffee and listen to the fountain. How wondrous it was to simply sit, to not have to say anything or to be anything but in the moment. This was a precious ease of companionship Gwen had not thought to experience with anyone again. Too bad it couldn't last. But perhaps that was what made it so precious, supply and demand being what it was.

After a long, peaceful interval, Dev spoke. 'I don't know which crisis troubles me more. The contretemps with Bish or the matrimonial mess with my aunt. Arguably, on the surface, Bish poses the greater threat, but in reality, he can be empirically settled and filed away. All that is needed is jumping through the hoops of legality and rolling out the necessary documents. Bish will be managed.' He gave a shrug, dismissing his cousin. 'Bish is an annoyance, nothing more.'

'But your aunt?' Gwen prompted sensing there was more to be said on the matter.

'The issue of my marriage is inevitable. It is only a matter of when and on whose terms.' Dev took another bite of the *maritozzi*. 'It has occurred to me that my aunt's desire to see me wed quickly is not only about the need to secure the succession. That is what she'd like to have me believe. But it is also about her need to have a hand in selecting my bride.' He leaned forward, his words coming fast as he laid out his thoughts like a general planning counter-manoeuvres.

'My aunt is worried about what the mourning period does in delaying my marriage because of the part she can play in it. If my uncle dies before I wed, it is a help to me. Mourning etiquette requires me to mourn for three months, during which time, because I am male, I can still carry on public duties as long as I am respectfully circumspect in my conduct. This buys me time to truly seek out a bride and marry perhaps next spring or summer.

'But for my aunt, this would remove her from the process except for indirect measures. While a nephew need only mourn for a few months, a wife is expected to mourn for at least a year. It would be unseemly for her to come up to town next spring. As a newly bereaved widow, she cannot direct my bridal search.'

Gwen nodded her understanding. 'You need the other portrait as a stop gap, a bridge that will get you from this Season to your uncle's passing.' She sighed her sympathy. 'Is there truly no chance of his recovery?' The Duke of Creighton was a well-liked man, highly respected.

Dev shook his head. 'None. It is just a matter of running out the clock, much to my regret. He's a good man. I'd like to have known him better and for longer. In some ways, it's like being with my father again, in ways I couldn't be with him, a second chance of sorts.'

Gwen unobtrusively split the last *maritozzi* and moved a halve on to his plate, wishing she could do more to ease his hurt. 'If you would like, I could paint him, or do a sketch, perhaps? Something to remember him by. Something honest, not trumped up with robes and busts in the background,' she was quick to add. 'Just something for you. If he's up to it, of course.'

The hardness of Dev's features softened. 'I would like that and I think he'd like it, too. Perhaps you could come with me to one of our afternoon meetings. You could sketch while he and I talked.'

'Then consider it done.' Gwen smiled at him over her coffee, her mind already moving to the other portrait that needed to be done. She would need silks for draping, something low for him to recline on. She began a list even as she began the process of removing Dev's clothes in her mind. Perhaps by the time he actually did remove them, she would be inoculated against the thrill of his body.

'You're doing it again, that thing you did in the carriage the first day I met you.' A slow, knowing smile curved on his lips.

'So I am,' she admitted freely. 'Occupational hazard, I suppose.'

'I don't mind. Strip away,' Dev drawled. 'When can we start?'

Gwen ran through her appointments in her mind. The schedule was getting busy as the Season got into full swing. She had the Rosemont girls sitting later this morning and preliminary sketches with Lord Bilsham for the orphanage.

'Tomorrow afternoon when you finish with your uncle,' and while all the decent ladies were at tea. 'Meanwhile, if you could send over some of your silks and pillows I would appreciate it. But,' she added as an afterthought, 'don't send them until later this afternoon. Your aunt is coming by for her last perusal of the formal portrait before I finish it.'

'I'm sure she'll be pleased with it.' The tension returned to Dev's eyes at the mention of the painting. 'The work is good, Gwen.' Even if it was a reminder that time was passing. May was slipping away from them and the reveal approached. The pressure to marry would be tenfold once the portrait was out.

He rose. 'I must take my leave then and let you get to work. Thank you for breakfast, Gwen. It was a delightful way to start the day.' Silence stretched between them as if he wanted to say more. 'I need that portrait, Gwen,' he said at last, desperation evident in his words.

She touched his sleeve with her hand. 'I know. You will have it, I promise.'

Chapter Eleven

This was promising to be a very interesting development. Bish Bythesea sat back contentedly and listened to the report of his two hired men. 'So you're telling me my cousin spent the night at Mrs Norton's home?' he summed up when they'd finished. He found that a little difficult to believe given her reputation, but perhaps less difficult when considering Dev's.

'Yes, Sir, it appears that way. Your cousin arrived at half past ten last night and left this morning at half past nine—' one of the men gave him a sly look '—wearing the same clothes.'

'He went straight to her house after leaving the musicale?' Bish organised the chain of events in his mind. He had not gone to the musicale, choosing to keep his distance from his cousin after his own interview earlier with the Duchess. By now, Cousin Dev would know he had voiced concerns over the succession.

'He didn't stay long, only an hour.' The other man, who appeared smarter than his sly counterpart, affirmed. 'Just long enough to make an appearance and satisfy obligations, no doubt.'

Or, Bish mused, long enough to ascertain that Guinevere Norton wasn't in attendance and wasn't going to be. He'd sensed there was something between them at the Camford soirée. There'd been something in the way they'd stood together and then they'd gone out to the garden for an extended period of time. He'd been careful not to assume too much given Mrs Norton's reputation for being in a quiet, perpetual mourning for her late husband. The woman was challengingly aloof and rumoured to be quite immune to flirtation as a result. And yet, if his men's reports were to be believed, Dev had found a way to pierce her impenetrable armour and quickly, too.

Bish pushed two bags of coins towards the men. 'Get some sleep. The day shift will take it from here. You're back on duty at dark.' He dismissed them and settled in for a good think. This piece of information was far more than he'd hoped for. He must consider how best to make use of it.

Bish crossed the room to the console holding the decanters and poured himself a celebratory brandy even though it was barely past the stroke of noon. Things were going far better than planned. He'd spent last evening at various entertainments, dropping careful insinuations veiled as familial concern about Cousin Dev's ability to meet the requirements for succession. He'd been cautious to keep those worries worded objectively so that no one would say he was grasping for a title himself. Instead, they would say he was showing admirable concern for the family.

His efforts had been enough to light the flames of gossip. When an enterprising matron would nod in commiseration and whisper confidingly, 'I have had my own concerns about Everham, being raised abroad. He hasn't even attended English school. Who knows what he's learned.' Bish had been all too happy to supply further kindling in nuanced phrases such as 'he was practically raised at his grandfather the Raja's palace'. It was the sort of comment that on the surface seemed to come to his cousin's aid as if Dev being raised in the palace should assuage concerns over an education, but in reality implied Dev was not like them. 'The Raja's palace?' the eager matrons would gasp in scandalised horror. 'The one with the sixteen wives?' Yes, Bish affirmed, the very same. Whatever conclusions they might draw from that, Bish could not control any more than a wildfire could be contained.

He felt certain the rumours would soon be out of control. He needed them to be. Dev would produce documents proving his legitimate succession. It would be a question of whether or not the Heralds' College would *want* to aver those documents or if they would choose to find them lacking in some regard, having been signed in a provincial location by perhaps someone less than an expert at their job. If the Heralds' College had concerns over Dev, they could choose to find loopholes, could choose to invalidate Dev's claim. Bish needed these rumours to 'encourage' them to do so. They owed Dev Bythesea nothing. He was not one of them, but Bish was. If they had the tools through which they could choose to denounce Dev, Bish needed them to do so.

This latest finding wasn't rumour, though, it was truth. Dev was not helping his cause by spending the night at Mrs Norton's. It was tantamount to announcing he was starting an affair with the woman who was painting his portrait. It would prove every wild thing being said about him. Dev was digging his own grave there. Bish tossed back his drink. The Creighton Dukes didn't have affairs. The Duchess wouldn't like it. He would relish informing her of that little development when the time was right. It wasn't just her who wouldn't like it. He could think of a few others who would find Dev's little escapade distasteful as well, primarily the fathers of the girls the Duchess was trying to wed Dev to. 'Blood will tell,' he murmured to himself. And when it did, he would be there to pick up the pieces. He would be ready.

'Are you ready to make your selection?' Rafe asked over drinks at the Travellers. He handed the list of candidates back to Dev with a wry smile. 'If only all matchmakers were as efficient as your aunt.'

Dev sighed. 'I am far from ready.' He was perhaps even less ready to succumb to matrimony now than he had been three weeks ago. But that was before he'd met her—Guinevere Norton with her bravery and broken heart, her strength and her determination to make a life of her very own. Dev took a swallow of *maireya*. 'How did you know Elspeth was the one?'

Rafe chuckled. 'She wasn't afraid to challenge me.

Not on silly things like a horse race in the park, or wicked dares, but on real issues, things that mattered like how my father and I were running the shipping company, how we had strayed from our initial mission into doing things for profit, not necessarily for decency. She said things to me no man working for the company, no member of the board of directors, dared to say even if they thought them.

'Because of that, she forced me to think about the business in a different way, conduct business in a different way. I will be grateful for ever. She is my partner in all things, Dev. She knows my goodness and my bad. She knows my darkness and loves me anyway. How could I not want the one person who sees me for who and what I really am, flaws and all?' He raised his glass in a toast to his absent wife.

'I was afraid you'd say that.' Dev drank to the toast, but it didn't help the turmoil growing within him. 'I don't think such a woman is on my aunt's list of twelve.'

Rafe offered him a commiserating smile. 'No, I don't think she is either.' He played with his glass. 'But she's not in India either, Dev.'

Dev straightened, alert. 'What does that mean, Rafe?'

Rafe gave him a knowing stare. 'Sometimes I think you've not got over Aanchal, that she's the measuring stick you hold other women to and perhaps idealised in the extreme. You forget, I was still there, in India with you, when you had certain hopes. And I have your letters from when those hopes were dashed. I know how it broke you to lose her.' Not just to lose her, but to lose her to Raynesh, a man he'd grown up with, counted as a best friend as surely as he counted Rafe.

'That was a long time ago.' Dev shook his head. 'I loved her, but she would not have been suited to the life I have now.'

'Suited or not, she has made you wary. What happened with her has left its mark.' Rafe gestured for another drink.

'True, but perhaps a very necessary lesson was learned. She made me see for the first time what I was really up against with my mixed blood. It was one thing to know the East India Company didn't hire mixed-blood clerks regardless of who their fathers were. I told myself that was a corporation talking, it was what had to be done for business. But with Aanchal's father, when he refused my suit on grounds of my birth, I was forced to take it personally, to *face* it personally. It has toughened me for England, for what I face here with these peers and their daughters. It readied me for this. And I thought I *was* ready. A few weeks ago, I might have been more accepting. But things have changed.'

The waiter came and Rafe took his drink from the tray, his tone an ominous drawl as if he had already guessed. 'What things might those be?' Dev said nothing, holding Rafe's gaze steady, letting Rafe come to his own conclusion. 'Oh. I see. Mrs Norton.'

'Yes. The girls on my aunt's list don't hold a candle to her.' He'd been grappling with the realisation since breakfast, realising that what disturbed him most about his aunt's list was that Gwen wasn't on it, that these girls weren't her. When he thought of choosing one of them, he thought of losing her.

'When I think of marrying, of seeing myself with a wife, I see her beside me,' he told Rafe. 'She understands me on an elemental level before I even speak. And, yes, she challenges me as Elspeth challenges you.'

'Will she have you?' Rafe asked bluntly. 'I was not aware she was open to such discussions.'

Dev grimaced. 'I don't know We've grown close. So, maybe.'

'It's impressive to have got a maybe from her. Perhaps I underestimated you.' Rafe toyed with the short stem of his snifter. 'I suppose it's not impossible. She's not entirely unacceptable. She is the granddaughter of an earl. It's just that she's not entirely acceptable either, as you are aware.' He was aware. The Birdwells and others like them did not receive her.

'She's not what my aunt wants for the dukedom, I know.' Dev offered. 'But *she* is what I want.' Hearing himself say those six words out loud was powerful, clarifying.

'But what do you want her for? Just for you or for the dukedom? Perhaps you cannot serve both in this choice,' Rafe cautioned. 'Is Guinevere Norton Duchess material?'

That was the question. Could Gwen be his Duchess? Would she *want* to be? Or would she see it as too large of a sacrifice? The cost of her freedom too great? Her life *would* change, there would be no avoiding it. But duchesses were powerful women. They could shape society to their liking if they chose. Dev reined in his thoughts. The cart was well ahead of the horse at this point. She'd spent one night in his arms—platonically—and he was already walking her up the aisle despite what he knew she wanted and didn't want. He needed to take it one step at a time with her. Too much too soon and Gwen would run the other direction without a backward glance. He and Gwen had made progress, but that didn't mean she was ready yet for what he had in mind. They both needed time.

Gwen had the studio ready for the work of the afternoon—that work being Dev's visit. She toyed with the new pencils, their flat tips awaiting the sharp refinement of her penknife beside the fresh pad of sketching paper, acutely aware that the thrill of anticipation running through her now at the prospect of the upcoming appointment had less to do with the new art supplies than it had to do with her client himself. A very disturbing thought indeed, and one worthy of reflection given the events of two nights ago.

She reached for the penknife and began to sharpen the pencils. Usually, the excitement she attached to the beginning of a project was attributed to new supplies—a pristine page, the crisp, sharp tip of an unused pencil, both of which represented the endless possibilities always present at the start before she second-guessed the line of a nose or the tilt of a head. '*La petite lune de miel*...' 'the little honeymoon,' Christophe had laughingly called it, that point in a painting where perfection whispered its promise before the war between paper, paint and artist began.

The penknife in her hand slowed its motion. She could almost hear Christophe's voice as if he were in the room. 'Painting is like a marriage,' he would say, a twinkle in his eyes. 'Sometimes a beautiful dance, sometimes a heated fight.' Then, he would give a shrug of his shoulder. 'Like you and me, my darling.' He would draw her to him and painting would be forgotten for a while.

They did indeed have their fights. They'd fought over her art—she didn't like his interference, his bossiness about how she ought to portray a subject; they fought over money and how to spend it. He was far less frugal than she was, having been raised in a wealthier household where he hadn't had to economise; they'd quarrelled over the home in Florence, a place she felt stretched their budget too far in the early days when they were newly wed and not yet established there. But it had all worked out in the end.

She set down the penknife and wiped at a tear. Those fights, which had seemed so important in the moment, seemed a waste of time, ridiculous and petty even given what she knew now. In hindsight, knowing the shortness of their days together, she would not have begrudged him a single suggestion about her art, a single new waistcoat, or an expensive present bought spontaneously. Gwen fingered the delicate links of the gold necklace at her throat, a beautifully wrought piece Christophe had bought her for no reason except that he loved her.

'A beautiful woman should have beautiful things,' he'd said.

He'd seen it in a jeweller's window on the Ponte Vecchio one evening on his way home from Santo Spirito where he'd just won a commission for a new mural.

Gwen pushed the memory away, but gently so, as she reached for another pencil to sharpen. She knew why these memories were surfacing. They were her defences, her *best* defences, against the recklessness of loving. They were reminders that nothing, no matter how good, lasted for ever and that when the end came it would leave hurt in its wake. The better it was, the more devastating the loss of it when it was over. And yet, there was no denying despite her defences that the temptation of Dev Bythesea whispered loudly in the lonely silence of her life.

She gave a sharp swipe of the penknife against the pencil's nib, shaving off an edge. If that attraction was simply one-sided on her part, it would be easier to quell. One-sided attraction was merely infatuation. But he'd made it clear this attraction was mutual and that was a far more dangerous situation. He *would* pursue her if he was allowed.

The only thing keeping him in check was her permission. But permission for what? Permission would require her to be brutally honest with herself about what this was: a brief affair that would span the two weeks remaining until the Duchess's portrait party at which point Dev would be considered officially eligible and on the Marriage Mart. He would have no time for her or any need. She would, in fact, be the very last thing he needed once that portrait came out. The Duchess would want her as far from her coveted nephew as possible.

Perhaps the temporary nature of the affair was the best reason of all to allow Dev to give pursuit.

Temptation whispered insistently as she sharpened the last of the pencils. *You know it won't last. You know it will be temporary. You know how, why and when it will end, all the things you didn't know before with Christophe. That gives you complete control, control that will allow you to mitigate the hurt or pre-empt it altogether.*

That was the real temptation, to have all the pleasure of Dev's arms without the pain of parting. She knew in advance to give her body, but not her heart, to a man who understood her, who didn't want to change her or limit her. There was only the question now—to take the opportunity or to let it lie.

Dev's boots sounded on the steps leading up to the studio and she straightened, smoothing the folds of her work smock and summoning her professionalism, which was harder to do than she'd have liked. It wasn't the nudity in general that had her pulse racing. She'd seen several men naked or nearly so. It was the prospect of *his* nudity, of seeing Dev Bythesea in undress, that was not an event she could approach with her usual artistic detachment.

'Good afternoon.' Dev swept her a smile and a bow, looking dashing in a grey jacket and turquoise waistcoat that highlighted his eyes. She'd be lying to say that the thrill running through her at the sight of him had nothing to do with the idea of seeing the muscles rippling beneath the white linen of his shirt revealed. He set aside his black top hat on the console along with an elegant gold-headed walking stick of thick black wood. 'Shall we get started?' His hand reached for the knot of his cravat.

She was rather slow to pick up on his intention to disrobe right there in front of her. 'Wait,' she said, the word coming out in the half-strangled croak of a suddenly dry throat when she understood what he intended. 'Not yet. We must discuss the arrangements.'

She was stalling. How delicious it was to see the enticing, formidable Guinevere Norton off balance. She was nervous about the afternoon although she tried to hide it valiantly. Was she still thinking, as he was, about their night, of the things they'd shared that night and the following morning? It was the most exquisite evening he'd had in ages and it hadn't even involved sex. That alone was thought enough to keep him up at night.

Despite the mental energy he'd had to expend on the dukedom, on his errant cousin's contretemps and his aunt's matrimonial ambitions, his mind had still found room to contemplate and relive that night. Perhaps the difference between her and him, though, was that *he* was quite comfortable where his thoughts led, but she was not. He wanted her, complications and complexities notwithstanding. To that end, he would hazard the short affair.

Would she choose the same? He wasn't certain because *she* wasn't certain. She knew only that she was tempted. That temptation was written in her gaze every time she glanced his way. How close had temptation pushed her? What would it take to close the distance?

'Are you listening?' Gwen asked briskly, recalling him to his senses, 'Come and see what I have set up and tell me if you approve.' She gestured for him to follow her across the room to the window where a low bed had been set to the right side across from her workstation and draped with the silks and pillows sent over from the Evans Row house.

He surveyed the setting, seeing immediately what she'd done. 'You have recreated my bedroom.' He slanted her a look, a smile curling on his mouth as he ventured a little flirtation to test her mettle.

'It seemed the only place in the house that truly reflected you,' Gwen answered smoothly. They both might know what they wanted, but she wasn't going to make it easy for him. She was all business. 'I thought you could lay on your side, your head propped in your hand, perhaps one leg bent, your banyan strategically worn to both reveal and conceal. Is that something you'd be comfortable with? What were you anticipating?'

She was starting to relax now. Dev saw the signs. This was her territory. She was in charge here. This was a familiar routine, from showing her client the space they would work in, the pose she recommended and the questions she asked no doubt designed to put them at ease and to inspire confidence for this daring undertaking.

'I think the message we want the work to send is that you are a man who is not to be challenged,' she was saying, 'that in you there is strength and power which is symbolically represented here by your body, but it is a strength that doesn't come solely from muscle. It's a strength that comes from knowing who you are and who you want to be despite what others may suggest.' What a beautiful vision she had for the work. But it was a pointless consideration.

She moved about the space, straightening things that didn't need to be straightened. Dev stalked her with his gaze, with his silence, wanting her to be aware she had the full sum of his attention.

'You talk as if anyone will actually *see* the painting, Gwen.' He gave a rueful smile and crossed his arms. 'No one will care what message it sends. No one will ever view it.' What a shame that was—the thought flitted through his mind briefly. He'd like to see that piece of art…he'd like *others* to see that piece of work. How fruitless to create works of art that received such personalised consideration, but were never viewed, works that were made to be hidden instead. It seemed a sad waste of her talents.

'True, no one will see it publicly. It will never hang in a gallery and have hundreds stroll past it, study it. But *you* will see it, not just today or next year, but at some time in the future. Twenty years, thirty years from now and you will remember *what* you used to be, *how* you used to be. What do you want that memory to look like?'

'*Touché.*' He gave her a nod of concession. 'You have elevated my simple bid for insurance against my aunt into a memoir, a chance to capture a moment in time. You've made my endeavour noble.' He held her gaze for a long while in assessment and appreciation until she turned away, unable to endure his scrutiny no more.

He hid his smile. She'd waited too long, perhaps out

of pride, not wanting to show weakness. But it had cost her. She'd not want him to see the dilemma she'd been grappling with or what she'd decided to do about that dilemma. But he had and he filed the knowledge of it away. Temptation had her in its grip, her decision the source of her earlier nerves. 'Shall I change now? Strip down right here?' He worked the buttons of his waistcoat free.

'Not here. You may change behind the screen,' she instructed, gesturing to the trifold divider set in one corner of the studio. 'The banyan is already hanging there for you.' He flashed her a sardonic arch of his brow as if to say he did not need such modest consideration.

'I insist. We do not simply "strip down" in my studio. This is not a brothel where nakedness is common and low because it is easily attained in great quantities. What we undertake here is art where nakedness is revered and distinctive because it involves a single subject who is unique in themselves. Nakedness is not to be a cheap experience. It brings us that much closer to one's soul.'

He stepped behind the screen, his blood starting to sing with something that transcended lust and desire. This woman spoke to the very core of him, called to his soul. It was the rare occasion when he wanted to put himself in another's hands, to trust them. But Guinevere Norton had proven to be an anomaly to which he'd gladly surrender for the interim.

Chapter Twelve

The sight of Dev Bythesea emerging from behind the screen robed in russet silk was enough to make a woman surrender her good sense. The juxtaposition of the ripple of silk flowing unbelted over smooth bronze muscle on display where the banyan hung open was not lost on her artist's eye. Layers of contrast. And texture. Her hand itched to start sketching, to capture those layers. Layers, like the man himself.

Dev Bythesea was a complex man with unfathomable depths, a man who straddled two worlds abetted by an upbringing and education that were both of the east and the west. That was the man she'd attempted to preserve in some measure in the portrait for his aunt, but it was definitely the man she wanted to capture in full for this canvas.

Gwen's eye drifted over him, cataloguing the smooth glimpse of chest, the hint of a well-sculpted iliac girdle as her gaze dropped lower. She would want that on full display. There was the question of the dark mystery at his core as well, a promise of healthy male virility. How much of that promise to show? How much to leave to the imagination? She stepped towards him. 'May I?'

'Please.' Dev's voice was a rich rumbled invitation to touch, to acquaint herself with him. One had to feel textures to paint them. She pushed back the banyan, running her hands in slow exploration over his chest. 'Well? Will I do?'

He would more than do. Gwen took a step back towards her work table, searching for a small vial. 'I was thinking we might try some oil, if you don't mind,' she added. 'An oiled chest plays well with the afternoon light.' She poured a bit of oil into her cupped hand, letting it pool there before she blew on it. 'It helps warm it.' She gestured to the bed she'd created. 'Sit down and we'll get you oiled and arranged.'

'I am yours to command.' Dev's eyes glinted with mischief, though. The dratted man was enjoying this while it was taking all of her fortitude to maintain professional detachment as best she could. She knelt before him, pushing back the banyan from his shoulders, and began to rub in the oil, aware that her hands had already lost the battle for objectivity.

Her fingertips stroked and massaged, memorising the feel of the muscle beneath them, the long ridge of his clavicle, the fan-shaped definition of his pectoralis, the long lean lines of his abdominal obliques. Artistic anatomy had never felt so good, never looked so delicious.

'Perhaps we should do away with the banyan altogether.' Dev managed a low laugh, his eyes glinting a dark, dangerous green.

'Might we? I was thinking of that.' She stepped back

to survey her work, the oiling complete. 'It could be of more use to us as a drape than a garment. You don't mind? You understand quite a lot of you will be exposed?'

Dev stood and shrugged out of the banyan, a wicked grin on his face. 'Exposed to who? To myself? I assure you I've seen all I have to offer. And you, my dear, have seen far more important parts of me than my cock.'

He handed her the banyan while she fought to keep her gaze up and failed even though he was right. This was just a body. He'd shown her his heart, his mind. But it *was* a magnificent body. The sculpted musculature of his torso was mirrored in the strength of his long, muscled legs and the crown jewel of manhood displayed proudly and unabashedly at his core. She envied him his comfort with his naked state, especially when that state made her uncomfortably aware of her own desire, her own want, her own feminine appreciation of him.

'Do we need to oil anything else?' Dev was teasing her now, flirting wickedly on purpose.

She cleared her throat. 'No, we have enough oiled. If you could lie down, stretch out as we discussed and I'll arrange you from there.' It was a process that challenged her shredded detachment. There were fingers to run through his dark hair with its curling ends to muss it, to make it appear that he'd just awakened or completed a bout of something more intimate than sleeping in his bed.

There was the adjusting of his arm, his head, the tilting of his hips, the angling of his propped-up leg which brought her hands into tantalisingly close proximity with that ruddy crown jewel of his which was making no secret of how much it, too, was enjoying this. That didn't seem to bother Dev either.

'Why shouldn't my body enjoy this? A beautiful woman has her hands all over me,' Dev replied. 'It is a simple creature, it does not make distinctions for the reason your hands are on me. Work, pleasure, it is all the same for it.'

Gwen laughed, his frankness relaxing and refreshing. 'Why is it that men talk about their…um…anatomy…as if it has a life of its own? That it's somehow a separate sentient being?'

Dev chuckled. 'One of life's great mysteries, I suppose.' He held up his free arm. 'Where shall I put this hand?'

That was the current burning question. She'd left his other arm for last, unsure of what she might dare. 'Left to its own devices, it would rest at your stomach.' She moved his arm into position and studied the result, not entirely happy with how it obscured some of the musculature she'd taken pains to display. 'It will have to be lower,' she mused more to herself than to Dev.

'Like this?' Dev took himself in hand, the angle of his arm neatly drawing the eye to his phallus, the next logical stop on the journey down the lines of his body.

'Yes,' she breathed. 'Just like that.' Good lord, but he was a well-made man although that was not the sum of his appeal. She knew several physically attractive men who did not stir her because there was nothing beneath that surface. But Dev understood himself, was aware of himself, of his sexuality, and entirely comfortable with it. Such a combination was seductively intoxicating.

Guinevere retreated to her stool and took up her sketch pad. 'Don't move a single muscle,' she commanded. 'I have two hours of good light and I want to make use of them.' Because perfection didn't strike very often, but between the oil, the light and the man, she had it in front of her now. Dev Bythesea nude would be a masterpiece. The thrill of creating art, of creating something beautiful, hummed in her fingertips as she picked up her pencil.

'A masterpiece no one will see. Does that bother you at all? All this incredible effort that will be hidden away,' Dev asked.

'Public viewing is not the purpose of these works. That's no excuse to make them second rate. That would only turn them into something tawdry which is not the intent. This is not erotic work.' Gwen glanced up.

'The consequences might be erotic, though,' Dev suggested.

'That's up to the individual viewer's response.' Gwen shrugged. She could not control what people thought or how they reacted. It was one of the hardest lessons to learn about being an artist. One could not control subjectivity or a critic's review.

'Although I must admit, it was simpler in Italy. Perhaps because more people had more appreciation of the execution of work and their understanding of the work wasn't limited to the content. England is rather restrictive in that regard.' Positively stifling, really. She'd not had to do her nudes in secrecy in Italy.

Dev's gaze turned thoughtful and he let her sketch in silence for a while. 'Your husband didn't mind?' he asked at last.

'Of course not. He was an artist, too. He understood the work required it. He painted naked women on occasion. And, no, I did not mind. We were very secure in our marriage, in our faith in each other.'

Dev chuckled. 'I think he must have been quite extraordinary to allow his beautiful wife to oil up men and paint them nude. I think it would test my limits, to be honest. But as you say, I am not an artist myself.' He paused before asking his next question. 'Did you ever paint him nude?'

'Yes,' Gwen said quietly, sternly. 'But like this painting, it is private, for a single person alone. *Not* for public consumption.'

'Forgive me, I overstepped,' Dev apologised and Gwen relented. She'd been waspish just then, too protective.

'Forgiven.' She gave him a half-smile. 'It was the first one I'd ever done.' She offered the nugget of information as a truce, but then couldn't stop the rest of the story from coming out. 'It was up at the villa early in our marriage. He was asleep and I couldn't sleep, so I'd got out of bed and fetched my sketch pad. The moonlight was coming through the window, hitting his face with such perfection I couldn't resist. He was sleeping the sleep of the perfectly content bridegroom.'

Gwen gave a soft smile. 'I wanted to remember him that way always and that I was the one who brought him that contentment, that satisfaction.' She laughed.

'It helped to look at the painting when we'd quarrel and I was fed up with him and remember that there was more to us than the current disagreement.' She'd looked at that painting often in the early days after his death. She'd not looked at it recently, though.

'You quarrelled?' Dev arched a brow. 'I thought Christophe was perfect.'

'No man is perfect.' Gwen reached for a fresh pencil. 'The sooner a woman realises that, the happier she'll be. Perfection is a dangerous illusion.'

'Thanks. Good to know. I'll remember that.' Dev gave one of his low, seductive laughs. 'Tell me, Gwen. How did you meet Mr *Almost* Perfect?'

'You'll be disappointed,' she warned with a smile. 'In quite the usual way. My family went to the art showing at Somerset House that opens the Season and I saw him standing with a group beside a painting I rather admired, although once his eyes met mine I quickly forgot the painting altogether.'

She leaned forward, caught up in the long-ago memory. 'Something in me knew in that moment we were meant to be together, that we *would* be together. It was a *coup de foudre* for me *and* for him. I will never forget watching him cross the room, ignoring people who wanted to talk with him, cutting through the crowd to reach my side because it was the place he said he wanted to be the most.

'I think it proves that even on the most ordinary of days, extraordinary things can happen.' She felt herself blush self-consciously, feeling slightly foolish at the girlish confession, true though it was. 'What about you, Dev? Has it ever been love at first sight for you? Surely there must be someone in your past?'

She saw for a brief moment how uncomfortable the question made him before he could mask it and was almost sorry she'd asked. That had not been her intention. Her intention was only to learn a little more about him.

'There was someone once—a long time ago, it seems—called Aanchal,' he said at last. 'It was not a *coup de foudre*, at least not like it was for you. But perhaps it was in its own way. We grew up in the palace together. We were childhood friends in the summers until I turned twelve and, like the other boys in the zenana, was deemed too old to live in the women's quarters.

'Me, and my two cousins and friends, Raynesh and Aahan, moved to the palace with the other men. We had mentors who taught us the way of palace life, the different jobs that needed doing. It was a good education.' Dev diverged here to share, 'I was trained in languages and diplomacy. I was allowed to sit in the throne room when my grandfather met with foreign dignitaries and visitors from other provinces.'

'And Aanchal?' Gwen enquired, bringing the story back to its original topic.

'She, too, had growing up to do. I was told she was sent to other family in her home province. I did not see her for several summers. I was sixteen before I saw her again and it was like seeing her for the first time, yet it was also a reunion. We knew one another and yet we did not. We'd both changed, but there were strong ties between us. It was not hard to fall madly for her.

I was not the only one who fell. Raynesh was smitten with her, too.

A shadow moved over his face, his jaw set in a tense line. 'I meant to marry her. I saw no reason we should not wed when I turned twenty-one. I was the Raja's grandson, the son of a wealthy merchant. I could provide for her. I loved her and she loved me, but not the world I moved in. Her father refused my suit and chose Raynesh for her instead. I was too different, too much the outsider.' He sighed, making an effort not to ruin his carefully arranged pose. 'My story does not end as well as yours.'

Gwen studied him thoughtfully, trying to read his mind, but finding it guarded, hidden from her. 'Do you love her still?' She found herself irrationally both envious and angry with the mysterious Aanchal who'd captured Dev's heart and then rejected it.

'No, not romantically. It was a long time ago and it taught me some lessons I desperately needed to learn about the world and how it viewed me. It made me more aware, more alert, wary even, which is why I question whether I'll be able to find a woman among the *ton* who would be a suitable bride on my terms. But despite those lessons, I will always remember her fondly, though, for the role she played in my childhood and for our friendship.'

He held her gaze steady and she felt the tenor of the room shift. She braced, her pencil halting as Dev spoke. 'Aanchal chose another, our cousin and one of my best friends, and that choice hurt for a long time, but I learned I do not need to hate her for it. I do not need to close myself off from others because of it. Love has no limits, love does not have to be given only to one person and never given again. Love has room for others if we are willing to open ourselves up.'

There was a lesson in that for her, Gwen thought, her pencil starting to work again. Loving another didn't require she love Christophe less.

'There is risk in that, though. Risk in being hurt again,' she countered. What he proposed was nice in theory, but perhaps not entirely realistic.

'Without risk there is only compromise and compromise assumes the loss of something,' Dev answered smoothly. 'Consider your own situation. You want to paint nudes so you compromise and do it in secret, producing beautiful work that cannot be seen by the public. Is it worth it? Why do it?'

'The nudes aren't for the public, but for the individual. They help others see themselves. I had not planned on making it a side business, if you will, when I came to England. But one of my first clients needed it.' Gwen sharpened the pencil, brow furrowing as she recalled that young girl. 'She was eighteen, a wealthy merchant's daughter who was going to marry a baron's son. It was a trade of wealth for a handhold on the rung of the aristocracy. She was a quiet girl who had little confidence in her own charms. I could not let her go into that marriage thinking her father's money was her only asset. She'd be eaten alive by her new husband's family.' Gwen shrugged. 'So, I showed her what she could be. I showed her her power.'

Dev's eyes glinted with interest. 'Did it work?'

'Yes, but that is all I will say on the matter. What happens in the studio stays in the studio,' she scolded. 'Which is why I am a bit put out with Lord Eden. He should not have told you.'

'He knew he could trust me,' Dev assured her.

'It's not that,' Gwen corrected. 'It's that I don't want a third party deciding where my trust is bestowed. I can't have it and ensure that no one finds out about my little enterprise.'

'I've been wondering about that,' Dev drawled in all seriousness. 'How do you really expect to keep this a secret for long? In my experience the more people who know and the naughtier the secret, the more likely it is to be put about.'

Gwen flipped the sketch pad to a fresh page. She had time for one more quick drawing. 'It's the power of mutually assured social destruction. People don't want these portraits seen any more than I do. Besides, I don't do them for just any one, only those who truly need them.'

'Like Lord Bilsham? Why does he need one?'

'He's a shy man who has devoted his life to public service.'

Dev laughed. 'Shy? I may have only been here a month or so, but the man talks incessantly. He is not shy.'

'Yes, he is. Sometimes the more bombastic a man is, the more insecure,' Gwen insisted. 'Listen to him talk. He talks about the orphanage, the children, but never himself. Talk is his protection. He deserves to see himself, to recognise himself as a man.'

'And Eden's bride? She doesn't seem the type to need your services.'

'Doesn't she?' Gwen offered cryptically. 'Perhaps you should ask *her*. It's not my story to tell.' She set aside the sketch pad and flexed her hand. 'There, I think I have what I need. You did well. Feel free to relax. You must be stiff.' She regretted her choice of words immediately and blushed.

'Yes, I rather am, come to think of it.' Dev flexed his own hand about himself, testing and laughed.

'You are incorrigible,' Gwen scolded, but she couldn't help but laugh, too, at herself, at him.

'It's fun to tease you, Gwen.' Dev said softly, nothing teasing at all in his tone, but something far more intimate. He rose from the improvised bed and reached for the discarded banyan, shrugging into it, an invitation in his gaze. She looked away, busying herself with her pencils and papers. But he was not deterred.

She felt him before he touched her, coming up behind her, settling his hands at her shoulders and massaging. 'You're tight. Occupational hazard? Hmm?' he murmured at her ear. God, his hands felt good.

'That feels great.' She rolled her neck and let herself indulge in the luxury of being touched.

'Do you know what else would be great?' He pressed his thumb against a knot in her shoulder and she sighed. 'Dinner. I'm starved. Modelling is hard work and it's late now. Will you let me take you to dinner? There's a little place I know run by a gentleman from Bengal that sells a delicious curry.' He continued massaging.

She'd never felt less like going out than she did right

now. She wanted more of *this*—more of Dev's hands on her, more of the slow hum running through her body. It was a hard-won admission, an admission to herself that she did not take lightly. It meant crossing bridges from which there would be no turning back.

'Or,' Dev continued in decadent tones, 'we could stay in. I thought I saw a chophouse down the street on my way over. Perhaps we could find an errand boy to fetch us some supper.'

She knew what consenting to that meant. It was the first step towards other affinities, other familiarities. She was inviting him, *permitting* him, to return to the intimacy that had been born a few nights ago, only this time those intimacies might take other forms. They would not be limited to talk and an exchange of stories. They'd likely venture into the physical, a natural culmination of an afternoon spent in the presence of a naked man.

One could not do such a thing and remain entirely unaffected by it, much like one could not watch a horse breed and not be at least somewhat aroused in the aftermath. How could things not take an intimate turn, eating dinner with a man clad only in a banyan?

Stop justifying it, she scolded herself. *You can just want it. You don't have to have a reason. You know what this is and what it will not be. Perhaps this is exactly what you need to take those last steps into the future.*

She turned to face Dev, to let him see her face, her decision. 'Let's stay in.'

Chapter Thirteen

Staying in was easily accomplished. Within three quarters of an hour, they were seated cross-legged on the wide platform bed, cradling bowls of steaming soup in their hands, a makeshift table pulled close to hold their wine glasses and the loaf of fresh bread, a lamp illuminating their space in the newly fallen spring darkness.

It was a simple supper in a simple space, but Dev could not recall a meal he'd enjoyed more. Because it was with her, this woman who'd teased and tantalised him all afternoon with her glances, her touches, the glimpses she'd allowed him into her life, into *her*.

He shifted on the bed, careful to keep his banyan arranged to hide the tell-tale signs of just how much she'd tantalised him. Even now, his body readily recalled the feel of her hands on him, massaging oil into his skin with a competent expertise that he found extraordinarily arousing. He hadn't her gift for detachment, nor her experience with it. If he'd been her husband, he would not have been as gracious as Christophe.

Yet, he did not think he was the only one struggling for objectivity today. And then there'd been the
way she'd sighed when he touched her this evening,
his hands at her shoulders. She wanted him, needed
him. She'd done battle with her demons to have him.
In what capacity, though? What had been the terms of
her victory?

Dev reached for the wine and poured them each another glass, indulging himself a bit tonight with a rare
second glass. 'What shall we toast to? To staying in?'

Her blue eyes were dark sapphires in the flame of the
lamp. 'To staying in with good company,' she amended.

'Of course.' He clinked his glass against hers. 'I
think you stay in far too often alone.' It had occurred
to him as she'd talked this afternoon that for someone from a large family, she mentioned them very seldom. 'Surely your brothers are in town,' he fished as
he sipped his wine. 'Do you not dine with your family
or with your in-laws?' Certainly the Earl was in town
during the Season.

She shot him a wry look over the rim of her glass.
'They're interfering. I prefer to keep them at arm's
length. Out of sight, out of mind, or something like
that. As long as I am no trouble, they're content to let
me be.' He knew what that meant. As long as she lived
discreetly, lived without scandal attached to her name,
she could remain independent. But she was always on
probation, a probation that could be revoked in their
minds any time.

'Loneliness is a high price to pay for freedom,' Dev
replied somewhat grimly. Her family had found a way

after all to keep their wayward daughter on a short leash, although somewhat more indirectly than dragging her home from Italy.

She shook her head in disagreement. 'It's not too high, though. I have my own house, my own business. I come and go as I please. I have agency over my own money and my career. I paint as I like. I take care of myself. How many women can say that?'

In secret. In risk of discovery. Living on the edge of a society that didn't know what to make of her.

Self-reliance was an expensive, lonely gift, Dev thought, but did not give voice to the idea. Tonight was not for arguing with her. Tonight was for setting loneliness aside for a short time for them both.

'The soup was good. I admit I am still getting used to the taste, or lack of taste, of English food. Are you finished?' Dev reached for her bowl and set it aside.

'There are far fewer spices in English food. It's less exciting than Italian food,' Gwen agreed. 'In Italy, we had fresh food almost year round. From basil our cook made the most delectable pesto.'

Dev smiled. 'We don't have pesto, but we have *dal*. It's a thick, lentil soup, I supposed you'd call it. We make it with coconut milk and vegetables, and lentils of course.' Dev smiled, an idea coming to him. 'There's a little place in the East End down by the docks that serves *dal*. We should go some time. I'd like to take you if you're up for such an adventure.' She'd be safe enough with him. 'After all, you've introduced me to *maritozzi*. The least I can do is reciprocate.'

She put a soft hand on his. 'Don't do that, Dev. Don't tempt me with things that will likely never be.'

Dev leaned forward with a teasing grin, breathing in the jasmine scent of her, evocative like a spring night. 'Who says they'll never come to pass? Don't we get to decide?'

'Dev, you know what I mean. Once the official portrait is revealed, your attentions will be required elsewhere.' One could always count on Gwen for an honest assessment of a situation. It was both heartening and brutally accurate. She was laying out the rules of their engagement—that was the heartening part. It was her timeline that was brutal—the idea that there was only two weeks left to them before she would no longer countenance an association between them.

Perhaps Rafe was right. She did not see herself as a duchess, did not want to be a duchess. She was probably the only woman in the *ton* who wouldn't want such an accolade. But that was part of her charm. She fit no mould. He didn't want her to, yet therein was the irony. By claiming her, he'd be asking her to take on that mould, to find a way to make it fit.

She was not the only one with conditions. He had rules to lay out as well. 'But before then, my attentions are all yours.' He reached for her hand and lifted it to his lips. 'Turn around and let me work on your shoulders some more.'

His hands were nothing short of magic, easing the tension from her shoulders with calm expertise. It had been an age since anyone had ministered to her, touched her for the sole purpose of her own benefit, and she sank too easily into the pleasure of it. 'If you were to slip out of your dress and lie down, I could do your back,' Dev whispered at her ear, his hands already sliding the sleeves of her gown from her shoulders and loosening the fastenings.

She did not think to protest it any more than he had protested her oiling of him earlier, even though, intuitively, she knew this was leading to a far different place, with a far different result. There would be pleasure of another sort at the end of this road.

Whenever she'd contemplated that particular pleasure, it had been with the tension of anticipation. Never had she'd thought she'd arrive at that point while in a state of utter relaxation, the moment surrounded by a sense of rightness, that this indeed was the most natural progression of their evening together, their relationship and for once there was no guilt.

Perhaps Dev was right. Love was infinite, it did not need to be exclusive. But that didn't change other realities, primarily that this thing between her and Dev could not last. Love or not, this was for the short term only.

She heard the soft susurration of his banyan as it slid to the floor, her cue that he was entirely nude now and she would be shortly, that the game had changed, ratcheted. His warm hands made short work of her underclothes. She felt the weight of his phallus and his sac against her buttocks where he straddled her, accustoming her to the heft and feel of him, his hands once more on either side of her spine, pressing, rubbing, releasing tension until she felt nothing but the thrum of desire humming through her.

Her entire being was fixed on that desire now from the race of her pulse to the pool of warm heat in her belly and the dampness below. How delicious, how intoxicating to feel desire again, to feel it filling her, not like a rushing stream flooded and swollen with the melted snows of winter, but like the steady, inexorable, unstoppable crawl of lava from a volcano, until she was filled with it and just as overwhelmed. He pressed a kiss to the back of her neck, whispering the seductive command, 'Roll over. Look at me and let me look at you.'

Even having sketched him all afternoon, she was not prepared for the sheer masculine beauty of him up close, for the burning green eyes, the muscled power of those bronze shoulders and the atlas of his chest. There was no protection of objectivity now, no pretence to hide behind. There was only them and their desire. Their eyes held and she better understood his request. There was to be no hiding, no using him and pretending he was another. This was to be honest. Of course. She expected nothing less from him.

Dev Bythesea was not a man who shared well. He was a man who possessed and protected. His comments this afternoon had made that clear. In his desire to protect he would protect her freedom and all that was important to her. Perhaps that was why she felt safe with him, safe enough to lay the ghost of her past.

His mouth was on hers with a kiss that teased and tempted. She could taste the wine on his tongue, could smell the patchouli of his soap as his body covered hers, warm and solid and welcome. 'You are my goddess,' he whispered, the roughness from his evening beard rasping against the tender skin of her breasts as he trailed kisses down her neck to the valley between them, every nerve in her body alert to every sensation he raised no matter how minute until all she wanted was him, in her, filling her, the ultimate joining, the ultimate completion.

'I must have you, Dev.' Her words were an impatient command. She shifted, the cradle between her legs widening, inviting, luring, echoing the message of her words.

He did not tease, did not play coy, or attempt to deny her, to be the master of their pace, to tame her. His body answered hers, levering between her legs and nudging at her entrance and finding her tight despite her evident desire. He eased from her and sat back. Instinctively, she reached for him, a sigh of disappointment escaping her.

He bent forward with a brief kiss to her lips. 'What's good for the goose, my love. Be patient.' He reached for the little flagon of frangipani oil she'd used earlier and took himself in hand, slicking his length with it, his eyes on her as he did. Her breath hitched at the intimacy of the act and his apparent comfort with it. Her pulse raced and then he was over her again, the scent of the oil mingling with the promising musk of sex.

This time, her body did not protest as he entered, his eyes half-lidded, his body in abject concentration on the act. His length reached terminus and Gwen sighed beneath him, a sigh of wonder, of completion even though she knew there was more to be had. In this moment, this seemed enough in itself, to have him sheathed within her.

Then he began to move, *they* began to move, she
with wanting, he with giving, the motion creating pleasure's inexorable tide. Every inch of her vibrated with
it, with feeling, with life itself. Her hands clawed first
for purchase in the silk draperies of the platform bed,
then her body anchored about him, legs about his hips,
hands at his back, as she held him close and she gave
voice to the sounds of pleasure.

'My love, you must let me go.' His words were a
hoarse rasp she could barely comprehend at her ear.

'Not yet,' she begged, her own voice raw with desire.
'So close…' And then she was more than close, she was
there, at the apex of pleasure, spiralling up into the sun,
Icarus at the height of his achievement, and then in a
brilliant burst, falling out of the sky in an explosion of
colour and sensation, Dev panting beside her.

For a long while all she could do was stare at him.
Had that really just happened? The intensity overwhelmed her, claimed her ability to think. There was
no guilt, no comparison, no echoes of the past in the
space between them as they lay on the silks. There was
only Dev and Gwen, the two of them and the extraordinary moment they'd shared.

Gwen reached out to smooth back a dark lock of his
hair, allowing her hand to skim his cheek. This had
been about them. Just them. That was the more honest
answer and the one that required she take agency of her
decision. She had done this because she'd wanted to,
because she was attracted to him, because he touched
her in some elemental way that had eluded her since

Christophe's death, a way she thought she might never be touched again.

'We're good together.' That was an understatement. They were extraordinary together. He reached for her hand and kissed her knuckles, his gaze lingering on hers with drowsy contentedness. 'What now, Gwen?' He was letting her decide, although he likely knew what that decision would be.

She pressed against him, a leg hitching over his hip. 'What do you think after that?' She gave a throaty laugh. 'Who would choose one night of Heaven when they could choose two weeks?'

His hand was warm at her back, his mouth hovering over her as he chuckled, 'Not me.'

'Nor me,' she whispered, sealing the agreement with a kiss.

Chapter Fourteen

Breakfast teased her senses, waking Gwen with the nutty aroma of strong coffee and the sweetness of fresh baked buns overriding the scents of art and the night. She gave a languorous stretch, eyes closed, letting herself feel the morning as it came to her: the smells of the studio, the pleasant ache in her bones of a night well spent.

'Coffee, my dear?'

She opened her eyes to see Dev squatting beside the platform with a mug in his hands, his banyan loose and flowing about him, his dark waves tousled, his jaw stubbled. 'Mmm, what a lovely way to wake up.' She smiled at him—how could she not? The sight of him looking as indecently rumpled as she felt sparked reminders of how they'd spent themselves in the night, making love until exhausted sleep was the only recourse open to them.

He pushed a strand of hair back from her face. 'I agree. A most wondrous way to awake.' He rose and retrieved a plate and his own mug before settling himself on the platform, sitting cross-legged, his banyan doing little to conceal him. She didn't mind. Clothed or unclothed or somewhere in between, Dev Bythesea was a sight to behold. He certainly kept a girl's eyes busy. 'See anything you like?' he teased, catching the trajectory of her gaze.

'Quite,' she flirted unabashedly, aware of how good it felt to play like this, with ease and confidence and life, because, yes, after last night she felt alive again in a way she hadn't since... No. She would not finish that thought. She would leave it there with just 'since'.

Dev passed her the plate of sweet buns. 'They're not *maritozzi*, but perhaps they'll do for the "something sweet" part of breakfast.'

She took one and bit into dough and icing. They were still soft and warm and she sighed her appreciation not only of the sweet bun, but of him. 'You remembered.' That mattered more to her than how the buns tasted, although these were quite good.

He grinned and laughed. 'Of course I did. You only told me a few days ago.'

She wouldn't allow him to downplay the utter thoughtfulness of his gesture. 'You remembered and you acted on it.' When was the last time someone had shown her such a thorough courtesy? It touched her, tightened her throat and threatened tears. She tore off a piece of her bun, determined to push the tears away. She was *not* going to cry over a sweet bun. She leaned forward and fed the piece to him. He took the piece from her, his mouth making a decadent act of it.

'These are delicious, where did you get them?' She

finished her bun and reached for another, finding herself ravenous now that she was fully awake.

'There's a bakery down the street and coffee from the chophouse.' Dev refilled their coffee mugs.

'You didn't go dressed like that, did you?' She took a careful sip, imagining with some humour and more trepidation Dev striding into the bakery, his banyan open, and asking for breakfast rolls for the art studio.

'No,' Dev assured her. 'I sent the errand boy who lounges at the front of the building.' He gave a grimace. 'Speaking of which, do you have clients this morning?'

'I do not,' she informed him with a saucy smile. She set aside her coffee mug, breakfast and sweet buns forgotten. She had another sweet treat in mind. She straddled his lap. 'Well, actually I have this one client, he's very demanding, stays all night,' she teased with a kiss, her teeth nipping his bottom lip.

'Minx,' he growled appreciatively. His phallus surged hard against her mons and she felt an undeniable thrill of womanly power at being able to extract such a response from him, this man who was always in control. His hands gripped her hips, steadying her as he instructed, 'Wrap your legs about me, it will be more… comfortable.' She did not think the word comfortable had ever been uttered with such naughty nuance.

He was absolutely right. Gwen gave a final wriggle, her body fitting to his like a piece to a puzzle. The position made it impossible to not also wrap her arms about him and for his arms to wrap about her, holding her close against his chest. It was indeed a comforting position, communicating a sense of safety and calm, even as it was also an erotic position. As comforting as it was, one could not overlook one's partner's arousal at this proximity. She could no more ignore the press of his erection than he could avoid noticing the damp invitation her body offered it. 'Shall I ride you?' She nipped softly at his ear. It would be no effort at all to push him backwards on the platform-cum-bed and have her way with him.

Shall I ride you? The words were a potent aphrodisiac and the minx knew it. She knew precisely how she affected him. How could she not? He'd taken no pains to hide her ability to rouse him. But if he wanted joy for her in their lovemaking, he wanted control for himself. If he didn't take charge of the situation soon, he would surrender control and that would not serve either of them when he had something more pleasurable in mind.

'Not ride, my dear. *Flow.*' He breathed the word against her ear, his mouth answering with a nip of its own as he gave his decadent lesson in low, seductive tones meant to entice her, arouse her. 'Riding suggests domination, which has its own attractions to be sure. But flow is about connection, about togetherness.'

He rocked against her in the gentlest of motions and slid effortlessly, easily, into her depths as he continued the erotic tutorial. 'As we are now, there is no beginning, no end to us.' His body ached with the closeness of it as he began to move within her, his hands at her back, his mouth at her mouth with a kiss that was infinity itself, long and full, tasting of coffee and sweet icing. All his senses were alive, bristling with it, in fact, until he nearly trembled with alertness. 'You are glorious.' His voice was not more than a hoarse rasp of desire.

He pressed into her and she gave a delicious gasp, her own body abandoning itself to the pleasures of the lotus, her legs about his waist tightening, holding him to her, helping him, guiding him to the destination of their mutual pleasure, his partner in all of it. He thrust once more and let the pleasure come, sweeping over them in a moment of wild recklessness, the desire to claim pleasure overriding practicality, her cries muffled against his shoulder as completion took them.

He held her in the intimate closeness of *padmasana* for a long while, feeling her breathing return to normal, her body relax with his as the intensity of pleasure was exchanged for a more comfortable, calming iteration of itself.

Only then did he lay her back on the bed, separate from her and stretch alongside her, replete and sated on the edge of a morning nap. Perhaps it was a good thing she did not have clients this morning. Dev seriously doubted his ability to rise from this bed, such as it was, and then find the strength to dress himself. Both seemed liked Herculean tasks at the moment.

Gwen's hand was light on his chest, a finger drawing idle circles on his skin, her voice husky. 'I keep thinking the next time will be less spectacular, that it can't possibly be that good all the time and then I am most delightfully proved wrong yet again.' She sighed contentedly and curled against him, her head fitted to the indent of his shoulder. 'What is *padmasana*?'

'The lotus. That's the name for making love in that

particular position. It emphasises pleasure through togetherness.' Even now, sated as he was, his body managed to rouse slightly at the memory of them locked together, seeking pleasure. It was not a position for the timid or unsure. It required confidence and participation. Guinevere Norton was a bold lover who had both. If he needed further proof that she was meant for him, there it was. But how to convince her?

Dev let out a deep, contented sigh. 'The morning is ours, what shall we do?' Gwen's hand stilled on his chest. His request had caught her by surprise, hopefully a pleasant one.

'I was going to paint. I thought you were eager for your portrait.'

'I am, but it has occurred to me that as long as I have the sketches you did last night, I have the leverage I need. My aunt would absolutely hate those sketches seeing publication in any form.' Prints at Ackermann's, for instance. 'I am due at Creighton House this afternoon for a session with my uncle. You could come and sketch him,' Dev suggested. 'Do you have any errands this morning?' Perhaps he should not press his luck. Maybe she wanted him to leave. He was rather surprised to discover he didn't want to. He was in no hurry for anything that didn't involve Gwen beside him.

She thought for a moment and then smiled. 'I do have errands. I need to go to the market. I've been putting it off on account of being so busy here.' She made a frown. 'Are you sure you don't mind the market? It's rather mundane and plebian, I suppose. Most ladies send their maids, but I prefer to do my own shopping.'

Dev grinned. 'It just so happens, I love markets. Then it's settled. The market for the morning, Creighton House for the afternoon. And the evening?' He was testing her. What would she say? Had she meant it last night when she'd chosen two weeks over a single evening?

She gave him a coy smile. 'I thought you already knew the answer to that, Dev. This evening we should try making love in a bed for once.'

Somewhere in the neighbourhood the bells chimed, sounding the hour. Nine. It was a long time until night. He was going to think about her words all day, which meant only one thing—he was going to spend the day fighting a constant state of arousal. Dev groaned and swung his feet to the floor. 'Sounds like a busy day. We'd best get started.'

'Wait, I have one condition.' She tugged at his arm. 'You may not leave the bed until you agree,' she teased him with a smile.

'Then maybe I'll disagree on the grounds that the punishment is better than agreeing.'

'After the market, we need to stop by my house so I can change. I cannot go to Creighton House in yesterday's work dress. Your aunt would know what we'd been up to.' Dev doubted that would stop his aunt from figuring it out. His aunt would only have to take one look at his trousers and know what they'd been up to. But it was easy enough to accede.

Slow down, boy, his inner voice cautioned. *You start giving up control on little things and then it will be bigger things*.

Dev pushed the warning away.

They only had two weeks. By those parameters there was only so much he could give her, but he would give it all to her in the hopes that he might change her mind. But her mind wasn't the only one that would need changing. There was his aunt's mind and perhaps even society's mind. But surely that would be the less difficult of the two tasks. As Rafe had pointed out, it wasn't that she was unacceptable. The bigger battle would be whether or not she'd believe it, allow it.

Dev Bythesea at the market was a revelation indeed. He'd not lied. He *did* love markets. Guinevere found herself studying him as much as she studied the wares displayed in the stalls. She'd watched him so much she'd walked right past the stall selling quills and had to go back. His green eyes took it all in, as if his mind was making avid notes. 'You seem happy,' she commented, tucking the quills into her market basket. 'I've never known a gentleman who actually enjoys a market.'

'But they were likely not raised in the markets of India.' His hand applied a light pressure to her back, drawing her aside to avoid a passing crowd of urchins. 'Keep your basket and reticule close,' he murmured. 'Light fingers in the area.'

'You have good eyes.'

'Again, I was raised in the markets of India.' He smiled. They found a less populated, quieter aisle to stroll. 'Tell me about it,' Gwen coaxed.

He was an infinitely fascinating man. Every time she thought she understood him, he displayed a new facet: nephew of a duke, grandson of a raja, a man born to nobility, yet the son of a merchant, a self-made man who'd passed that quality on to his son, a man who was determined to control his own destiny whether it be mercantile or marital. That man intrigued her, drew her because, for all their outward differences, he was like her.

They stopped at a leatherworks booth. 'This is good work,' Dev complimented the man at the stall before they moved on and he consented to answer her request. 'I followed my father on his rounds as soon as I could keep up. I spent my days running behind him, listening to him talk to the merchants, make his deals. Before I was born, of course, he worked for the East India Company. Later, when the company's policies were no longer tenable for him, he was able to buy out his contract and set up for himself. It was something of an unorthodox arrangement, but my uncle helped the situation along.'

They stopped at a stall selling brightly coloured ribbons. 'This blue matches your eyes.' Dev held it up before she could protest. 'Would you permit me this small token of my affections?' He produced two coins for the vendor and the matter was settled, much as all matters were settled with Dev. It was the action that mattered, not the words.

'Will you tie it on?' Gwen asked, giving him access to her neck. 'I feel like a school girl with her first beau.' She laughed as his warm hands skimmed the nape of her neck. He pressed a kiss to her skin before he stepped back and her blood thrummed. Being with him was intoxicating. She'd not expected that.

'And why shouldn't you feel that way—you are

hardly in your dotage?' Dev queried, moving to take the market basket from her.

She gave him a serious stare and contemplated her answer as she surrendered the basket. Nothing but the truth would do. 'Because I didn't think I would ever feel that way again.'

'But then you gave yourself permission and it was possible,' Dev said.

'Yes,' she breathed with a smile for him. She'd allowed herself to feel and the results had been extraordinary and different. What she felt with Dev was not a replica of what she'd felt with Christophe, that was truly gone. But both were intoxicating in their own ways. Perhaps it was because *she* was not the same. She'd been a girl when she'd married Christophe. Everything had been new. She was not that girl with Dev. She was a woman who knew her own mind and her risks.

They paused at a cinnamon stand and she ordered a twist of ground cinnamon for her cook. The vendor dug his scoop into a jar, but Dev stopped him with a shake of his head, polite but firm. 'I want to smell it first, please.' He sniffed. 'Do you have something else? This is not as fresh as I'd prefer.' The vendor begrudgingly brought out another canister and Dev sniffed again more approvingly.

'What was wrong with the first one?' Gwen's curiosity got the better of her as they walked away, the twist of fresh cinnamon tucked securely away.

'It was stale, the scent wasn't what it should be,' Dev explained.

'And what should it be?' Here was one more piece

of information to file away about this man who could tell fresh cinnamon from stale.

'Delicate, sweet, but also rich. He was trying to sell you cassia instead, too,' he added. 'You want Ceylon cinnamon, it's always the better choice. You can tell the difference from the colour. Ceylon cinnamon is a tan brown.'

'You are a marvel, Dev Bythesea. The only Viscount in England who knows the difference, I'd wager.' Gwen laughed. 'Let me guess, your father specialised in spices?' They stopped to buy meat pasties for lunch.

'My father's company began as a spice-exporting company. He worked with the local merchants and with Rafe's father to export spices back to England.' Dev guided them to a quiet spot where they could eat and talk, acutely aware that the morning had slipped away. Afternoon and Creighton House loomed.

'Why did he leave the East India Company? Most men don't. Surely the money was good enough and the company bears all the risk.' She'd been curious about that ever since Dev had mentioned the arrangement to leave the Company and his father's aversion to certain unspecified policies.

'The Company was changing. It was not the Company he'd come aboard with. Early on, it was not frowned upon for men to marry Indian wives, but by the time I was born, the Company had decided to distance itself from the Indian population, indirectly of course, through certain policies.

'The Company encouraged British girls to come out and marry the men. A woman who marries a Company

man, for instance, earns an annual allowance of three
hundred pounds for the duration of the marriage.' He
paused with a grimace. 'There were other policies, too.
Mixed-blood sons could not work for the Company,
not even clerking. The Company would never take me
on. There was no longer a future for our family there.'

Gwen took a moment to process the import of
those words when added to what he'd revealed about
Aanchal's father. 'So, your father formed his own company, a legacy for you.' What a father Dev's must have
been and he'd passed that consideration for family on
to his son, shaping the man his son had become.

'Not just for me, but for our family. How would I support my mother if anything happened to my father if I
couldn't work for the Company? Yes, my grandfather
would have taken us in, but suffice it to say, the palace
had its limitations, too, for me and for my mother,' Dev
said seriously and she saw for the first time the depths
of the worlds he navigated. He was multifaceted because he had to be, it was a matter of survival for him.

'It's much like the reasons you set up your studio.
Your family, your in-laws, would have taken *you* in.'
His thumb brushed at a drop of juice at the corner of
her mouth and he smiled softly. 'It is not so different,
Gwen. *We* are not so different.'

'I know,' she whispered. That was what scared her.
The longer she was with him, the closer she let him get,
the more she began to wonder how was it possible that
she might have met a man she could love but couldn't
have? 'We should probably go. I need to change and

your uncle is expecting us.' But her briskness didn't budge Dev.

His hand closed about her wrist and he gently tugged her to him, drawing her between his thighs. Her breath caught. For a moment she thought he might kiss her, here in public. His mouth hovered near hers, but there was no kiss, only the low rumbled privacy of his words as his green eyes held hers. 'It's all right to feel, Gwen. This thing between us is wonderous, glorious. Do not be afraid of it or of yourself.'

And when it ended, what then? Then, there would be plenty to fear.

Chapter Fifteen

Creighton House loomed like a mausoleum, columned and quiet off Portland Square. Large trees in full leaf shielded it from view by the casual eye. Stepping on to its grounds was like stepping outside the world. The busy London street with the clatter of carriages and the shouts of drivers disappeared, replaced by a stately solemnity not unlike the stillness found in a graveyard.

Dev slid her a look and reached for her hand as they took the steps. 'Are you ready?'

'I suppose I am.' She'd changed into a blue muslin afternoon gown trimmed in white ribbon. She touched a hand to the blue ribbon from the market, still about her neck in decoration.

He squeezed her hand as they waited for their knock to be answered. 'Thank you for doing this. I hope my uncle is having a good day.' He had changed, too. They'd found time to stop by Evans Row as well and he'd traded yesterday's attire for buff-coloured trousers, a dark coffee-hued coat and a bronze silk waistcoat. He'd brushed his dark waves into a semblance of order but immaculate grooming couldn't disguise the worry that lay beneath.

'If he's not feeling up to it today, I will come another time,' she assured him, realising too late how little she could control that promise. The Duke didn't have the luxury of another time—future days, planning for next week, were not guarantees for him any longer. 'I *am* sorry, Dev,' she said softly as butler answered the door.

Inside, Creighton House was silent, servants moving like wraiths. It was as if everyone was holding their breath, waiting for the inevitable to happen, but not wanting to do anything that might cause that inevitability to occur. The place had no life, no spark, no colour. No wonder Dev had insisted on his own home. She could not have lived here. Yet her heart went out to them, they were already in mourning, their hearts already breaking.

Guinevere swallowed around the sudden thickness in her throat as they climbed the stairs to the Duke's chambers. This pre-mourning, this sadness at watching it all slip away, was what Christophe had spared her that day on the beach in Naples. This was what it would have been like to watch him slide towards death and be able to do nothing but mourn what was to come.

'Are you all right?' Dev asked quietly as they reached the top of the stairs. His words were close to her ear, private and concerned. 'I know it's difficult to be here, to see everyone like this.' He nodded towards a set of doors where a man in livery waited. 'It will only get worse. If you'd rather not, I'd understand. You can leave now and I'll see you tonight.'

'No, of course not. I want to do this.' For him—for Dev. Now that she'd been here, it was more important to her than ever that she do this for him, to give him a remembrance of his uncle.

The footman held open the doors as they approached. 'His Grace is having a good day, Lord Everham. He is looking forward to your visit.' He offered the report in low tones appropriate for a library or…a morgue.

The Duke's chambers held some relief from the tone of the world outside his doors. The heavy curtains were drawn back, windows open to let in fresh spring air, but there was no mistaking that this was a sickroom and that the man in the enormous bed would not leave this room alive. For today, however, the Duke looked rather more alive than dead. He sat in the massive bed, propped up by pillows, clean-shaven and groomed, wearing a shirt, cravat and burgundy dressing robe.

Impending death haunted the Duke's features. Gwen had spent too much time staring at faces, sketching faces, to not recognise the over-prominent bones poking at the grey flaccid skin and the purplish bags beneath his eyes. It was in his eyes, Gwen noted, that life remained, where indeed, she might argue, that life had gathered all its strength and pooled there where it might look out on the world it was leaving. She would capture those eyes, green like Dev's, sharp and alert. The Bythesea eyes, she thought. Bythesea green.

'You've brought a guest today, Devlin. This must be the painter you've talked about so much.' Those green eyes twinkled and the man tried to sit forward. Dev was quick to restrain him with a gentle hand at his shoulder.

'I brought Mrs Norton, but you must not get over-excited,' Dev instructed firmly, 'Or Aunt will not let me bring her again.'

'I've come to sketch you, with your permission, Your Grace.' Gwen stepped forward.

'She's pretty, Devlin. Just like you said,' the Duke praised and Gwen felt herself blush. 'You're Lord Sandmore, Harry Parkhurst's, granddaughter.'

'Yes, I am.' Hardly anyone referred to her that way any more. Gwen smiled and settled on the edge of the bed.

'How is old Sandy? I haven't seen him in ages.' The Duke gave a dry cough that Dev answered with a glass of water, taking care to help the man drink without spilling. Dev was good with his uncle, considerate without smothering, without scolding.

'Neither have I,' Gwen confessed. 'He doesn't come up to town these days and I don't go to the country so our paths have very little opportunity to cross.' But perhaps she should make the effort, Gwen thought. Her grandfather wasn't getting any younger. Termagant head of the family he might be, he was still her grandfather. She flipped over the sketch pad and took a pencil from her satchel. 'Is it all right if I sit here while the two of you talk business?'

The Duke nodded and Dev pulled a chair to the bed and reached for the ledgers stacked on the table. 'Today, Uncle, I want to discuss the village at Taryton. It's a minor holding, but I think it could be much more.'

Gwen settled to her work as the men talked. Mostly, Dev talked. Too much speech for the Duke brought on fits of coughing and she could see Dev making the effort to spare him while still including him in the conversation. She spent much of her time on the eyes, wanting to get them right, this final glory left to what had once been a handsome man.

She could see that one-time handsomeness imprinted on Dev now that she saw the two men side by side. Dev had the family eyes, the long, straight, family nose. He was Bythesea through and through, except, of course, for his bronze skin as Dev had mentioned on two occasions now.

Today's mention had been more implicit. Gwen looked down at the sketch and added more shading to the Duke's jaw. That moment in the market when Dev had answered her question about why his father had left the East India Company had been…poignant. Telling, especially against the backdrop of his heartbreak with Aanchal. He was proud of the business his father had built, but there was also the awareness that it was a choice his father had *had* to make.

'It was something of an unorthodox arrangement, but my uncle helped that along,' he'd said.

He was acutely aware of what the family had done not just for his father but for him, *because* of him. Family above all else, the most important of duties and responsibilities. Dev had said that, too. No wonder he had come when his uncle had sent for him, no wonder he was willing to tolerate so much of his aunt's mechanisations.

The family had been there for him and now it was his duty to be there for them even though it took him halfway around the world and away from all he knew, even though it demanded he step into a tightly knit aristocratic world that did not know what to make of him, that did not always want to welcome him. That took a certain kind of rare bravery.

She finished her studies of the Duke and took a moment to do a study of the two of them together: the elder and the younger, the Duke and the heir, a new age and the old. The passing of a torch. They'd moved on from Dev's thoughts about updating the village at Taryton to his investment with the Duke of Cowden's new Prometheus Club. There were powerful themes underlying the already powerful recognition of closeness between the two men.

What a painting this would make, Gwen thought. It would be a different kind of work for her, it wouldn't be a portrait. It would be a scene, one that told the story of every title in Britain—the hope and fear of every heir that the apex of their lives, the achievement for which they'd been raised, rested on the demise of those who'd gone before them, ascendency and grief inseparable parts of their unique circle of life.

'Gwen, do you have everything you need? I think we're about finished here.' Dev broke into her thoughts and she startled, dropping her pencil, as she recalled herself to the present.

'We're not done yet, dear boy,' his uncle broke in. 'I want a word with Mrs Norton, alone. Why don't you go find your aunt and I'll send Mrs Norton down later.'

She'd not expected that. But perhaps the man only wanted a look at her sketches. Perhaps he wanted to harangue her about making him look like a man who had one foot in the grave. She braced herself as Dev left the room with a final admonition that the Duke not over-tax himself and a promise to see him tomorrow.

'Those promises are worth more than gold to me, these days,' the Duke said as Gwen took Dev's vacated chair. 'One more day, I tell myself. Devlin is counting on me. Devlin needs to talk about Taryton or the home farm at Creighton, or something else that cannot be overlooked.' He attempted a feeble wave of his hand and failed. 'I can't even make a simple gesture.' His sharp green eyes fixed on her, the sharpness gone, replaced by sad pragmatism. 'Devlin hopes I have the summer. My physicians equivocate—they tell me it could be months, thinking that gives me hope. It is a lie. I do not have months, I do not have a summer as much as I would wish to give Devlin what he wants.'

Gwen reached for his hand and clasped it between her own, choosing to stay silent. What could she add besides more lies?

'Are you not going to lie to me, too? Argue with me? Tell me that I have time?' He gave a rattly chuckle and Gwen hoped it wouldn't bring on a coughing fit. The afternoon had left him worn and exhausted.

'No, I am not, Your Grace.'

He smiled. 'I knew I liked you. My nephew likes you, too. I'm sure he's told you that by now. He's a very direct man, like his father. I was always the diplomatic one. My brothers were the headstrong ones. The three of us ambitious in our own ways. We were a good team. I missed my brother when he went to India. It was the right thing to do. There was nothing for him here but getting into trouble. But we missed each other's adult lives—weddings, births, he wasn't here when our father passed, when perhaps I could have used both my brothers to guard my back,' the Duke mused and paused, the long interchange leaving him winded.

'Devlin needs a wife who will guard his back,' he said at last.

Gwen didn't know what to make of that statement. Was it a warning to stay away from his nephew? A reminder that she was not a proper wife for him? Perhaps he was only seeking reassurance? 'The Duchess has made an admirable start on that front. She has a list for him and the portrait she's commissioned will be quite persuasive. I am sure by the end of June, he'll have his pick of London's best.'

'They will never make him happy.' Gwen felt an infinitesimal tightening of his hand in hers, an insistence on the Duke's part. 'He talks of nothing but you when he comes. It was the first sign of life in him, real life, since he arrived. I am so glad he brought you today, so that I could meet you and see you for myself. You make him happy.'

'Thank you, Your Grace. But I feel compelled to point out that we've only known one another for three weeks and even then only in a business capacity required for the portrait.'

The Duke raised a brow in a gesture reminiscent of Dev when he doubted her. 'You were at the Camford soirée with him. My wife told me and I have eyes, my dear girl. I am not so far gone that I cannot see what is right in front of me. There is something about the way you are together, how you stood when you entered the room, an innate closeness, comfort with one another.'

He seemed to sink further into the pillows, his eyes closing. 'I remember you better than you might think. You married the Earl of Benton's second son, the wild, handsome artist, and went to Italy. I was sorry to hear of his accident. Drowning, was it?' He paused for a long while and Gwen thought he might have drifted off. But his next words were spoken with surprising strength. 'It was something of a whirlwind romance as I recall. How long had you known Benton's son?'

'Just a month before the engagement,' Gwen confessed softly. The wedding had followed within two weeks of that announcement, but she kept that to herself. The Duke didn't need any more ammunition with which to make his point.

The Duke opened his eyes. 'Just one month,' he repeated with a smile flitting on his dry lips. 'And your marriage was a happy one? No regrets?'

'It was happy and the only regret is that it was much shorter than I'd anticipated.'

The Duke gave a sad, knowing nod. 'Life itself, my dear girl, is much shorter than any of us anticipate.' His eyes closed again and Gwen took her cue.

'I should go, we have worn you out today.'

'Not yet, please. Give me a moment. There's one more thing I'd like to say.'

And this might be my only chance.

The words lay unspoken, but no less present for their silence. Did Dev know the Duke felt time was running fast? 'My wife means well,' he said at last. 'She has always done her duty for Creighton. In her mind, marrying off Devlin is her next duty. Her list will not suit him and Devlin will not stand for it. Do not let protocol and archaic social expectations keep you from following your heart, Mrs Norton. It is in attempting the impossible that we truly discover ourselves. I would not want to see you and my nephew deny yourselves happiness because of some silly rules set by even sillier people.'

She smiled. 'I will keep that in mind, Your Grace.'

'I want your word on it, Mrs Norton. I am counting on you,' he said sternly. 'Will you come again?' She nodded and he sighed. 'I would like to live long enough to see your portrait of me, but I doubt I shall. In any event, it was never for me any way.'

She squeezed his hand and rose. 'Good day, Your Grace. I *will* see you soon.' Outside the room, she wiped at her tears. The encounter with the Duke had been emotional, conjuring up old grief and mingling it with the new—a grief for what she could not have no matter how earnestly the old Duke might wish for it. It wasn't just social protocol that kept her from Dev, it was her own heart. She could not risk opening herself up to such loss again.

She'd promised herself two weeks, and that she could protect herself if she knew from the start how and when and why it would end. But she could not take on the angst of 'until death do us part', never knowing where that ambiguous line was—today? Tomorrow? Ten years? Thirty years from now? And even then, she knew instinctively thirty years or fifty wouldn't be enough.

The Duke's words whispered to her. *'Life is shorter than any of us anticipate.'* How could she deliberately put herself through that again? Yet she wondered if the choice was really up to her? That perhaps that was what she told herself—that she wouldn't do it—because it had already been decided that he wasn't meant for her regardless of what she wanted. All she had was two weeks.

Chapter Sixteen

These two weeks might possibly be the most perfect two weeks of his life to date, Dev mused as he watched Gwen sleeping beside him, her blonde hair a tousled halo on the pillow, the coverlet draped across her hips, spring sun pouring through her bedroom window's gauzy white curtains. Below in the back garden, he could hear the burble of her fountain. She looked like Botticelli's *Venus* come down from Olympus to walk among the mortals.

He loved waking up here beside her in her little piece of Italy. Dev breathed in the sweet jasmine scent of her and sighed contentedly. How was it possible that she was both calm peace and wild passion, the perfect paradox of the ideal woman?

They had managed to carve out a bit of paradise for themselves amid the complexities and tensions of his daily life. Their days had taken on a rhythm of their own after the night she'd drawn him in her studio. Their nights had advanced to being spent in beds, alternating between his and hers, usually hers. He preferred the latter. In the mornings he escorted her to her studio where he either stayed while she painted or he would discreetly leave so she could meet with clients and return for her in the afternoon. She would accompany him most days to his uncle. That reminded him of his uncle's portrait. If he wanted a sneak peek at Gwen's sketches, now would be his chance.

Dev slipped out of bed and threw on his banyan as he strode towards her little writing desk where her portfolio and sketch pad lay. He cast a last look at Gwen asleep and quietly opened the sketch pad. A soft smile curved on his lips as he took in the drawings, his mind filling with remembered images of her with his uncle: Gwen listening to the older man's slowly told stories; Gwen holding his uncle's hand while she waited for them to finish discussing business.

She was kindness and patience personified, begrudging his uncle no moment of her time. She'd been good for his uncle, had brought that Bythesea sparkle back to his eyes. Perhaps, Dev thought, she'd even bought the man a little more time. She'd captured that sparkle perfectly in the eyes that stared back at him from her drawings.

Dev had not asked what his uncle had talked with her about that first day and Gwen had not offered any insight on what had been discussed. Whatever it was, his uncle had meant for it to be private. So, Dev had let it be. He could imagine what it might have been though, if it was anything like what his uncle had said to him yesterday.

'Don't let her get away, my boy. Don't lose her in the crowd.'

He knew the crowd his uncle spoke of: the debutantes, their mothers, their ambitious fathers who were already crowding around. With the exception of the Travellers, he couldn't even go to his clubs without those ambitious fathers begging a moment of his time to advance their daughters. Word had got out that his uncle had worsened and the vultures were getting their ducks in a row.

He would fend them off, of course. He would not be coerced into anything. He was more worried about Gwen slipping away at the stroke of midnight like Cinderella. She would slip, too, simply allow herself to fade into the crowd when he wasn't looking, allowing herself to be swallowed up. It was something she was much practised at from the discreet art of her plain, unadorned gowns to her more direct choice to eschew teas and social circles for the afternoon light of her studio.

He would not permit it. Such brave, foolish words. What did he think he was going to do about it? Whatever it was, he would have to do it soon. His aunt's portrait party was tomorrow night, the unofficial end to the two weeks. They'd not talked about it. But they must.

Did she really think he would simply kiss her goodbye tomorrow night and let her walk out of his life? Did she want that? But would she want the alternative? Some might say it was the question of which was the lesser of two evils. That was a poor analogy. He'd prefer a woman not think of being with him as an evil. He must discuss it with her today.

Gwen stirred and sat up sleepily across the room. 'You're peeking, shame on you,' she teased drowsily. 'I can't believe you're awake already. Apparently, I didn't wear you out enough last night.'

'Well, you can always try again,' Dev drawled. He closed the sketch pad and made his way back to the bed. 'You've captured his eyes beautifully.' He dropped his banyan and slid beneath the sheets. 'You know, in Hinduism, the eyes are the gateway to the soul. Religious art always makes the eyes last because they are holiest, and when we go to the temple, we invoke the *darsan*, the two-way vision where we see the god and the god sees us.'

Her hand stroked through his hair, her gaze soft on his. 'We. Us. Do you think of yourself as Hindu, Dev?' she asked, a little furrow forming delightfully at the bridge of her nose.

'I was raised Hindu and Christian.' He smiled and pressed a kiss to her furrowed brow. He settled her against him. He loved mornings like this, just the two of them snuggled in bed, talking, discovering one another, exchanging their stories.

'When I was young, my father took me to a talk in Calcutta given by the missionary, William Carey, who spoke of Hindu Christians and how there was room for Jesus within Hindu culture. I was almost ten at the time, old enough to be impacted by his words even if I was not necessarily fully aware of his politics and he certainly had his own agenda.

'Still, at the time, it helped me to see myself not as a person caught between two worlds, straddling two

spheres, but as a whole person who wasn't a contradic-
tion. I saw that it was possible to be Christian by faith
and Hindu by culture. It wasn't until the episode with
Aanchal that I realised the rest of the world didn't necessarily reconcile things in the same way.'

'You are absolutely a most fascinating man.' Gwen
smiled and the words warmed him, thrilled him. Where
much of London found him odd, she found him intriguing. Where London wanted to push away from him, she
wanted to draw close. Part of him wanted to crow, to
gloat, to even press her and ask if he was more fascinating than Christophe. But that was not the point. He
wanted her to recognise that she could have them both,
love them both completely.

He drew her atop him, 'How fascinating?' he teased,
only to have his overture interrupted by an urgent knock
on her door. 'Or not,' he groaned as Gwen got out of bed
and slipped into a robe to answer the door.

He adjusted the sheet so as not to offend her maid
should the girl peep into the room. There was a brief
discussion at the door and then Gwen returned to bed,
a note in her hand. 'This is for you. Your man brought
it from Evans Row, apparently with some rush.'

He took the note and unfolded it. They exchanged a
worried look and he knew what she was thinking: His
uncle. That day was coming. One morning that news
would greet them, or it would find him as he sat for
drinks at the Travellers with Eden, and when it did his
world would complete its upending.

He shook his head, wanting to ease her worry. 'It's
not him.' But there were other worries besides his uncle,

worries that he'd been able to hold in abeyance these past two weeks, although they hovered on the periphery of his happiness.

He'd been waiting to hear from the Heralds' College, waiting to be able to go on the offensive with Cousin Bish, waiting for the swarm to officially descend after the portrait party, which meant going another round with his aunt over how he would live his life and approach his responsibility to the dukedom. He was not much good at waiting. 'It is my aunt. She requests my presence immediately at Creighton House.'

Guinevere came to sit on the edge of the bed. 'Does she say why? For what reason?'

'She doesn't say, only that there is an immediate need.' Which, knowing his aunt, could be anything from a true crisis which might involve his uncle, to a minor slight of protocol that she felt must be addressed promptly. Dev swung his legs over the side of the bed and sat up with a sigh. 'I'm sorry, I have to go.'

This was not how he'd imagined the last day before the party. He'd awakened this morning thinking of the things he'd meant to discuss with her, about how this didn't have to be the end. No matter what happened, in the next days, things *were* going to change and he wanted to be in charge of the direction those changes took, not his aunt. He leaned forward and stole a kiss. 'I'll send a note and let you know what has happened.'

His aunt was waiting for him in the breakfast room, the breakfast laid out on the sideboard untouched in the chafing dishes, newspapers waiting beside pristine white place settings while she paced before the window, agitation radiating from every pore. She turned when she saw him.

'The worst thing possible has happened. The timing could not be more inconvenient.' His aunt gave him a hard stare and approached the table. 'I trust you haven't seen the papers this morning?' She shook her head. 'Of course not. You've probably been with *her*. The footman I sent over to the Evans Row house said you were not at home, that a message had to be relayed to a certain address.'

'Where I go and who I am with is my business, Aunt. I am a grown man.' Dev shot her a censorious look as he strode to the table and picked up the first paper folded back to the society page, bracing himself for the usual—that he was a stranger infiltrating the exalted ranks of the *ton*, or perhaps complaints about his absence from events the past two weeks.

Even early in May people had complained that he'd not thrown himself whole-heartedly into the social whirl—the gravest of missteps given that he expected to marry. How was one to find a wife if one did not actively look for a wife at the balls, musicales, suppers and card parties? He had to read the column twice to fully digest it.

Lord E., who is supposedly on the hunt for a wife, needs to show more enthusiasm for that hunt than he is currently showing for a current amour who is rumoured to be a widow of the ton. *Our sources confirm he has spent the last fourteen nights en-*

*joying her charms, which explains his notable
lack of attendance at key entertainments.*

Dev felt himself freeze. The paper was blaming
Gwen. Without naming her, of course, but how could
anyone know even this much? They'd been discreet.
There was nothing untoward about how they'd conducted themselves in public. He'd behaved with her as
he would escorting any lady. There'd been no stolen
kisses, no inappropriate touches or unnecessary closeness. Well, except for the day at the market. But the *ton*
didn't frequent the Strand markets. No one could have
seen them unless they'd known he and Gwen would be
there. The only way to know that would be if someone
had followed him.

His mind began to work. If someone had followed
him to the market, it stood to reason that they'd known
he was at the studio and that he'd not left it. They would
have had to have followed him the day before when he'd
left his uncle's. *Followed.* That was nearly as chilling
of a thought as the thought of someone knowing what
he and Gwen had been up to.

He grabbed another paper. The report was much the
same. He supposed he ought to be thankful for small
mercies. They had not named Gwen in any way or al-
luded to her in any fashion that might incriminate her
or her business. But the threat remained. If they knew
where he'd been, they knew who he'd been with. They
were simply holding back. It was only a matter of time
before they broke that little bit of news as well. Gwen
would not thank him for it.

'I have to go.' He turned for the door. He wanted to reach Gwen before the papers did. This was what she feared, what she'd warned him against, the reason she said she didn't mix business with pleasure. Now, because of her association with him, she was in risk of exposure.

'You have to go?' his aunt almost screeched. 'To her? I should say not. You have to think about your family. We have to figure out how to handle this.'

'Aunt, we *are* handling this. The portrait party will quell any legitimacy anyone might give a piece of gossip they read in the papers.'

'If you think that, you are not taking this seriously enough,' his aunt snapped. 'It's been remarked upon in no less than four papers. People will not so easily discount that.' She stamped a foot in an uncustomary show of anger. 'I did not expect this of Mrs Norton. She's a woman of good character, not one of those loose widows.' She glowered at him. 'I did not expect you to be so naive either, so easily caught in her web. Perhaps because I did not expect her to spin a web at all. She's been adamant about not marrying again.' His aunt snorted. 'Well, now we see that for the lie it is. She's been playing coy.'

Dev's patience stretched. 'Whatever do you mean?'

'Don't be obtuse, Devlin. She saw a chance to entrap you, to take advantage of all the time you would spend with her while she painted. It's such an intimate setting, painter and subject, alone for hours, talking, sharing. It creates a bond that is dangerous because it's false, but it seems true at the time. This is why we can't let young men and women be alone together.'

'Aunt, I am hardly a young man overwhelmed by a young lady's charms,' he reminded her. 'That is not at all what happened with Mrs Norton.'

'How was it then?'

'It is none of your business.'

'It is if it concerns your ability to marry well and do your duty to the dukedom.' His aunt would not back down. 'You are carrying on an affair that has now become public. What young girl will be swept off her feet if she knows your affections are quite obviously engaged elsewhere?'

'That is what fathers are for. These are not real marriages, Aunt, as you've pointed out. They are alliances.'

His aunt crossed her arms. 'It's the scandal I don't like, especially with Bish making difficulties over the succession. It doesn't look good, *you* don't look good. Those fathers you spoke of will think twice.'

'I am sure, Aunt, that the dukedom will speak for itself when it comes to it.' Privately, though, Dev agreed with her. This came at the worst possible time, or perhaps, at the best possible time depending on who you were. 'Now, I really must go. I need to make sure there are no further rumours printed.' And he needed to prepare Gwen.

His mind had arrived at a very disturbing conclusion. He had been followed. But who would want to follow him? Who had an interest in where he went or whom he saw? Or was even just interested in fishing for something potentially damaging? Who would want that? He'd not been in town long enough to acquire truly aggressive enemies. But he did have one.

'Bish is behind this.' He flicked at the newsprint. It was all he could do. Confronting Bish would accomplish nothing. Bish would deny his accusations and, if Bish thought he knew, it could cause Bish to escalate his discrediting campaign. Escalation would expose Gwen. As much as he'd like to plant Bish a facer, he simply could not.

His aunt pursed her lips. 'I suppose that's very possible. I also suppose you're right. The party is our opportunity to change the narrative. You will need to be very attentive to the young ladies in attendance and it would be best if Mrs Norton wasn't there. Best for her, so that no one connects the two of you together, but also best for you to prove to everyone that your attentions are on matrimony.'

'She's the artist. It is customary to have the artist on hand for the unveiling of their work.' Dev shook his head. 'Excluding her is unacceptable. It's bad manners on our part.' He thought for a moment. 'Also, excluding her might risk it looking like a case of protesting too much. The oddness of excluding her might put others on the scent.'

His aunt contemplated the idea. 'Very well, she can come. But you can give no one cause for comment on your association with her. Especially since after tomorrow night, there is no reason to continue associating.' Dev chose to make no remark. He alone would decide whom he associated with. He picked up the papers. Gwen would want to see them and he would not hide anything from her. But she would not be pleased. This was definitely not how he'd expected their last day together to go.

Things were going well. Bish paced in front of the window of his library as he listened to his secretary read the latest papers to him. His cousin was going to look like a regular rake once he had finished with his discrediting campaign. Men might keep mistresses, but they did have a double standard when it came to the men who married their daughters. Fathers of the *ton* did think twice before betrothing their innocent girls to known rakes and that could not be what his aunt wanted. The dukedom needed Dev wed and soon.

'Is that it?' he asked when his secretary fell silent.

'Yes, Sir. All four papers.'

He nodded, thinking. The pieces were in play: his complaint lodged with the Heralds' College and his rumours circulating among the *ton*. Now, it was time for act two. The curtain would come up on that with the portrait party. It wouldn't so much be what happened at the party as what happened away from the party. While everyone was watching Dev, Bish would have his men conduct a little reconnaissance to feed the rumour mill. The best part was, what could his cousin do? First, he had to figure out it was him and, second, even if he knew, what did it mean?

There was no way Dev could threaten him without risk to himself and to Guinevere Norton. That lady was absolutely a liability to his cousin for several reasons, but mostly because of how his cousin obviously felt about her. It made him vulnerable and it made everything negotiable. Bish hummed to himself. This mad play to capture a title might actually work. It was certainly much more feasible than when he'd begun.

Chapter Seventeen

It was the beginning of the end—an end she'd known would come, which was why it seemed illogical to be upset. So much of this was anticipated and yet she felt unprepared for it, shaken by it as if this was a bolt from the blue.

After Dev left, Gwen dressed in a morning gown of aquamarine muslin and put her hair into a quick twist. Whatever news Dev sent, she did not want to receive it here in the bedroom, a place charged with memories of nights spent in indescribable pleasure, nights rediscovering passion, rediscovering herself, feeling alive. She wanted nothing to taint that. She hoped, too, that by getting out of the bedroom, she would think better and feel better in a less emotionally charged space.

She took up vigil on her little patio, hoping the sun and the fountain would soothe her and bring the equilibrium she was looking for. But today, the peace of her little oasis was elusive and her breakfast sat untouched. Even the sweet *maritozzi* failed to tempt her.

Reason suggested she was behaving ridiculously.

She'd had two weeks to steel herself, to find perspective for this moment when it arrived. Reason also suggested that whatever news Dev sent, it wouldn't be good and it would require action. She didn't need an imagination to know what that action would be. Separation. Effective immediately.

She sipped absently at her coffee and made a face, surprised to find it cold. She'd not realised that much time had passed while her mind had frantically wiled away the morning, coming back to the only conclusion that mattered. The affair was over and she'd been wrong. Losing Dev was going to hurt.

The shortness of the affair, the pre-knowledge that it would end and when, even if the how had been ambiguous, had not protected her as she'd been sure it would. Perhaps it had been nothing but a lie she'd told herself to justify going to bed with him simply because she'd wanted to.

Surely it was worth it, though? Some small part of her prompted wistfully. No matter how short the affair had been, it had been genuine. There was something undeniably sincere between them, although she dared not name it. Perhaps there was no name for it or perhaps there was and she didn't want to confess to it, give it power. It would make giving him up that much harder.

She tossed out her cold coffee and poured a fresh cup. She'd not gone to bed last night thinking that would be their last night. She hadn't been thinking about last nights at all, as she recalled. She'd been too focused on other things, such as what Dev was doing with his tongue in the most decadent of places. Now she was paying for it. She'd come back to life just in time to feel the aches of hurt and loss.

'Gwen, I thought I'd find you out here.' Dev's voice broke into her reveries as he strode out to the patio, a set of newspapers beneath one arm. He gave her a soft smile as if it did his heart good to see her, but she could not smile back, even as her mind sought to capture one more image of him, one more remembrance of when he was hers.

'It must be even worse than you thought if you've come back in person instead of a note.'

Dev gave a wry smile. 'Well, let's just say I'm glad you have your *maritozzi*. Its magical properties will definitely be tried.' He took the wrought-iron chair across from her and sat, setting the papers aside.

'Is your uncle all right?' She poured him a cup, relieved when he nodded. 'That's good news.' She found a smile for him. 'Then the worst hasn't happened. All else, I am sure, can be managed.' She said the words as much for herself as for him.

Dev's green eyes were serious as he held her gaze. 'It can be managed, that is true, but not without some expense to ourselves.' He blew out a breath. 'I hardly know where to begin, Gwen. Perhaps I should start with an apology. I tried to rehearse one on the way over and nothing came, nothing adequate anyway.'

She reached for his hands as he continued. 'I am sorry, Gwen. What has happened is my fault. I take full responsibility for it and I will do whatever I can to protect you from the fall out, I swear it.' He disengaged one of his hands and pushed the newspapers in her direction. 'I was followed. Our affair has been noted in four different social columns. You were not named in any way, but the affair has been noticed.'

He sat back, releasing her, allowing her time to read the columns. Gwen set the last paper aside. 'You could have done without the attention,' she said at last. 'Your aunt must be furious—to have this happen right before her party is a great blow to her.' She furrowed her brow in contemplation.

'I don't mean to be cavalier, Dev, but while it is not pleasant to be mentioned in the columns for such behaviour, I do not see this as the crisis you purport. You will weather this. You're a man and soon to be a duke. Once you marry, you will be forgiven. Your aunt is a secondary character in all this, her part will be forgotten. I've not been named. So, I think this is imminently survivable.' Even as she said it, though, Gwen felt naive, as if there was some piece she was missing.

'That is my aunt's plan, as well, to pick my bride quickly and overshadow the rumours with the wedding of the Season,' Dev said grimly. 'But that's not what I want. Moreover, these rumours are not idle speculations by bored gossip columnists. I could live with that. Instead, these were maliciously gathered and placed intentionally in the newspapers to harm me. It is a shot fired at the succession.

'I was followed, Gwen. My every move was deliberately tracked in the hopes of gathering something unsavoury. Now, think who would be so motivated to do that and why.'

Her footman brought a fresh pot of coffee and a new

tray of *maritozzi*. Gwen waited until he'd retreated before she spoke, letting her thoughts settle. 'You're sure you weren't followed out of general curiosity? Perhaps it was nothing more than an intrepid reporter looking for a good story, something different.'

Dev shook his head. 'Not when I have a cousin who is rabid for a title, rabid enough to break the dukedom for it. A reporter would have published the story sooner. These mentions all highlight that this affair had been going on for two weeks. This was deliberately released to coincide with my aunt's party, when all eyes will be turned towards Creighton.'

She caught the angst in his voice and it cut at her heart to hear it. He took his role seriously as the soon-to-be titular head of the Bythesea family. He would see all of this as his fault. She reached for his hand and threaded her fingers through his. 'Have you talked to Bish? Told him that you know what he's done? He seems a cowardly sort, only willing to engage in contretemps behind people's back. If he were called to public account, perhaps it would scare him off. His career, his integrity would be at risk if others knew of his behaviour. Society would not respect or condone his actions if they understood his true motives.'

Dev gave a bitter smile. 'I can't do that, Gwen. It would escalate things. If I were to threaten him, he would retaliate.'

Gwen gave him a quizzing look. 'With what?'

'With the name of the woman I've been seeing,' he offered quietly as if soft tones made the news less devastating. Gwen felt herself freeze. She'd been so caught up in what this meant for Dev and his family, she'd not stopped to consider the implications for herself.

'So that's why I've been spared thus far.' It made sense now. Why give away all of one's information in a single showing? Bish had wagered on Dev's sense of protectiveness and responsibility working against him, of wanting to keep her name out of the papers as leverage. Bish needed a little something to sweeten the pot, to ensure Dev remained vulnerable. The more vulnerable Dev was, the better Bish's chance at negotiating.

That last made her think. Bish didn't know Dev very well if he thought his cousin would trade the dukedom for her. 'He can't really believe you would let him wreck the dukedom over a woman.'

'That's not why he'd do it,' Dev ground out. 'He wants to discredit me, to add it to his case with the Heralds' College that I am not worthy of having the title bestowed on me. I know what you're thinking. Living a moral life is not one of the three criteria, who I associate with cannot sway the decision. You're right. It can't. But it can influence the College. If they don't want to approve me, they can suggest my proofs are somehow incomplete, that my legitimacy is not ironclad.'

She was to be a liability then, either way Bish used his information. Dev would see her protected, she knew that. But perhaps it would be better if she protected him instead. There was only one way she could do that.

She rose with brisk movements, her tone business-like. 'Then this is goodbye. It's hardly the way I pictured it and it's slightly earlier than anticipated', but only by a day—how much could a day really matter? 'Your aunt is right. The best way to mitigate the rumours is to pretend you're untroubled by them and pick a bride, perhaps even from the girls there tomorrow night.' She would resign herself to reading about all of it in the papers.

Dev's eyes narrowed to green slits. 'Will you not come tomorrow and see your own painting unveiled? It is customary to have the artist there. I discussed it with my aunt and insisted she follow protocol.'

'Only when the artist hasn't been sleeping with the subject,' she snapped, anger getting the better of her. Hadn't she known it would hurt? Hadn't she known this would happen? That someone would find out? And she'd gone ahead and done it anyway. She'd been selfish. Now, the things she valued most were at risk. 'I have things to protect, too, Dev.' Her career, her reputation, her family, her independence. All of it could come toppling down because of one unfortunate instance.

'I have no intention of being coerced into a rushed marriage with a stranger simply to save appearances and I want you there for your career.' Dev met her arguments with equal sternness. 'You deserve your moment of greatness. Besides, if Bish already knows we're lovers, there's nothing new for him to discover.'

Dev made it sound so easy. In the end maybe it was. Going or not couldn't change anything in the immediate future. They'd always planned on the party being their last night. Perhaps it would be best to just stick with that plan.

'All right, I'll come,' Gwen said, relenting. 'But you

have to promise to behave. We mustn't give anything away.' When the evening was over, she'd fade from his life, making it clear that whatever affair he might have conducted had been ended, solidifying his serious intention to marry.

Dev flashed her a curious stare. 'What if it could be different? What if it doesn't have to end? Would you let us go so easily? Will you not fight for us?'

She felt as if the world was shifting at his words. This was dangerous talk, changing plans here at the end. 'Fight for us?' she echoed hollowly. 'I have fought for us, for these two weeks. What more do you think there is to fight for, Dev? I have my freedom to preserve and you have a dukedom to secure. This is where our paths must diverge. It is what was discussed.'

'Do you wish it could be different? Don't you want it to be different?' Dev pressed her.

'The romantic in you is showing, Dev,' she scolded gently, a crack forming in her heart. 'How could it be otherwise? I am not what you need.'

'You are everything I need, everything I've ever looked for and despaired of finding.' Dev's eyes burned with the intensity of his words.

'I am not duchess material.' She infused her words with steel. 'And that's what the Duke you will be needs. Do not make this harder than it has to be, Dev. We promised ourselves two weeks and now we've had them.' She strode past him. 'Now, if you'll excuse me, I am expected at the studio. Movers are coming to transport the official portrait.'

It wasn't the most glamorous of leave takings, but

she had to go or she'd find herself capitulating to the impossible. There were only so many battles she could fight in a day. She needed to save her strength for the battles to come.

Chapter Eighteen

Tonight, his clothing was his armour. Bish tugged at his cuffs as his valet completed the final touches on his evening attire. Tonight he wore dark trousers and a new, tightly fitted coat in deepest teal, beneath which he wore a bright peacock-blue waistcoat with a rolled collar. Both new. Both expensive. Both necessary, in his opinion, for the battle to come. His cousin's portrait would be revealed tonight and he would be on hand, ostensibly to lend his support to quelling the rumours that had surfaced in the papers yesterday.

It would be akin to walking into the lion's den, though. He'd have to be careful. He was not naive enough to think Dev wouldn't figure it out. The question was what did Dev think he could do about it? His valet draped a length of silk about his neck and Bish lifted his chin.

'I think an oriental knot tonight would be best. It's simple, unique, but won't distract from my waistcoat.' Noticeable but not overpowering elegance was the image he wanted to cultivate this evening. He needed to cultivate the illusion of supporting the family while he did the exact opposite. He needed people to see him acting more ducal than the man in line for the title.

There was a knock at his door. 'Come,' he instructed.

'Sir, there's a man to see you downstairs.' The disdain on his footman's face told Bish all he needed to know. It was one of his hired men. 'He says it's urgent.'

'Well? What have you found that is urgent enough to interrupt my toilet?' Bish strode into the sitting room with an air of casual aloofness as if his every nerve wasn't primed for the report.

'This.' The man tossed a few pages torn from a sketchbook on the console. 'You'll be interested in the pictures. Seems your cousin is something of an exhibitionist.'

Bish picked up the book and thumbed through it, eyebrow hooking. Nude sketches of Dev. Well now, this was juicy. Not just because his cousin was naked, but because of who'd done them. They'd come from her studio.

There was no question Mrs Norton was the author of them. The more he dug, the more he found she was hardly the upstanding widow she proclaimed to be. If that got out, it could hardly do her or Dev any good. He closed the sketchbook with a contented smile.

What might Dev be willing to do to make sure that never happened? To make sure the Heralds' College didn't find out about it? Because while he had a long game to play he also had a short one. The key was in making Dev believe he could actually take the dukedom from him. These sketches would go a long way in that direction. It was going to be an interesting night, just the kind of night he thrived on.

To the untutored guest unaware of yesterday's news, the evening gave every appearance of being a typical unveiling ceremony. The Duchess's five daughters and their husbands were all on hand to lend further countenance to the event and the guests were in the mood to play along. Even with the unsettling news having had a day to circulate, the guests at Creighton House were doing an admirable job of pretending they had not turned out for the Duchess's party simply for curiosity's sake.

Still, Gwen thought, as she stood beside the draped portrait, Dev ramrod straight on her right, waiting for the Duchess to finish her speech, there were definitely signs this evening was something out of the ordinary. For one, there were far more guests than one might expect at such an event. This was an event where it only mattered *who* came, not *how* many came.

When the Duchess had envisioned the party, it had been with an elite but reduced guest list in mind. Since the news in the papers, people had been begging for invitations and the Duchess had provided them, thinking that it would be better to have everyone here to see for themselves how marriage minded and marriage eligible her nephew was. 'If we don't invite them, they'll think we have something to hide,' she'd told Dev.

So, here they all were, dressed in finery, drinking champagne and putting on a show, disguising their curiosity behind good manners while they waited for something to happen. And something might indeed happen. The knowledge of that gave the evening its sharp edge. Gwen looked out over the guests as they listened to the Duchess. Bish was here in the crowd, handsomely dressed and circulating all night, but he'd not approached Dev or her. She was glad for that. If she could last another half-hour, she could flee the event unscathed, reputation intact.

Gwen shifted discreetly on her feet and slanted a cautious glance at Dev. Did he feel it, too? The Duchess was getting long winded now. She wanted this done. Once the portrait was revealed, she would only need to mingle a few minutes longer and then she could disappear. No one would notice. They would be too focused on Dev and Dev would be too busy with the guests to come after her. It would be best that way, to spare them the pangs of an official parting. A formal good bye could change nothing now. It could only bring more hurt, more fruitless argument about the impossible.

'Gwen, won't you fight for us?'

The words haunted her, but she could do nothing about it. What did he think a fight would accomplish besides hurt and scandal and more disappointment?

The Duchess raised her voice, perhaps signalling her speech was at an end. 'Now, I am proud to present *Fortitude et Familiam.*' Strength and family. Her Grace had insisted on giving the portrait the Bythesea family motto for a title. The Duchess gestured for a waiting footman to drop the velvet draping covering the portrait. The curtain fell with a soft whoosh.

In that interim between revelation and response, Gwen held her breath, the usual nerves fluttering hard in her stomach. Would they like it? Would they find it not just a picture of a man, but a piece of valid art?

Usually, her portraits were revealed at much smaller, more private events as they were hung in a family gallery. In some ways, she was as much on display tonight as Dev was. The only difference was that this was temporary for her, a moment of fame until she was overlooked once more.

An artist's life was like that. If one did not produce publicly displayed and acclaimed work regularly, one was quickly forgotten, which suited her ideally. She told herself to be grateful for small blessings. She could walk away from it all. For Dev, this was only the beginnings of a life he would never be able to walk away from. It was he she should be pitying, not herself.

The applause began in the first row and rippled towards the back of the drawing room. Gwen felt herself breathe again. Dev's voice was at her ear. 'They love it, my dear. Just look at their faces.' His hand dropped to the small of her back as the first of the guests approached for a closer inspection of the painting. 'Enjoy this, Gwen. You deserve it,' Dev whispered. 'You've outdone yourself. The portrait is magnificent, exactly what my aunt wanted and what I wanted. I did not think it possible to combine them both, but you've accomplished it.'

She felt herself at Dev's lavish praise. She glanced at the portrait, trying to see it through his eyes as opposed to her own. He'd only seen the finished product when it had been brought over to Creighton House, whereas she'd seen it for weeks on end, knew every stroke, every hue she'd anguished over.

Eden and his young wife approached. 'Congratulations, Mrs Norton. The portrait is a triumph,' Eden enthused. 'The colours are vibrant and yet subtle.' He peered closer at the painting, 'I'm not sure how you achieved that.'

'Thank you, Lord Eden.' She had been pleased with the colours, the burnt golden brown and olive hues of the books and other objects in the painting contrasting against the red ducal robes with their miniver fur. It had taken careful mixing of her paints to achieve the shades she'd wanted, shades that did not distract from the man who ought to be the focal point of the painting, but, at the same time, captured the east–west essence of who that man was.

'We would love to have you to dinner,' young Lady Eden offered sincerely. 'Both of you, of course. We see too little of you, Everham.' she tapped Dev on the sleeve with her fan. Lady Eden's invitation froze Guinevere. Gwen hoped no one else had heard it or the linking of her with Dev. Had Lady Eden not read the papers? Or was this an attempt on her part to show support?

Lord Eden intervened, having obviously read those papers and understood the implications. 'I am sure Everham will come if it's possible, my love, but his schedule is quite full these days.'

Full of debutantes to woo, Gwen thought uncharitably. Dev probably would go to Eden's for a supper, but not with her. He would go with some other lady by his side, perhaps to have Eden vet her suitability as his future duchess. She shouldn't be so sulky over it. She knew this was coming. This had always been the plan.

'Smile, Gwen.' Dev urged quietly as a line formed, everyone eager to meet the artist and her subject— mostly the subject, Gwen thought, based on the number of families with daughters in line. The Duchess stood on Dev's other side, making introductions. Dev's manners were impeccable, greeting each lord with pleasure and each daughter with polite enchantment, each lady wife with a compliment. She hated seeing it.

'Lord Carys, this is my nephew, Viscount Everham,' Dev's aunt all but crooned as a tall, older gentleman came forward with his wife and stunning daughter.

'Everham, good to meet you at last,' Carys said, drawing the girl forward. 'This is my daughter, Lady Mary Kimber.' Gwen wanted to discount her. The other girls had been easily discounted—too young, too naive. But this girl was all poise and shining dark hair, tall like her father and composed like her mother.

Gwen's stomach sank with the knowledge that this was the girl the Duchess had hand-picked for Dev, the girl at the top of the list. They would make a striking couple with their dark hair and their height. It was too much. Too much to stand there and give him away, this man who'd brought her back to life, shown her that passion and pleasure had not died with Christophe.

You knew this was coming.

Yes, but she didn't have to stay and watch it.

'Excuse me,' she murmured, not certain that anyone heard, or that Dev heard. Perhaps it was best that he didn't. She took a quiet step backwards, slipped into the crowd and into the night, anonymous once more. Alone once more.

She did not go home. She couldn't. Not yet. There would be too many reminders of Dev there. She went to the studio first, wanting to take refuge with her brushes, to lose herself in the familiar. She would work on her painting of the Rosemont girls who were inseparable even in art, insisting on having their portraits painted as one.

At the studio, she paid the hack driver and climbed the stairs, letting her mind turn itself over to the details of the Rosemont portrait. She wanted to use rose hues to honour the girls' favourite colour—pink. A part of her mind registered vaguely how lonely the studio was tonight. No errand boys waited at the bottom of the steps, lingering in the hopes of making an extra penny.

At the top of the stairs, Gwen fished in her reticule for the key and fitted it to the lock, but before she could turn the key, the door pushed opened. Her mind took a moment to register the import of that.

Her studio door was unlocked.

Had she not locked it when she had come to instruct the men from Creighton House on moving Dev's portrait? She was sure that she had. She was always so careful. But that seemed the most logical explanation. Gwen stepped inside and lit the lamps, trepidation growing with each wick as the space became illuminated. Was it her imagination running wild over the unlocked door or was something wrong here?

Something was definitely off. Her things had been

touched. Drawing tablets had been left open on the work table. Works in progress that she'd propped against the wall had been uncovered. Someone had been here. Her panic ratcheted at the sight of a drawer pulled from the work table, its contents spilled on the floor. She pushed back the panic. Whoever had been here wasn't here now. She needed calmness, needed to assess the situation.

Gwen lifted a lamp to throw light about the room, doing a quick visual inventory. As best she could tell, no large items were missing and she had nothing small of any value worthy of enticing someone to commit burglary. People didn't steal oils and paints and brushes. She set the lamp on the worktable, an alternate scenario coming to her: if it wasn't burglary, it meant whoever had been here had been looking for something particular. But what? She had half-done portraits of debutantes in demure white dresses, some sketches of the old Duke…and sketches of the new Duke. In a state of undress. *Complete undress.*

The panic she'd tamped down came roaring back as she tore through her sketchbook. They were gone. The pages ripped out. On the wave of that panic came stark realisation. Someone had come looking for something, anything, that might prove the affair, that might act as proof of an intimate connection and they'd found it. Only, they'd found much more than that. Those sketches would ruin her if they were made public. They'd do Dev significant damage as well. And she knew who that someone was.

She needn't pretend this was a random act perpetrated by a faceless criminal. Bish had done this. He'd sent men to do this. It must have happened after the portrait had been moved. She hadn't been here and Dev had been certain he'd been followed. If so, Bish would know the studio was unoccupied, that his men would have access to it. *There were no errand boys tonight.* No doubt, there'd been no errand boys last night either. Bish had bought them off with shiny coins and sent them packing so they couldn't report what they'd seen.

She sat down hard on a stool, letting the realisation sweep over her. This was devastating. She had to tell Dev. Right away. It wasn't a question of how Bish would use those sketches, it was a question of when. She had to go back to the party. Had to warn Dev. Bish was there, on the prowl, perhaps he even had the sketches with him.

Her gaze moved about the room, searching the dark corners more diligently now. Her eyes snagged on a shelf in the corner where she kept the jar of Christophe's brushes and a cry ripped from her throat. Ruined. Every last one of them. She rushed towards them, hoping it was a trick of the shadows. It was not. The bristles had been cut off each of them.

'No, no,' she breathed, her hands starting to shake. She took down the jar, irrationally looking for a way to save them. Then the tears came. They'd ruined Christophe's brushes, her one connection to him, to a time she'd never get back, a person she'd never get back. Gwen sank to the floor, cradling the jar of ruined brushes and sobbed. Tonight, it was simply too much. For four years she'd fought back the pain of loss, guarded her reputation, tried to live again and she'd failed spectacularly. And now she was losing Dev just as she'd lost Christophe. Only this time, she couldn't blame Dev as she blamed Christophe.

'Won't you fight for us?'

No, the only person to blame this time was herself. This was a loss of her own making. *She'd* lost him, she'd made the thing she feared come to life by deciding what happened to them.

Her inner voice stirred: *Just as Christophe took it upon himself to decide for you both how your life together would end. This is no different. The one thing you resent about Christophe is the one thing you're inflicting on your relationship with Dev. You feared losing Dev and now you've lost him anyway. Fear didn't stop it from happening. The deals you made yourself didn't stop it from hurting and Dev is lost to you any way. You could have saved him, saved what you had together and you didn't.*

Worst of all, it didn't have to be that way—something she saw too late. Loving Dev didn't need to come at the expense of not loving Christophe. Dev had been trying to tell her this all along, show her this and, now that she understood, it was too late.

In the space of a few weeks, she'd jeopardised everything she'd worked for, all because she'd tried to claim the impossible. Dev's cousin had sent a powerful, malicious message. She was not safe. No one associated with Dev was safe. Bish knew what she'd done and he would not hesitate to expose her. He did not care what he ruined as long as he got what he wanted. She'd been so foolish to give in to her heart and now all was lost.

Chapter Nineteen

Dev was quite close to losing his temper. In fact, he would have lost it if he didn't think it was exactly what Bish wanted: further proof that Dev didn't have the desired breeding of a true Englishman. And, of course, he wasn't going to lose his temper in front of his aunt's coveted guests.

'It's a nice portrait.' Bish surveyed the painting with a casual eye before dismissing it. 'But a few props touting the western canon are hardly going to be enough to convince anyone to forget your antecedents.' He gave Dev a sly smile. 'I hope you have another trick up your sleeve, Cousin, if that was your intent. But perhaps Lord Carys's daughter is the other trick? A marquess's daughter would be an impressive catch if she didn't come with so much debt. But everyone has their price, I suppose.' Bish included.

It was tempting to rise to the bait, to ask the question Bish was deliberately leading him towards: what is your price? What will it take to make this unholy mess go away? But to ask such a thing would be to validate that Bish's claims had any legitimacy to them. He would not give Bish the satisfaction, not here where everyone could see.

'Your lovely artist has left the party,' Bish said in low tones. 'That's too bad, I had something I wanted to discuss with her. But perhaps I can discuss it with you? Privately, of course, unless you'd prefer a more public setting.'

The smugness in Bish's tone put Dev on edge. He'd noticed Gwen had left an hour ago and he'd been powerless to stop it short of insulting Lord Carys and his aunt and alerting anyone paying attention to the fact that he'd chased after the portrait artist, an action that would be out of character for someone whom one associated with neutrally. He'd had to stay put in the reception line in order to protect her reputation and it had taken all his willpower.

'The estate office, then. Shall we?' Dev led the way to his uncle's office. In too short a time, this would be his office, this home his home. He would have to give up the Evans Row town house. Not that it bothered him to do so. Neither place felt like his. Although Bish had no problem making himself at home. Bish went straight to the decanter.

'I'd offer you a drink, but I hear you don't imbibe, at least not our British stuff.' Bish poured himself a full glass of brandy.

'What do you want? You've been prowling all night, no doubt up to no good.' Dev didn't mince words. Here in the privacy of the estate office, he needn't be polite.

'Depends on whose side you're on.' Bish gave the

brandy an experimental swirl. 'Perhaps from where you sit, it doesn't look so good. But you have only yourself to blame.'

'I know what you've done.' Dev took a seat behind the huge desk, taking up a position of authority, and went on the offensive. 'You were the one behind the gossip in the social column. You had me followed for no reason except to dig into my private life. I don't think people would care to know that—family spying on family. That's hardly the image you want to cultivate.'

Bish did not even bother to deny it. 'I disagree, Cousin. I think people would be very grateful for what I did. A man like Lord Carys should know the sort of man he's marrying his daughter to—a foreigner with a taste for licentious behaviour, carrying on behind everyone's back while he searches for a wife. It's hardly the stuff on which a stable marriage is made. Most men swear off their mistresses early on to make a good impression at least at the beginning.'

He arched a brow and smirked before taking a swallow. 'But perhaps it's different where you come from. After all, a man can have sixteen wives.'

'You know nothing about where I come from and you will not malign my grandfather because you are too senseless to know anything about which you speak.' Dev levelled a challenging stare at his cousin. 'I will not sit here and allow you to speak slander about the family, any part of it.'

'What will you do about it? You're not the Duke yet.' Bish laughed. 'Call me out? Are you any good with pistols?'

'You said you wanted to talk, so talk. What did you need to discuss with Mrs Norton?' Dev redirected the conversation. Bish did better when he thought he was the centre of attention. Dev would not give him the chance.

A smug smile curled on Bish's lips. He reached into his coat's inside pocket and pulled out a folded square of paper. 'Something I came across.'

Dev reached for it, feeling the texture of the paper. It felt like…sketch paper. One edge was jagged as if it had been torn from a book or tablet. He opened the folds and flattened out the sheet, a sense of horror filling him. 'Where did you get this?'

Bish drawled, 'It's an excellent likeness of you. I don't think anyone who sees it would mistake you for another, even without the clothes.'

'That's not what I asked you. Where did you get this?' Dev repeated, temper rising. His first thoughts were for Gwen. If he didn't contain this right away, she would suffer. For him. Because of him. She did not deserve that. She'd taken an enormous chance in being with him and she would not thank him for it if this was how she was repaid.

Bish gave a harsh laugh. 'Stop with the stupid questions, Cousin. You know exactly where I got it.'

'You went to her studio.'

'In a manner of speaking.' Bish was enjoying this. It took all of Dev's self-control not to leap across the desk and throttle him. That would be one way to solve the problem. The man deserved more than a throttling for what he'd done. He'd sent men to break into Gwen's studio. That would devastate her. Her studio was her sanctuary, like her home.

'How did you know the sketches were there?' Dev tried for calmness, willing his mind to stay cool, to keep working, keep thinking. If Bish had one sketch, he possibly had the others: Lady Eden's bridal sketches, the sketches of the young merchant's bride and the rest. Nudes in the hands of someone who wouldn't respect their privacy was exactly what Gwen feared, the very thing she'd asked him to give his word on when they'd first met. Now, the thing she'd protected herself against for four years had come to pass through no fault of her own.

Bish waved his glass. 'I didn't. But my men noted that you went into the studio in the afternoon and didn't come out until the next morning. It made me curious as to what might be up there. So, I sent them on a little fishing expedition and we caught a big one.' He gave another smirk. 'Posing nude, Cousin. How...exotic.'

'Why do you care? I assure you no one else will care. It might be the "rumour of the week" but it won't last.' Dev added slyly, 'The Heralds' College won't care. They *can't* care. It's beyond their purvey. Nothing says one can't pose nude and not inherit their title. It does not impact one's parentage or one's church membership. Surely, as a successful barrister, you must know that,' Dev goaded coolly. Bish was the sort of man who could be tempted into disclosing his agenda especially if he thought he was in an ironclad position.

Bish took up residence in the chair across the room, slouching elegantly. 'It's called character, dear Cousin.

I simply want to show everyone your character, posing for nudes, carrying on with an artist, and you have only been here a short time.' He made a mock-frown of concern. 'Exactly what one should expect from someone who wasn't born to this life. Who knows what you might do to the dukedom.'

'That might set back Aunt's plans for a quick wedding, but it will not stop anything else from going forward.' He did not think he'd heard all Bish had in mind. A man as smart as Bish would not have believed such an indirect assault on the succession would carry any weight.

'In fact, your scandalmongering might just be doing me a favour. I'd prefer to wait to marry, pick my own bride, instead of having Aunt pluck one for me.' Bish wouldn't like to think of actually having come to his aid. 'Perhaps I should be thanking you,' Dev couldn't resist rubbing a little salt into the wound.

Bish didn't flinch. 'I don't think Mrs Norton would share your sentiments. You might brazen out such a scandal and come back next year for a wife. She won't survive the scandal, if anyone knew it was she and that she'd been alone with you.'

'Widows can do as they please,' Dev cut him off, his temper starting to show in Gwen's defence.

'Some widows. She runs a business that relies on the *ton*'s patronage. I can't imagine matrons being all that pleased to have their daughters' portraits painted by a loose woman. Now men, they might decide they all suddenly need portraits, so perhaps I'm wrong.'

'Stop it. You will not reduce her talent to a harlot's

trick with your insinuations,' Dev growled. His hand flexed. They were coming to it now, what Bish really wanted.

'If I cannot get what I want, I will expose her and the drawings,' Bish said simply.

'Why do you think that would matter enough to me to give in to blackmail?' Dev ground out in tones he hoped were neutral enough to sell his words.

Bish gave an all-knowing grin. 'Because you care for her, you like her. Without your protection she will be ruined and it will be your fault. Besides, you are hopelessly loyal to the family, a veritable lapdog coming when called. You want to protect the family, too. You can't bear to think of your uncle hearing about all of this on his deathbed.'

'I will not let the dukedom go, I will not allow you to break it up simply to save face.' Not even to save Gwen's face. She wouldn't want that. But he did need to find another way to protect her. He would think about that later.

'That's not up to you or me to decide,' Bish said blandly. 'The Heralds' College will decide it. All we can decide is what I am owed for not publishing the sketches and naming Mrs Norton. I think the estate at Taryton and an annual allowance would be compensation enough.'

Bish stood up and set down his empty glass. 'Take twenty-four hours to think about it and let me know what you decide. If I don't hear from you, I'll assume it's a no and I'll send the sketches straight to the papers.'

Dev let him get to the door before he spoke. 'Why

are you so insistent on bringing the family down, Bish? What have they ever done to you?'

Bish turned. 'Why, nothing, dear Cousin. The family Bythesea has done nothing *for* me and that's the problem.'

Dev stared at the door a long while after Bish departed, letting his thoughts settle, letting a plan form, one that would allow him to protect the family, the dukedom and Gwen while mitigating the harm Bish could do. Scandals would blow over. Blackmail would not. If he gave in to Bish now, Bish would be back asking for more next year. First things first, though—he needed to find Gwen.

Every second he had to wait for the coach to be readied chafed at Dev. He paced impatiently in the alley outside the mews as the horses were brought. That patience was tested further when he arrived at her little town house only to find the house dark and a footman, grumpy at having been awakened, who told him she wasn't there.

He thought for a moment before giving the instruction to the driver. 'Mrs Norton's studio on the Strand,' he said grimly. If she was there, she likely already knew what had happened. He would have spared her that discovery, alone at night, already carrying the emotions of the last days with her on top of this. 'As fast as you can manage,' he leaned out and called up to his coachman.

Concern for Gwen gripped him. How the studio had been left would be quite telling. Had Bish allowed his men to leave a wake of destruction or had they been more discreet? He didn't hold out much hope for the latter. Discretion would only be useful if Bish had wanted his possession of the sketches to remain undetected as long as possible. But Bish had wasted no time in making it known that he had the drawings.

Dev leapt down at the kerb, instructing the coachman to wait. He took the steps up to the studio two at a time, calling for her as he came, announcing his presence so that she would not be startled. She'd had enough shocks tonight. The door to the studio stood open and he stepped inside, his gaze taking a moment to adjust to the dim interior. He scanned the room, noting the destruction. His anger rose. Bish's men had been obvious and careless, showing no regard. His gaze found her, huddled in a corner, head buried on her knees.

'Gwen!' She lifted her head as he approached. She'd been crying. Her eyes were red, her cheeks stained. He could see that in the lamplight. He went to the floor beside her and gathered her to him.

Words failed him at the sight of her so undone. He'd seen her in command, sternly scolding him, firmly giving direction to his aunt, he'd seen her flustered from flirtation, vulnerable. He'd even seen her in tears that night she'd told him about Christophe. But those tears were not these tears. These were tears of hopelessness and they stirred the warrior in him. Too bad they lived in a civilised age where he could not settle this with a sword. But that would not undo what had been done here, to her.

She turned her face to his. 'I am so sorry, Dev. They took the sketches. The drawings I did of you are gone.'

'Shh, I know.' He wrapped his arms about her, dropping a kiss into the silky depths of her hair. 'Bish has them. I've seen them.'

'I am so sorry. It will ruin everything for you.'

'It's not your fault. You're not to think about it,' Dev soothed, the splendidness of Gwen washing over him once again. Despite the trials of the night, the personal devastation she'd experienced, her first thoughts were for him.

She leaned into him and he felt her relax. Her arms loosened enough for him to see that she held something. 'What is this?' he asked softly, taking the jar from her.

'Christophe's brushes…' She choked on the words. 'All the bristles have been cut.' That explained why she hadn't gone home, why she'd lingered here after discovering the wreckage. She simply couldn't leave.

Anger surged. Bish would pay for this. His cousin's men couldn't possibly have known how horrific of a crime they'd committed in ruining those brushes, how much they'd meant to her. But in doing so, they'd broken her, the woman he loved. The woman he'd failed to protect. It would not go unpunished.

Dev rose and helped her to her feet. 'We need to get you out of here.' She sagged against him, exhausted, and he swung her up into his arms. 'I am taking you home.' To her little oasis in the city where she would be surrounded by the things that brought her peace and comfort, where there would be hot tea and a bed, his undivided attention and in the morning she would have her *maritozzi*. He would put his plan to her then and start to put her world back together.

Chapter Twenty

Morning light helped only marginally in that it drove back the emotions that surged in the dark. Gwen had found over the years that morning brought a certain sharp clarity to issues that eluded one in the night as well as a dull resignation to accept that clarity. Sometimes all one could do was accept.

She woke slowly, not wanting to open her eyes, not wanting to reach for the morning and all it would hold. It would mean facing the night all over again: the unveiling of the portrait, standing beside Dev watching fathers and daughters fawn over his favour, her heart breaking because she realised too late how much she wanted to keep Dev for herself, that two weeks with him would never be enough; of retreating to the studio only to find it vandalised, Christophe's brushes destroyed, her sketches of Dev gone. Her world had unravelled.

Dev had come, though. She remembered sobbing against him, remembered him carrying her down the stairs, bundling her into his coach. The rest was a blur of soft voices and kind hands—Eliza, her maid's, and

Dev's. She was grateful to them, for getting her home, for helping her when she couldn't help herself. If not for Dev, she would still be there, hunched in the corner. Perhaps it didn't matter. It was still too late.

The door to her bedroom opened, followed by the jingle of morning china on a tray and the restoring scent of strong, nutty coffee. She groaned, tempted to send Eliza away. Was she ready to be restored? If she opened her eyes and drank that coffee, she'd have to face the day, have to find solutions for the twin disasters that had befallen her: a broken heart, and social ruin.

She heard the tray being set down on the table by the window, the sound of coffee being poured into her demitasse cup and then the sound of a second cup. A second cup? She was not here alone.

Her eyes flew open of their own volition. Dev stood by the tray, demitasse and pastry in hand. *'Maritozzi?'* He favoured her with a warm smile and approached to serve her breakfast in bed, which raised the other question of where had *he* slept? Her hand reached out to the other side of the bed, looking for proof. The pillow beside her held the indents of having been slept on and the sheets were still pleasantly warm.

'I spent the night.' Dev sat on the edge of the bed, handing her the coffee. 'I didn't want to leave you alone. I hope that was all right?'

It was absolutely *not* all right, her heart cried. Now, she'd have to go through the trouble of saying goodbye to him again. This was exactly the kind of goodbye she'd left the party to avoid. 'You have to leave me alone, especially now,' she said sharply. 'Being seen with me can only do more harm.' Particularly to her. She was being selfish there. The one strategy left to her was mitigation.

'I think we should talk,' Dev countered. 'I am not sure separating is the best defence.' He offered her the plate of *maritozzi*. 'Eat first, though. I have it on good authority these can make any situation look better.' His green eyes lit briefly with a teasing sparkle. But she didn't want to laugh with him, didn't want his smile or his eyes to conjure her feelings. She just wanted to let him go and yet it was also the very last thing she wanted to do. What she wanted was impossible.

Dev let her finish eating before he began to pace, long, slow strides eating up the length of her room and back again as he began to define the situation. 'Bish will make the sketches and their artist public in twenty-four hours if I don't turn over a small estate and an annual allowance to him.'

Gwen clutched the warm coffee cup to hold back the panic those words inspired and the anger. Yes, anger. There *was* fury along with panic. After four years of living independently, her independence wasn't going to be decided by her but by two men, the very thing she'd set out to avoid. If she was going to let men run her life, she would have gone to the country and lived with her in-laws or allowed her father to arrange a marriage to a nice, widowed squire. She had not asked for this, yet it was happening anyway and she could not stop it, could not be the source of her own protection, and it galled.

'You can't give it to him.' That much was obvious to her. It must also be obvious to Dev. 'He'll just ask for more. This only stops him from publishing the pictures. It doesn't stop him from using the incident to try and sway the Heralds' College about the succession.' Her ruin was imminent. She could not save herself, but she could mitigate the damage to Dev.

Dev paused at the window and looked down into the garden. 'You are right. I cannot give in to his request and I have no intentions of doing so. However, that leaves us both open to the scandal that will follow. I have a solution for that which will enable us to reduce the damage and perhaps even redirect the gossip. We both know that scandals, like fire, need a certain oxygen to maintain themselves. If we take that away, the scandal will extinguish itself all the more quickly.'

Against her better judgement, Gwen felt her pulse quicken. Was there indeed a magic solution after all? She leaned forward as he turned from the window. 'I would like for us to marry, Gwen.'

She was glad her cup was empty, or she might have spilled it on the coverlet. He strode towards the bed and took the cup from her before taking her hands. 'I know it's not the most romantic proposition in the world, but that does not mean there isn't romance between us. I wasn't sure what you'd appreciate more—something flowery and flattering, or just the plain truth. I want to marry you and, in light of recent events, it makes sense to marry now instead of later.'

'Dev, that is absolute madness. Our marriage would be a scandal. I am not what your aunt has in mind. I'm independent and older. I am no Lady Mary Kimber.'

Dev chuckled. 'Thank goodness. I don't want to

marry a young woman who has seen nothing of life, or who will rely on me for everything including her own thoughts. I've waited my whole life to find *you*. And here you are, just when I needed most to find you. The universe is a marvel that way.'

'There will be scandal, Dev.' Had he not heard her say it the first time? Had he not thought of that? And yet her heart was not immune to his words. Oh, how she wished it could be true, though. It would mean she didn't have to mourn him yet, that she could stay with him a while longer. But that was the stuff of impossibility.

'I should hope so. I am counting on a marriage announcement to divert people's attentions from whatever Bish might stir up. I am also counting on the announcement to reshape how the public might view those sketches if he publishes them. The nudity might be scandalous for a short time but not the artist if she is merely painting her lawfully wedded husband whom she sees naked anyway.' Gwen sighed. Mitigation, of course. 'Don't you see, Gwen, as my future Duchess, my name, my station, will protect you and your business.'

'You make it sound so easy. For the price of a little scandal we get what we want. It sounds too good to be true,' she questioned, her eyes on Dev. 'You know what they say—when something is too good to be true, it probably is.'

Dev's features hardened. He did not care for her rebuke. 'I don't want to hurt you, Dev,' she offered softly. 'I appreciate your offer but I think you'd come to regret it.'

Green eyes turned stormy. 'You do not give yourself enough credit, Gwen. You are suitable for marriage. You are the granddaughter of an earl and, if that was not enough, you were married to an earl's son. Your rank *is* enough for those who might concern themselves with such things.'

He paused, the storm in his eyes receding. 'There might be another more personal reason for choosing marriage that trumps all of these machinations. Have you considered that?' He paused again. 'We were not careful the morning of the lotus.' No, they'd not been careful. They'd both been too lost to passion. He'd not withdrawn before reaching his climax.

'It was just the once,' she argued. They had been careful all the other times but his gaze said he didn't like those odds, that once was all it took. But here, he was too much the optimist.

Gwen looked down at their hands, entwined and gripping each other hard as they each made their case. 'Have you considered why in all the years of marriage to Christophe that we had no children? It wasn't for lack of opportunity.' Although to be fair, children had not been discussed explicitly beyond a dream for the distant future. Still, one did wonder why no children had happened as a natural result of their sustained passions.

Dev was not deterred. 'I assumed there were no children by choice.'

'In part.' She would not lie to him. 'But it could have been more than choice. It could be that I cannot conceive. That is not a risk you can afford to take. The whole reason for your marriage is to produce an heir.' She softened. 'Dev, I could not live with myself if I was the source of such a disappointment to you.' She knew how important his family was to him, of all he'd given up to come to England and rescue that family. It was noble that he wanted to rescue her, too, but the cost was too great.

'Besides, I think you've overlooked a key element in your grand plan,' she said seriously. 'Your title can't protect me or anyone if it's not yours. The Heralds' College has not confirmed you. That means they are still considering Bish's complaints.' And whatever bribes Bish was offering to have them disassemble the dukedom.

Dev's eyes went cold. 'Are you determined to thwart me at every step of the way? Is marriage to me such an unpalatable idea that you won't fight for it?' His anger was turning towards her now. Perhaps she deserved it. He'd offered her his name, his heart, and he did not feel she had responded in kind.

'I *am* fighting for you, trying to help you see reason. The first step towards any managing of the scandal has to be securing the dukedom. Without it, you have no weapon. Without it, there is no family to protect. You could go back to India.'

'I will not go back,' Dev said firmly. 'Because you are here. You have changed everything.' He hesitated, eyeing her as a new thought occurred. 'Do you say I must secure the dukedom first because you will not marry without it? Has it been my title you've been hunting all along? My aunt has suggested as much.'

Fury gripped her. She wrenched her hands from his and scrambled from the bed, wanting to put distance between them. 'How dare you suggest I am a fortune hunter. After all these weeks, what we've shared, every conversation we've had, do you not know me better than that? I could have remarried long before this if I had wished.'

Dev crossed his arms. 'But not to a duke and here I was, alone in a new place, perhaps over-eager to make a connection, and you saw an opportunity. The art of catching a duke, we might call it.' They were both angry now, their fury a refuge from which they could hurl fire.

Gwen threw a pillow at him. 'I was perfectly happy with my life until you came along and now look at the mess it's in.' They stood, the bed between them, glaring at one another, Dev clutching the pillow.

'I see we're at an impasse.' Dev said steadily, setting aside the pillow. 'We will resolve nothing right now. We will discuss this later. I will call this afternoon for your answer once you've had a chance to cool down.' He straightened his shoulders and strode from the room as if he were departing a drawing room, or leaving a business meeting instead of leaving a lovers' quarrel.

She stood frozen, the heat of her anger leaving as she watched him go. Of all the endings she'd predicted for them, ending in anger and accusation had not been one of them. She and Christophe had had their fights, but they'd always found their way back to each other and never had their fights attacked one another's personal integrity the way Dev had today.

He's hurting. He offered all he had and you refused him. Every man has his pride. He struck out because you wounded him. Yes, because I had to protect myself, because I had to protect him from me.

If all they could do was hurt each other, it was best they weren't together. She could hear Dev's voice in her head from those early days.

'All pleasure is attained at the existence of pain. One cannot exist without the other.'

This was their pain then, to only be able to love because they were also capable of hurt. She would not accept that. She had to put herself beyond Dev for both their sakes.

Gwen rang for her maid, her resolve set. Her mind formed a list of tasks. She could not do this alone. She needed an ally. At her writing desk, she took out a sheet of paper and wrote hastily. Only Kieran and Caine were in town at the moment. The other two were at Newmarket for racing this week. But it would be enough. She folded the note.

'Eliza, I need this note sent immediately to Parkhurst House and my travelling trunk brought down from the attic. Make sure Kieran knows haste is necessary.' Kieran had come for her once, in Italy. He would come for her again and see her safely to the security of the countryside where no one would know what had happened here. When Dev returned this afternoon she would be gone.

She was gone. Dev knew it from the way the footman let him into the town house, from the way the house felt, as if it, too, knew its mistress had fled. Her things were still here, he noted, following the footman into the little drawing room where they'd spent the night before the fire, where she'd told him the story of her marriage, showed him the love scars on her soul, the night he'd probably fallen completely in love with her, truth be told. That was the beauty of hindsight. One could see the patterns that led to the current moment so much more clearly.

He had been too much in the moment this morning. He'd said an awful thing to her. He'd been angry and hurt. That was no excuse, of course. It was when one was angry and hurt that one had to mind their words and thoughts even more closely. He should have known better.

'She's not here, is she?' He put the question to the footman bluntly, handing him the flowers he'd brought.

'No, my lord.' The question made the footman uncomfortable. The answer made Dev suspicious. If she was not here, why show him in? Why not turn him away at the door?

'When do you expect her back?' Perhaps she'd gone to the market, perhaps he was making too much of this because of the quarrel.

Boot heels clicked on the floors. 'I don't know that she's ever coming back.' A tall, black-haired man dressed in riding attire stood in the doorway. Despite the differences in hair colour, Dev knew immediately who this was. This man and Gwen shared the same blue eyes.

'Ah, one of the famed Four Horsemen,' Dev met the man's steely gaze with a stare of his own.

'I'm Caine Parkhurst and you must be Creighton's heir.' Parkhurst slapped a riding crop against his thigh. 'My sister sent round a note this morning saying she had to leave the city immediately. Kieran is with her.

Taking her home. Where she belongs, in my opinion, to avoid entanglements such as this.' There was a censorious tone to Parkhurst's words. 'You've done her no favours, apparently. I gather there is to be some trouble that goes beyond the privacy of a broken heart, although I also hear that is involved as well.'

'I asked her to marry me. I think it is a suitable resolution that will stop the trouble,' Dev said, studying Caine Parkhurst and wondering if he'd have to duel him. He hoped not. Parkhurst was a fellow he thought he'd like under other circumstances—as a friend—he was definitely not the sort Dev wanted for an enemy.

Whack went the crop against Parkhurst's thigh again. 'Without asking her brothers or her father for permission? You are not winning any points with me, Duke.' He paused. 'I forget, you're not Duke yet, are you?'

'No, my uncle, rest his soul, still lingers and I am glad for each day,' Dev replied.

Parkhurst arched a brow 'That's part of it, I suppose. I hear there's other reasons, too, though. You've got a nasty thorn on the family tree in the form of your cousin.' He shrugged. 'Rumours have been trickling through the clubs. I'd not want to see my sister messed up with the likes of him.' He paused. 'I do not like what you've done to my sister, yet I see that she cares for you, that she's alive again. For that, I must give you thanks and credit.'

He pointed the crop at Dev. 'But you have no business proposing to her until you have your own house in order. I can help with that. Bish Bythesea must be dealt with. To that end, I have sent him a pre-emptive challenge this morning. If he releases anything defamatory about my sister or anything that can be traced back to her, I will meet him on the field of honour.'

Oh, Bish was not going to like that. He did not strike Dev as being very good at pistols. This particular horseman of the apocalypse was more like an avenging angel, an ally in the nick of time. 'You don't need me to tell you that you've done me a great turn here. I am in your debt. How can I repay you?'

'Waste no time in securing the dukedom and then convince my sister to marry you. That will be repayment enough.'

'I do not know if she'll have me. This morning, we said some things—' Dev said.

Parkhurst interrupted. 'I am sure you must have. She looked awful when we arrived. But if the depths of her misery is in any way equal to the enjoyment she takes in your company, then you must try. I cannot bear to see my sister unhappy. So, I shall deal with Bish Bythesea and you will deal with Gwen.'

Caine smiled. 'Between the two of us, I think you will have the harder job. *Bonne chance.*' Good luck indeed, Dev thought. If he failed, the odds seemed strong that he'd be the next person Caine Parkhurst 'invited' to the duelling field.

Chapter Twenty-One

Dev envied Parkhurst the simplicity of his solution. He, however, could not challenge his cousin to an actual duel for several reasons—one did not duel one's cousin and then suggest one put family above all else; or because duelling was illegal and the last thing he could afford at the moment was arrest or exile. But he could 'invite' his cousin to a duelling field of a different sort. He was done waiting for the Heralds' College to do their job and affirm him. They'd had two weeks with the documents and that was twelve days longer than they needed.

The first thing he'd done upon returning to Creighton House that afternoon before meeting with his uncle was to send two notes. The first, informing the Heralds' College—not asking them, he was done with waiting—that he and Aldrich Bishop Bythesea would be in their offices at ten sharp the next morning to settle the question of succession.

The second note was sent to Bish, stating that if he wanted to contest that succession, tomorrow was the day to do it. All would be settled by noon on the morrow. He would see to it that the news made the papers for the following morning in order to quench the rumours once and for all. He would give society a week to readjust their opinion of him, a week to secure a special licence and a few other projects he felt honour bound to undertake before he could approach her, and then he would go for Gwen.

The sooner the better, Dev thought, too, when he saw his uncle. Some days his uncle sat up in a chair, or dressed, as he had the days Gwen had come. Not today. Today, his uncle looked grey and impossibly exhausted. 'It's nothing, dear boy,' his uncle assured him as he reached for one of the ledgers. 'Just a rough night. A few days of rest will restore me.' Although by now, they used the term 'restore' subjectively. 'You didn't bring Mrs Norton today. How is my portrait coming?'

'It's going well.' Dev had no idea how it was going. Regrettably, the last few days, the last week even, had been too focused on him. He realised he'd not even asked after the portrait since the morning they'd laid in bed talking of the *darsan*. It was one more black mark in the balance against him. One more thing he would have to make up for. And he would.

'At least something is going well.' His uncle gave him a knowing, scolding look. 'Your aunt has confessed all. The two of you should have come to me sooner about Bish.'

'We didn't want to worry you. In the beginning it seemed nothing more than smoke, nothing to be concerned over,' Dev tried to explain.

'I have nothing left to do but worry, so let me worry,' his uncle scolded. 'And now we have a bona fide threat to the succession and blackmail? What do you propose to do?' His uncle's still-sharp eyes studied him. 'This will be your first test as Duke.'

'I am meeting with the Heralds' College tomorrow to settle the nonsense and Caine Parkhurst has been an effective deterrent for the blackmail business in ways I could not be because of my position.'

His uncle smiled. 'Good.' He nodded towards the table cluttered with pills and bottles. 'I have written a letter for you to take with you tomorrow that should settle any question the College may have. It took my secretary and I all morning to get it done, but there it is.'

Indeed, it would have taken extreme effort for his uncle to dictate a missive. That he'd chosen to spend his strength on it touched Dev deeply. 'Thank you, Uncle. I am sorry. I can't help but feel this is all my fault.'

His uncle's hand groped for his. 'It is not your fault, it is merely a consequence of your position. People are envious, covetous of what they don't understand—that the dukedom is not all wealth and parties. It is a grave responsibility, an enormous undertaking for life. People's livelihoods depend on your ability to do it well, to protect them and their families.' His uncle coughed. The spasm passed.

A few more weeks, please, Dev whispered in his mind to whatever powers might listen. *Let him live long enough to see me wed, to know that all will be well.*

Dev cleared his throat. 'Shall we start with the ledgers?'

'No ledgers today. I want to talk about Guinevere Norton and why you should marry her no matter what your aunt says.' The old man settled back against his pillows, a smile on his face.

No one was smiling the next morning when Dev was shown in to the Heralds' College offices that occupied an old U-shaped redbrick building near Blackfriars. Bish had arrived ahead of him and was looking pale but well-turned-out in a grey morning coat. The pictures had not run in the evening news or in the morning papers, proof that Caine Parkhurst's challenge had done its job.

'Good morning, Cousin.' Dev took the chair at the head of the table, forcing Bish to sit to his left alone while the college's panel of heralds, headed by no less than the college's head, the Duke of Norfolk, arrayed themselves on the right. 'Thank you all for meeting. I do not think this shall take long given that it is merely a review of documents I supplied the college over two weeks ago.'

Dev wanted to make it clear that he was in charge of this meeting. The panel was only here to affirm matters. He nodded to Bish. 'And of course to answer any questions.' *Not* to answer concerns, *not* to address attacks. Bish would not be allowed to rant, to bring up issues that should have no bearing on the process.

'Let's begin with the first criteria, the legitimacy of my birth. As you can see from my birth certificate, as well as from my parents' marriage certificate issued by the Church of England, I was born over a year after my parents' marriage. I believe this more than suffices on the account of the first standard. Heralds, are you satisfied?'

He glanced at the Duke of Norfolk with a look that said this was de rigueur, that he was not expecting opposition. 'Moving on, then, to the second requirement, being a member of the Church of England. You have my baptismal records. So, that too should be of no concern.'

Norfolk nodded, but a few other members squirmed in their seats. Ah, so this was where Bish was going to hang his hat. And clearly, it *was* instigated by Bish because the panel was obviously waiting for *him* to speak. Dev turned his stare towards his cousin. 'Do you have something to say?'

Bish cleared his throat nervously. Of course, the coward didn't work well when called on the carpet. His specialty was behind the scenes where no one could see. 'There is some concern about your membership. You've not attended church since arriving, you've been heard to make references to Hindu gods like Ganesha and you speak freely about Hindu beliefs, so freely that one might believe you espouse them for yourself. Suffice it to say, you seem more Hindu than Christian.'

Bish reached for a glass of water. 'Please understand how difficult it is to represent these claims to you, Cousin. I do not mean to make trouble,' Bish said in a tone that bordered on pleading as if somehow he was the wronged party here being forced to such testimony.

'You *do* mean to make trouble, Cousin,' Dev said baldly. 'You've played the snake in the grass all Season thus far, whispering poison in society's ear. For myself,

I would not care what you said about me if it had not been done in an attempt to undermine the succession. My armour is thick. But when you attack my uncle's dukedom, I cannot let that go unnoticed,' he said evenly.

Dev eyed the panel, staring each of them in the face as he delivered his next message. 'Nor can I stand by while bribes are offered and perhaps tolerated to see the dukedom dismantled. Which, you well know, is the consequence of not affirming my legitimacy.'

Norfolk looked alarmed. He glared at the panel. 'Is this true?' He swung his gaze towards Bish. 'Have you attempted to corrupt the Heralds' College?'

Bish turned a whiter shade, but his barrister's mettle stood him in good stead. 'I think that would be very difficult to prove. Perhaps my cousin has misunderstood, foreigner that he is and unfamiliar with our ways.'

He was not wrong. No prize money or lands had been delivered as of yet and it was quite the confederacy of thieves. The panel wouldn't out themselves and Bish would not confess. But Dev wanted one last word on the subject.

'Your Grace, I might suggest for your consideration that the idea of holding my documents for over two weeks for a situation that is usually all but rubber stamped within a day, supports the claim that something was afoot. I might also suggest that it would be time for a review of your personnel. I hope to be mistaken in my suspicions, but actions often speak louder than words. I do feel that to be the case in this situation.'

Bish looked livid, his green eyes flashing fire against the stark pallor of his skin. 'You are distracting us from the real issue—that you're a Hindu by practice. You don't drink, no one has seen you eat beef. It's not natural.'

'My lifestyle is not at issue here.' Dev broke in before Bish could get up a head of steam. 'Whether I am Hindu or not is irrelevant. I might suggest that several Englishmen in India have adopted Indian ways because it makes sense to live as the country lives. But that is not on trial here. I am baptised Church of England. That is all that is required.'

He stared hard at Norfolk. He needed the Duke to get his panel in line, to prove his panel was not corrupt. 'Might I remind the Duke, if it is of any note, although it should not be, that other peers have been affirmed for succession as recently as the last century even though they allegedly practised satanic rituals. Shall I name them?' He opened the file before him.

Norfolk shook his head. 'That will not be necessary.' He shot Bish a withering look. 'What you have is hearsay and it is not relevant.'

Bish returned Norfolk's stare. 'So that's how it's to be? You will allow the title to be turned over to a foreigner who knows nothing of our ways, who has never set foot on English soil until two months ago, was not even educated here, who is not even a true Englishman raised abroad but who is the product of a mixed marriage with a native.'

Bish's voice rose. 'Who is not even fit to serve the East India Company. He cannot even be hired as clerk, but we are willing to endow him with a dukedom? Take a moment and think about the sheer irony and ridiculousness of that. All I have done is try to give you an option to prevent such ludicrousness from occurring in the highest echelons of our society.'

Dev had never wanted to hit someone as much as he wanted to hit Bish. Rage tore through him. It was the nineteenth century, men had made technologies that allowed them to circumnavigate the world, to produce goods at rapid speeds previously unbelieved. And yet they'd come not far at all in understanding the world they explored and lived in. It galled him to think it was possible that mankind could be in possession of such grand intelligence and also such great narrowminded stupidity. He reached in his coat pocket for his uncle's letter. 'The Duke of Creighton sent this for you, Your Grace. He felt it might offer clarity.'

It was a long while before anyone spoke as Norfolk read the letter and passed it down the line, each herald reading it in turn. At last Norfolk spoke. 'I believe I speak for the Heralds' College in the decision to affirm Mr Devlin Bythesea as the heir to the Duke of Creighton.'

He held up his hands to indicate he had more to say. 'We offer an apology to Mr Bythesea in regards to the delay when the matter should have been perfunctory. We apologise for whatever hardship may have been accrued. Secondly, I feel the need to address the last remarks made by Mr Aldrich Bythesea in regards to the quality of the heir. The College does *not* control or judge who inherits. Hereditary inheritance protects against such potential for fickleness. Devlin Bythesea is heir for the same reason that every man before him has been the heir. A man is born to the succession, nothing more and nothing less.

'As for you, specifically, Aldrich Bythesea, I am ashamed by your endeavours to cast aspersions on a man's character all for the sake of your own personal gain. This situation is closed. You are all dismissed.'

When Dev stepped out into the sun of latest May, he felt renewed. One dragon slain, one more to go. Gwen.

Chapter Twenty-Two

Had it only been a week since she'd fled London? It seemed an eternity. Days passed slowly, filled with mundane tasks, or simply staring out the window of Willow Park, her family home. Only it didn't seem like much of a family home now with everyone gone except her parents. She'd been the first and only one of the Parkhursts to marry. She'd not lived here with all of her brothers gone. She remembered the house being noisy, crowded, all the time. The boys had all shared rooms so that she could have one of her own.

Growing up, she'd coveted that small room, a tiny island of quiet. Now, she could do with some noise. Too much quiet meant too much time with her thoughts. To break the solitude, she spent her afternoons as she was spending this one: rambling the countryside on wide-ranging walks, but, as usual, her thoughts had found a way of coming, too.

These days, those thoughts all had one central theme: Dev. Dev's proposal. Dev wanting to make a life together. Dev accusing her of wanting his title. Surely he hadn't meant that last. He couldn't have meant it and still wanted to come back that afternoon for her answer.

Not that it would have changed anything. She would still have been gone. She couldn't allow so much sacrifice. He would resent her for it. She knew. She resented Christophe for leaving her, for not making that decision with her. As much as she missed him, loved him, resentment was there, too. She didn't want that for Dev.

And yet resentment seemed inevitable on that front as well. She'd taken control of the situation from him. She'd decided to end things unilaterally when he'd been clear it was not what he desired or what she'd desired now that she knew there was room in her heart for two. It simply wasn't possible.

She stopped to pick wildflowers, gathering an arrangement she thought she might paint. She hadn't painted anything in a week although all her old art supplies were still in the attic. She hadn't drawn anything either. Every time she started something, it always took the shape of Dev's face. She was spending too much time with him in her mind, reliving their time together, carrying on imaginary conversations full of things she'd like to tell him.

Gwen wondered what he was doing today. Was he driving Lady Mary around Hyde Park? Would he be dancing attendance on the rest of Her Grace's list at a ball tonight? He'd have girls lining up to have him write his name on their dance card. She'd seen a three-day-old newspaper yesterday that proclaimed him as heir. The issue with the Heralds' College was settled, Bish defeated.

Gwen sighed. She supposed she could go back now. Caine and Kieran had managed it so that Bish could not defame her. Caine had the sketches safely locked away. She could continue on as she had before. Clean up her studio, paint more portraits.

But it would be a half-life just as it had been before Dev. She couldn't stay here, though, not indefinitely. Her parents were being patient, but they wanted her to have a plan. She could go to Italy. It was cheaper to live in Italy than here. She still had friends there who would help her get settled. She could paint and not have to watch Dev marry and become the Duke. That might be best.

The house came into sight, the sprawling jumble of chaotic architecture that made up Willow Park, named for its ancient willow trees, and it made her smile. She was safe here for a while. She would sort it all out and she would carry on. She'd done it once, she would do it again, but there would be no joy in it.

Her mother met her in the hall, eyes bright as she reached for her daughter's hand. Gwen was instantly suspicious. 'We have a guest, Guinevere. Please come and say hello.'

'Mother, I don't want to meet anyone. I'm not dressed for it, I've been out for a ramble,' she improvised. Her mother was not above inviting an eligible man from the neighbourhood in for tea if she thought there was a chance.

'You look fine.' Low, familiar tones drawled from the front parlour. Gwen froze. How often had she heard that voice at her ear? She would know those tones without looking. But there he was in all his dark-haired, green-eyed glory, lounging against the door frame. *Dev.*

'What are you doing here?' She nearly stammered over the words, so complete was her surprise.

'I've come for you, Gwen.' He pushed off the door and came to her. 'The business with Bish is finished. The title is mine. I've done as you've asked and secured the dukedom.' He gave a wry smile. 'I've also done as your brother asked and sought your father's permission and *his* to marry you.'

He grasped her hands and went down before her on one knee. 'I'll do it right this time, Gwen. I've asked your father and I'm down on my knee, asking you, not telling you. We can marry for ourselves now. So, Guinevere, because I love you, because you complete the circle of myself and I am not whole without you, will you do me the honour of being my wife?'

Her father had come to stand beside her mother and Gwen was aware that they stood waiting on the periphery of her world, a world that was fully centred on nothing else in the moment but the man kneeling before her. 'And the art of catching a duke? Did you mean that?' she asked quietly.

'No, they were rash words that should never have been spoken.' She felt his grip tighten on her hands as if he feared she might slip away. 'Do you believe in second chances, Gwen?' Not just for him, she realised. He was asking if she believed in second chances for herself—second chances to love, to trust, and even to risk the inevitable loss that would come. But for him, she'd believe.

'Yes. Yes, I do.' There was a sigh somewhere from her mother and then she was in Dev's arms, laughing and crying over her good fortune and he was laughing, too. 'Just an hour ago I didn't know what I was going to do.' She smiled at him. 'I was lost.'

'Lost things are meant to be found, the balance of the universe requires it, my dear.' Dev stole a kiss. Her father handed around quickly uncorked champagne and offered a toast. They laughed and drank, but Gwen sensed there was something more Dev was holding back.

'What is it?'

'I have a special licence and I think we must make haste. My uncle insisted I claim you against my aunt's wishes if need be. I want him to see us married and I think his time is near.'

Gwen nodded. 'I'll get my cloak and we can be off.'

'We will all be off.' Her father sprang into action, calling for the family coach. 'We can be in London by nightfall.'

'A candlelight wedding will suit me very well.' Gwen squeezed Dev's hand and went for her cloak.

The two coaches were off within a quarter of an hour, perhaps the fastest departure in the history of departures. But that's how love worked. No sacrifice too great for those you loved. Dev had crossed oceans for his family. She could do no less.

'It won't be a big church wedding, it won't even really be a small wedding,' Dev apologised as they bowled towards London.

'It will be our wedding and that's all that matters,'

Gwen assured him. She'd not even stopped to change her gown. She laughed. She'd be married in her pink walking dress and half-boots. Oh, well. What did a silk gown matter when she was marrying the man she loved? The man who'd brought her back from the grave?

But they needn't have worried. The Duchess of Creighton had not spent a lifetime being a leading hostess for nothing. Anticipation was her strong suit. Upon their arrival at Creighton House, the Duchess had hot water waiting in guest chambers and a clean dress laid out for Gwen, one of the gowns Gwen had left in her rush to flee the city. It was blue and it would do well. The Duchess had a bouquet of blue forget-me-nots and pink roses for her, too.

Dev met her outside his uncle's bedroom door, refreshed from his own brief ablutions. 'Will I do?' she asked with a smile, giving a twirl.

'You will more than do. Shall we?' Dev held the door for her. It would just be the two of them and Dev's aunt at the bedside ceremony so as not to overwhelm his uncle. But her family waited downstairs to celebrate afterwards, the Duchess having sent messengers to Parkhurst House.

The room inside was dark, lit only by candles, but the setting was peaceful. The Duchess perched beside her husband on the bed, holding his hand while the old man's eyes gleamed with unshed tears at the sight of them. Gwen and Dev stood at the foot of the bed, hands clasped together as the vicar began the ceremony, 'Dearly beloved, we are gathered here...'

It had been short and lovely and over quickly as Dev

slid a ring on her finger and placed a kiss on her lips. The old Duke beamed as they came to him, taking his hand. He could barely utter any words and Gwen's happiness broke a little. Dev had not exaggerated. His end was near, but their life together was just beginning. The happy with the sad. 'Love one another,' he whispered, looking at his wife, 'as we have loved each other and you will not go wrong.'

They left the Duke and Duchess and made their way towards the stairs, but Dev drew her past the stairs and further down the corridor to 'our room', he said cryptically. 'I want a moment with you first, before I have to meet *all* of your brothers.'

'It will be fine, we're already married. There's nothing they can do. Technically, they're your brothers now, too.' Gwen laughed as he shut the door behind them and pressed her to the wall, stealing a kiss. She wrapped her arms about his neck. 'Do we have to go downstairs?' she flirted. 'Maybe we can just have dinner brought up.'

'No, we must go down. But that's not why I brought you in here,' he scolded, disentangling her arms and stepping towards the bed where a big box waited. 'I have a gift for you, a wedding present.'

'"A gift"? Is that what we're calling it now?' she teased.

'*That* gift comes later. Come, open this one,' he urged, a touch of solemnness in his tone.

Gwen sat on the bed and opened the lid, a little gasp of surprise and delight escaping her as she lifted the Italianate artist's case from the stationer's out of the box. 'Oh, it's lovely. What's even more lovely is that you remembered. We hardly knew each other that day.' She looked over the box at Dev. 'You were trying so very hard to engage my services.'

'And you were busy undressing me with your eyes, already plotting if I were worthy of your nudes.' Dev smiled wickedly.

'Thank you, it's perfect.' Perfect for all the reasons literal and symbolic, she thought. 'I will treasure it always.'

'Look inside,' Dev urged gently. 'Try this drawer.'

She opened the brush drawer. A small smile played at her lips at the kindness of the gesture. It contained a new set of brushes to replace the brushes lost in the break-in. She ran her fingers over the bristles of a filbert. 'Good brushes, too. These are expensive.'

'They're one of a kind. Look more closely, at the shafts perhaps.'

She smiled suspiciously at him. What was her husband leading her towards? Her smile froze, all playfulness leaving her as she recognised them. 'These are Christophe's, but how? All the bristles had been cut off.'

'I had the bristles replaced. Your friend, Mr Witty the stationer, was beside himself when I told him what had happened. He had a friend who could do the work.' He paused. 'I know it's not the same, but perhaps it helps.'

'Thank you, I think that's the kindest, most thoughtful gift I've ever received.' She tried for a smile and wiped at her eyes. 'You're going to make me cry, Dev. I don't have anything for you. I didn't know I was getting married tonight.' It sounded so ridiculous they both laughed. 'But you did,' Gwen said once they'd recovered. 'You must have been quite sure of yourself, or of me.'

'I would have given you the box regardless. That first day, I knew you had to have it. I just didn't know I'd be giving it to you as your husband.' Dev smiled and held out his hand. 'Well, Guinevere Bythesea, Viscountess Everham, future Duchess of Creighton, shall we go down and introduce me to your family?'

'If we must.' Gwen gave an exaggerated sigh.

'We must. But there will be champagne. You can look over the rim of your glass and practise undressing me with your eyes.'

'Better get used to it. I'll be doing that for the rest of your life,' she teased.

Dev grinned, but he wasn't teasing when he said, 'There's nothing I'd like more.'

Epilogue

One year later, spring 1826

What a year it had been. A year full of extremes, of immense sorrow, yet there'd been moments of immense happiness and pure joy. Never once through the emotional tumult of the year had Gwen thought she'd be standing here, surrounded by friends and family as they celebrated the opening of her art gallery. But today, on a sunlit Wednesday afternoon in May, that was exactly what she was doing, her dashing husband beside her.

The gallery had been Dev's idea when the place next to her studio had become available for lease. It was a long, narrow space, whose best features were the windows overlooking the Thames. It was not large, but it did not need to be. This was to be her space, a place where she could display and show her work to those closest to her.

Dev's hand rested at the small of her back as he lifted his voice to call the little crowd to attention. 'Does everyone have champagne?' A waiter moved among them serving the stragglers. A small glass of *maireya* was brought for Dev, who still adhered to the customs of his grandfather's palace.

Certain that all had been served, Dev raised his glass. 'Thank you, friends, and thank you, family, for being here with us today to celebrate the opening of my wife, the Duchess of Creighton's, gallery. To mark the occasion, she is unveiling her latest work, *The Heir and the Duke*, and of course, featured today are the final portrait and preliminary sketches of Charles Arthur Bythesea, my uncle, who sat for my wife, shortly before he died.' He slid a glance in her direction. 'Gwen and I hope that you will enjoy these works of art in the spirit of celebrating family.'

Gwen looked about the room at the faces of her family. Her parents and her four brothers—all of whom were badly in need of marriage in her opinion—were there today, as were Dev's five cousins with their husbands, and his aunt, who was still in mourning but had consented to attend this quiet occasion, although it wasn't too quiet. Between the Parkhursts and the Bytheseas, they could certainly fill a room.

There were friends here, too. The Duke of Cowden and his wife, Rafe and Elspeth and Cowden's friend, the Viscount Taunton, and his wife filled out the party. They were making friends, she thought. Dev was an active and successful partner in Cowden's Prometheus Club and that had helped smooth their transition into London society somewhat. It was a start. They had agreed early on they would not compromise themselves in exchange for acceptance. The *ton* could come to them when the *ton* was ready. It was not an attitude Dev's aunt had appreciated, but she'd supported them none the less.

Gwen moved to the draping over the painting that hung on the wall and pulled the cord, revealing the work she'd envisioned last May when she'd sat and watched Dev and his uncle work. *The Heir and the Duke*. The new and the old.

There was a poignant, bittersweet quality to the painting which showed the old Duke in bed, the ravages of time and illness evident as he shared the ledgers with his young, strong heir in the image of Dev. It was a portrayal of the inescapable facts of the circle of aristocratic life. The little group applauded and she encouraged them to move about the gallery to look at the paintings more closely. Among the pictures displayed today were also paintings of Dev's cousins' children, too. Everyone was celebrated today.

Dev stood beside her as she studied *The Heir and the Duke* more closely. 'It turned out beautifully, Gwen,' he spoke low at her ear. 'You have a real talent. I wish he could have seen it. He'd be proud of you.'

Gwen swallowed around the thickness in her throat at her husband's words. 'I miss him, too, Dev.' His uncle had passed away a week after the wedding. They had been beside him at the end as were his five daughters, five sons-in-law, ten grandchildren and his beloved wife. That was the real legacy of his life more so than his dukedom, Gwen had thought at the time. She'd spent the year paying tribute to that legacy with the paintings of his grandchildren. She'd done it for Dev's sake, too. It was a chance for him to get to know his family.

'What shall you paint next?' Dev asked. 'You haven't painted me nude for a while. I'm always up for that,' he teased.

She flashed him a mischievous grin. She had a surprise for him and this seemed the perfect time to tell him. 'I was thinking of adding to the family portrait collection.'

He nodded. 'Who? My aunt, perhaps? Or maybe my cousins?'

'You're not very imaginative, Dev. I was thinking perhaps I'd paint our child. Of course, I can't do that until December.' She let her voice casually trail off, watching the surprise and delight ripple across Dev's face.

'Our child?'

She squeezed his hand. 'Yes, *our* child.' She would have a child at last, a family of her own, all because she'd given herself permission to love again thanks to this man who had shown her, among other things, that love had no limits, that it was worth the risk.

'I love you,' he whispered against her ear. 'Shall we tell them all now?'

'Yes, let's.' She smiled up at him and they stood together in their own world, savouring the moment, the joy of the future they'd created together. But there was no chance to share with the crowd.

A footman approached. 'Your Graces, we have guests. Some gentlemen who are enquiring about *The Heir and the Duke*.' He made a small bow and handed Gwen the three cards.

Gwen scanned the cards. 'The Duke of Tintagel, The Duke of Newlyn and Lord Darius Rutherford.' She looked up at Dev. 'Rutherford is an art critic—his wife runs the women's art academy in Seasalter.'

'And the Dukes are two of the Cornish Dukes known for their social justice crusade. I know them through Cowden. They're good men,' Dev told her, a look of acknowledgment passing between them. The *ton* was coming to them.

'Show them in, Peter.' Gwen nodded to the footman. She beamed at Dev. 'This is what we hoped for, acceptance on our terms, for being ourselves.'

Dev stole a kiss. 'That's not all I hoped for. I hoped for a woman who would love me for who I am, who would see me, who would build a life with me.'

'What about a woman who undresses you with her eyes?' Gwen laughed up at her husband.

'Well, now, that's been quite the bonus.' He turned serious. 'And what did you get, Gwen?'

She smiled softly, her hand dropping to the flat of her stomach. 'More than I ever dreamed possible.'

* * * * *

*If you enjoyed this story, why not check out
Bronwyn Scott's Daring Rogues duology*

Miss Claiborne's Illicit Attraction
His Inherited Duchess

*And be sure to read her
The Peveretts of Haberstock Hall miniseries*

Lord Tresham's Tempting Rival
Saving Her Mysterious Soldier
Miss Peverett's Secret Scandal
The Bluestocking's Whirlwind Liaison

COMING NEXT MONTH FROM

HARLEQUIN
HISTORICAL

All available in print and ebook via Reader Service and online

WOOING HIS CONVENIENT WIFE (Regency)
The Patterdale Siblings • by Annie Burrows
Jasper's out of options when feisty stranger Penelope offers him a lifeline—
marriage. It's a practical match...until an inconvenient desire to share the
marriage bed changes everything!

AWAKENING HIS SHY DUCHESS (Regency)
The Irresistible Dukes • by Christine Merrill
Evan is stunned when Madeline takes a tumble fleeing a ball...and
accidentally falls into him! Now the situation forces them somewhere the
duke didn't want to be—the altar!

THE GOVERNESS AND THE BROODING DUKE (Regency)
by Millie Adams
Employed to tame the Duke of Westmere's disobedient children, Mary
should avoid entanglement with their widower father. If only she didn't
crave the forbidden intimacy of their moments alone...

HER GRACE'S DARING PROPOSAL (Regency)
by Joanna Johnson
Widowed duchess Isabelle's wealth has made her the target of fortune
hunters. A convenient marriage to mercenary Joseph will protect her but
could also put her heart in danger...

THE EARL'S EGYPTIAN HEIRESS (Victorian)
by Heba Helmy
Ranya's mission is clear: restore her family's honor by retrieving the deed to
their business from the Earl of Warrington. Until she finds herself enthralled
by the new earl, Owen...

A KNIGHT FOR THE RUNAWAY NUN (Medieval)
Convent Brides • by Carol Townend
Having left the convent before taking her Holy Orders, Lady Bernadette
is horrified when her father wants her wed! The only solution—marrying
childhood friend Sir Hugo.

**YOU CAN FIND MORE INFORMATION ON UPCOMING HARLEQUIN TITLES,
FREE EXCERPTS AND MORE AT HARLEQUIN.COM.**

HHCNM0523

Get 3 FREE REWARDS!

We'll send you 2 FREE Books plus a FREE Mystery Gift.

FREE
Value Over
$20

Both the **Harlequin® Historical** and **Harlequin® Romance** series feature
compelling novels filled with emotion and simmering romance.

YES! Please send me 2 FREE novels from the Harlequin Historical or Harlequin Romance series and my FREE Mystery Gift (gift is worth about $10 retail). After receiving them, if I don't wish to receive any more books, I can return the shipping statement marked "cancel." If I don't cancel, I will receive 6 brand-new Harlequin Historical books every month and be billed just $6.19 each in the U.S. or $6.74 each in Canada, a savings of at least 11% off the cover price, or 4 brand-new Harlequin Romance Larger-Print books every month and be billed just $6.09 each in the U.S. or $6.24 each in Canada, a savings of at least 13% off the cover price. It's quite a bargain! Shipping and handling is just 50¢ per book in the U.S. and $1.25 per book in Canada.* I understand that accepting the 2 free books and gift places me under no obligation to buy anything. I can always return a shipment and cancel at any time by calling the number below. The free books and gift are mine to keep no matter what I decide.

Choose one: ☐ **Harlequin Historical**
(246/349 BPA GRNX)

☐ **Harlequin Romance Larger-Print**
(119/319 BPA GRNX)

☐ **Or Try Both!**
(246/349 & 119/319 BPA GRRD)

Name (please print)

Address   Apt. #

City   State/Province   Zip/Postal Code

Email: Please check this box ☐ if you would like to receive newsletters and promotional emails from Harlequin Enterprises ULC and its affiliates. You can unsubscribe anytime.

Mail to the **Harlequin Reader Service:**
IN U.S.A.: P.O. Box 1341, Buffalo, NY 14240-8531
IN CANADA: P.O. Box 603, Fort Erie, Ontario L2A 5X3

Want to try 2 free books from another series! Call 1-800-873-8635 or visit www.ReaderService.com.

*Terms and prices subject to change without notice. Prices do not include sales taxes, which will be charged (if applicable) based on your state or country of residence. Canadian residents will be charged applicable taxes. Offer not valid in Quebec. This offer is limited to one order per household. Books received may not be as shown. Not valid for current subscribers to the Harlequin Historical or Harlequin Romance series. All orders subject to approval. Credit or debit balances in a customer's account(s) may be offset by any other outstanding balance owed by or to the customer. Please allow 4 to 6 weeks for delivery. Offer available while quantities last.

Your Privacy—Your information is being collected by Harlequin Enterprises ULC, operating as Harlequin Reader Service. For a complete summary of the information we collect, how we use this information and to whom it is disclosed, please visit our privacy notice located at corporate.harlequin.com/privacy-notice. From time to time we may also exchange your personal information with reputable third parties. If you wish to opt out of this sharing of your personal information, please visit readerservice.com/consumerchoice or call 1-800-873-8635. **Notice to California Residents**—Under California law, you have specific rights to control and access your data. For more information on these rights and how to exercise them, visit corporate.harlequin.com/california-privacy.

HHHRLP23

Get 3 FREE REWARDS!

We'll send you 2 FREE Books plus a FREE Mystery Gift.

PRESENTS
His Innocent for One Spanish Night
CAROL MARINELLI

PRESENTS
Bound by the Italian's "I Do"
MICHELLE SMART

Blue Blood Meets Blue Collar
One Stormy Night

The Rancher's Plus-One
Stranded with a Cowboy

FREE Value Over **$20**

Both the **Harlequin® Desire** and **Harlequin Presents®** series feature compelling novels filled with passion, sensuality and intriguing scandals.

YES! Please send me 2 FREE novels from the Harlequin Desire or Harlequin Presents series and my FREE gift (gift is worth about $10 retail). After receiving them, if I don't wish to receive any more books, I can return the shipping statement marked "cancel." If I don't cancel, I will receive 6 brand-new Harlequin Presents Larger-Print books every month and be billed just $6.30 each in the U.S. or $6.49 each in Canada, a savings of at least 10% off the cover price, or 3 Harlequin Desire books (2-in-1 story editions) every month and be billed just $7.83 each in the U.S. or $8.43 each in Canada, a savings of at least 12% off the cover price. It's quite a bargain! Shipping and handling is just 50¢ per book in the U.S. and $1.25 per book in Canada.* I understand that accepting the 2 free books and gift places me under no obligation to buy anything. I can always return a shipment and cancel at any time by calling the number below. The free books and gift are mine to keep no matter what I decide.

Choose one: ☐ **Harlequin Desire** ☐ **Harlequin** ☐ **Or Try Both!**
(225/326 BPA GRNA)   **Presents**   (225/326 & 176/376
                        Larger-Print   BPA GRQP)
                        (176/376 BPA GRNA)

_____
Name (please print)

_____
Address   Apt. #

_____
City   State/Province   Zip/Postal Code

Email: Please check this box ☐ if you would like to receive newsletters and promotional emails from Harlequin Enterprises ULC and its affiliates. You can unsubscribe anytime.

> **Mail to the Harlequin Reader Service:**
> **IN U.S.A.:** P.O. Box 1341, Buffalo, NY 14240-8531
> **IN CANADA:** P.O. Box 603, Fort Erie, Ontario L2A 5X3

Want to try 2 free books from another series! Call 1-800-873-8635 or visit www.ReaderService.com.

---

*Terms and prices subject to change without notice. Prices do not include sales taxes, which will be charged (if applicable) based on your state or country of residence. Canadian residents will be charged applicable taxes. Offer not valid in Quebec. This offer is limited to one order per household. Books received may not be as shown. Not valid for current subscribers to the Harlequin Presents or Harlequin Desire series. All orders subject to approval. Credit or debit balances in a customer's account(s) may be offset by any other outstanding balance owed by or to the customer. Please allow 4 to 6 weeks for delivery. Offer available while quantities last.

Your Privacy—Your information is being collected by Harlequin Enterprises ULC, operating as Harlequin Reader Service. For a complete summary of the information we collect, how we use this information and to whom it is disclosed, please visit our privacy notice located at corporate.harlequin.com/privacy-notice. From time to time we may also exchange your personal information with reputable third parties. If you wish to opt out of this sharing of your personal information, please visit readerservice.com/consumerschoice or call 1-800-873-8635. **Notice to California Residents**—Under California law, you have specific rights to control and access your data. For more information on these rights and how to exercise them, visit corporate.harlequin.com/california-privacy.

HDHP23

Get 3 FREE REWARDS!

We'll send you 2 FREE Books <u>plus</u> a FREE Mystery Gift.

FREE
Value Over
$20

Both the **Romance** and **Suspense** collections feature compelling novels
written by many of today's bestselling authors.

YES! Please send me 2 FREE novels from the Essential Romance or Essential
Suspense Collection and my FREE gift (gift is worth about $10 retail). After receiving
them, if I don't wish to receive any more books, I can return the shipping statement
marked "cancel." If I don't cancel, I will receive 4 brand-new novels every month and
be billed just $7.49 each in the U.S. or $7.74 each in Canada. That's a savings of at
least 17% off the cover price. It's quite a bargain! Shipping and handling is just 50¢
per book in the U.S. and $1.25 per book in Canada.* I understand that accepting the
2 free books and gift places me under no obligation to buy anything. I can always
return a shipment and cancel at any time by calling the number below. The free
books and gift are mine to keep no matter what I decide.

Choose one: ☐ **Essential**   ☐ **Essential**   ☐ **Or Try Both!**
              Romance   **Suspense**   (194/394 & 191/391
              (194/394 BPA GRNM)   (191/391 BPA GRNM)   BPA GRQZ)

Name (please print)

Address   Apt. #

City   State/Province   Zip/Postal Code

Email: Please check this box ☐ if you would like to receive newsletters and promotional emails from Harlequin Enterprises ULC and
its affiliates. You can unsubscribe anytime.

Mail to the Harlequin Reader Service:

IN U.S.A.: P.O. Box 1341, Buffalo, NY 14240-8531
IN CANADA: P.O. Box 603, Fort Erie, Ontario L2A 5X3

Want to try 2 free books from another series? Call 1-800-873-8635 or visit www.ReaderService.com.

*Terms and prices subject to change without notice. Prices do not include sales taxes, which will be charged (if applicable) based
on your state or country of residence. Canadian residents will be charged applicable taxes. Offer not valid in Quebec. This offer is
limited to one order per household. Books received may not be as shown. Not valid for current subscribers to the Essential Romance
or Essential Suspense Collection. All orders subject to approval. Credit or debit balances in a customer's account(s) may be offset by
any other outstanding balance owed by or to the customer. Please allow 4 to 6 weeks for delivery. Offer available while quantities last.

Your Privacy—Your information is being collected by Harlequin Enterprises ULC, operating as Harlequin Reader Service. For a
complete summary of the information we collect, how we use this information and to whom it is disclosed, please visit our privacy notice
located at corporate.harlequin.com/privacy-notice. From time to time we may also exchange your personal information with reputable
third parties. If you wish to opt out of this sharing of your personal information, please visit readerservice.com/consumerschoice or
call 1-800-873-8635. **Notice to California Residents**—Under California law, you have specific rights to control and access your data.
For more information on these rights and how to exercise them, visit corporate.harlequin.com/california-privacy.

STRS23

HARLEQUIN
PLUS

Try the best multimedia
subscription service for romance
readers like you!

Read, Watch and Play.

Experience the easiest way to get
the romance content you crave.

Start your **FREE TRIAL** at
<u>www.harlequinplus.com/freetrial</u>.

HARPLUS0123